# A PLACE CALLED FREEDOM

## BOOK 6 OF THE RED JAVELIN CHRONICLES

**BY ROSS HARRINGWAY**

**OMEGA PRESS**
**EL PASO, TEXAS**

# A PLACE CALLED FREEDOM

# COPYRIGHT © 2017 ROSS HARRINGWAY



OMEGA PRESS

An imprint of Omega Communications Group, Inc.

For information contact:

Omega Press

5823 N. Mesa, #839

El Paso, Texas 79912

Or http://www.kenhudnall.com

FIRST EDITION

Printed in the United States of America

**OTHER WORKS BY THE SAME AUTHOR
FROM OMEGA PRESS**

**THE CLOVIS ACADEMY LEGACY**

**Reign of Death
The Forbidden Region
Shadows in the Dark
Weakness is Provocative
Illusion of Freedom
Burdened With Morality**

**THE RED JAVELIN CHRONICLES**

**Red Javelin
Shroud of Cleopatra
Doctrine of Avoidance
The Undaunted
Obstacles From the Gods**

# CHAPTER ONE

How many Astronomical Units have we passed by, he wondered, as he sat down for his breakfast? Alan Anderson was sitting alone at a four-seat metal table in Take Ten. The seats were made of metal except for the cushions on the backrest. The walls were metal with several painted pictures of the Royal Family displayed here and there. He had been coming to the same establishment every day for the past few months at the same time. All his education and training had led to this, an assignment to go to an uncharted solar system in search of another ship full of scientists and astronauts that had vanished without a trace several years ago. He smiled when the robot resembling a human female approached with his first cup of coffee of the day. The robot looked human except for the grey metallic eyes. The manufacturers just did not seem to care about the eyes, or perhaps it was to ensure that humans could always tell robot from man or woman and thus avoid any awkward social moments such as making a pass at one of the mechanical constructs. Anderson sipped from his stainless-steel coffee cup, thinking that he was in for another boring day after the boring day before and the one before that. The recruiters made space travel sound so romantic and exciting. Anderson and his friends that left Australia of old Earth had been taken in by the propaganda and joined up. Many of his friends joined the military and went off into deep space as Marines, Military Intelligence or Army service men and women.  Others, like Anderson, elected to study at a military academy and become an officer.

He smiled when his constant breakfast companions finally showed up. Two were pilots and the third a nurse.  They were all women and each one was quite attractive in her own way. But Anderson was more interested in hearing their voices and to have the time to learn from each of them. Anderson had slept with one of the pilots, a lovely lady from planet Athena named Rita Del Valle Rusk. She was funny and loud and the sex with her was enjoyable. But Anderson mainly wanted to hear her voice as well as the voices of the others to end the monotony of being on the massive Battle Cruiser with a small skeleton crew. He had wondered if he made a mistake by volunteering to be on the skeleton crew. Sometimes the silence on the ship was unbearable. He found that it was more common that not when he would walk the five large levels of the Battle Cruiser and not run into any other crew member. On one day he walked the halls for eight hours straight, worked out in the gymnasium for an hour, ate three meals at the cafeteria and never saw another soul. He only heard the hum of the engines and the oxygen regeneration machines working. So, Alan Anderson savored all the human contact he could find during the long voyage to a place that mankind had visited only once before, and the fate of that prior mission was still a mystery.

Anderson smiled as he greeted the three women. It was good to see them and hear their voices. He hoped that the day would not end up being another boring day as the last several had been.

Anderson was not the only one that was having the feelings of restlessness. It seemed to be an endless voyage for the crew of the *Pegasus*. They had been flying into deep space for several months and no longer had contact with the rest of humanity or their friends and loved ones. The last communication had been received by the crew in early December. The silence of deep space could lead one to depression and despair without activities to keep one's mind off the loneliness. The protocol on deep space flights was to place most the crew into cryo-sleep tubes and have them sleep for the months of travel while a skeleton crew was left awake to monitor the progress of the flight and ensure that the safety and security of the space craft was maintained.

Those that were selected for duty found a wide variety of activities to keep their sanity. Most of the crew would spend their off-duty hours sleeping or keeping their physical fitness regimen by pushing themselves to the limit in the gymnasium. Others would read or watch old movies. Some would drink to excess or take drugs that had been smuggled on board. Sexual liaisons would occur frequently between crew members as sex was the best entertainment value on a long voyage into deep space. Due to the excessive number of women to men, the odds were enhanced that a man with Anderson's good looks and personality could find willing sex partners whenever he desired it.

Even with all the training and testing given to astronauts and crew, some humans found long distant space travel mentally challenging. Separation from family and friends, the lack of familiar surroundings and the endless darkness around them also challenged the psyche of each person. Each Battle Cruiser employed a few psychiatric doctors to treat the men and women to avoid the depression or despair that would eventually visit some of them.

Five Battle Cruisers from the United Nations Space Command had been ordered to search for a lost ship named the *Bismark* and bring her home. The *Bismark* had last been seen several years ago when she left the eight solar systems controlled by humanity to make first contact with an earth-like planet named Adanac. The *Bismark* should have returned to Earth years ago.

But she did not.

But it was as if the historic space craft and her crew disappeared. Seven years ago was the last time any communication had been received from the *Bismark*. In an effort to locate the ship and crew, the Space Command sent an entire fleet of Battle Cruisers to locate her. The command of the mission was assigned to Admiral Gerald Harrison and his first order was to take his seat as Admiral of the Third Fleet. He moved his wife and two of their children that were already officers to the flagship named the *Pegasus* to begin the mission. They began the long space flight in June after assembling a full crew for the five large space ships.

Harrison had been a graduate from the Space Command Academy located just fifteen miles away from Chicago, Illinois. He met his wife there and they began their lives together as a military family. They had several children and each had joined the Space Command save one daughter that had elected to become a school teacher. Harrison had placed himself and his family members into cryo-sleep just after he told his other son, Drew, good bye. He left each of the five ships under the command of their assigned Captain while he slept in peace.

The Captain of the *Pegasus* was named Yuschenko and he was hardly ever seen by the crew of the *Pegasus* as he was somewhat reclusive and preferred to give his orders from his private quarters. He normally would defer the day to day decision making to the commanders of the individual sections of the ship. He had his ground invasion commander, Major Carina Idris, take command while he relaxed in his private quarters and read classical novels and listened to classical music. When Idris contacted Yuschenko to inform him that the long range scanners detected an unidentified space craft, he waived it off and instructed her to handle the situation. He was too preoccupied with listening to Franz Liszt at a loud volume in his private quarters.

Idris had been born and raised on Mars. She had served in the Military Intelligence Branch of the Space Command and had a stellar career. She had additionally trained as a weapons officer in the Academy. She had married twice. Her first husband had died on a mission many years ago. She had three children, none of whom she had in her possession as she had left them all with their paternal grandparents on Mars so that they would be safe and she would not be worried about their well-being. She was asleep in the Captain's seat when she heard the computer alert that there was an unidentified space craft approaching.

Idris looked up at the third balcony of the Command Station and saw civilian computer technician Ginger Collins

O'Grady typing furiously on her holographic computer keyboard and speaking into her tear drop microphone that was hanging from the headphones around her neck.

O'Grady was one of a few hundred non-military civilians, also known as civil servants that served on the *Pegasus*. She was the computer technician of the day and her normal station was on the third balcony level. O'Grady was married to one of the weapons officers named Eamon O'Grady. They had both volunteered to go on the mission to Adanac and help in locating the Bismark. The couple met on New Edinburgh and married after a whirlwind romance. Ginger O'Grady was one of the best operatives on the laser canon and other weapons functions. She also was a talented computer programmer with skills that were far advanced from her peers in that field. She had red hair, light skin and a smile that made everyone like to be around her. After studying her computer screen, she stood up and leaned over the protective metal railing that surrounded the outer part of the balcony.

"Major, the ship that computer has spotted is a similar design to one of our very own Raumschiffs," O'Grady reported, her voice was steady and firm.

Idris frowned as she was under the impression that no other man made ship had gone this far into this specific quadrant of space other than the *Bismark*. "Is it from the *Bismark*?"

O'Grady shrugged, "I can't tell, Ma'am. Computer scans indicate that the ship is an older model Raumschiff, about twenty years old. I would say that it is possible."

There was only one other person on the Command Station and that was the pilot of the day, Lieutenant Karl Breckenridge. He was also scanning the ship in the distance and cleared his throat.

"Major, the ship looks like it went through a meteor storm or something. It has some hull damage and I am detecting no power." Breckenridge reported as he read the three-dimensional scan conclusions that the computer broadcasted before him.

He had joined the Space Command from the Space Command Academy in Reno, Nevada. He had been serving under Captain Yuschenko for five years as a member of the pilot team. He was tall, skinny and had thick dark hair that was generally a little too long for military regulations. He felt that the rules should be bent for him since he was a member of the wealthy Breckenridge family and that should afford him extra favoritism. Captain Yuschenko did allow him to bend the rules a little, but not because he was a Breckenridge but because he was perhaps the best pilot on board the *Pegasus*.

O'Grady typed in an order for the computer to show a visual of the damaged Raumschiff in the distance. "Major, I have the ship on screen."

"Thank you," Idris said and looked over the large three-dimensional view of the space craft.

It certainly was a Raumschiff and she had certainly had better days. Breckenridge had been correct in his assessment. The outer hull was black and grey with some scorch marks evident on the west side of the view. The ship had several holes in the outer hull and there was nothing visible in the way of lighting or other power sources. The ship was dead in space.

Idris contacted her Captain. When Idris informed Yuschenko of the contact, she was not surprised by his instructions that she handle the situation and not bother him again. She could barely hear his orders over the loud music from his room.

Idris asked the ship's computer to notify her as to the officers that were not in cryo-sleep that had received training in Search and Rescue.

The computer gave her two names: Alan Anderson and Mary Lincoln.

Idris instructed O'Grady to notify those officers to take two Allen Type Fighter space ships to the location of the unidentified ship and report in.

Anderson was elated to hear his name called out for a mission, he needed the change of pace. Anderson had earned a Doctorate in Search and Rescue from his Academy and had been commissioned as a Lieutenant. He had also attended the prestigious Spetsnaz Training course on Old Earth and was one of the few graduates. There were many advanced courses available to cadets and service men and women, but the Spetsnaz graduates were the best of the lot. He had learned survival skills, advanced military tactics, advanced hand to hand combat, advanced marksmanship, sky diving, scuba diving and advanced weapons training.

He finished his four years of study at the Academy in the astronaut program and was proficient in piloting any form of manmade space craft. He entered the doctorate program to study and practice advanced procedures on outer space search and rescue. It was a limited field that had grown in importance and need as humanity began to use space travel more and more. He was physically fit, handsome, intelligent and a good fighter.

His near-death experience when he was impaled by the poisonous tail of an alien Saharakaree on the Blood Moon had given Anderson a new view on the sanctity of life and how precious each second to live was. He was grateful that Julia Steiner had been there to save his life and was forever in her debt. Each day, Anderson would go to the Gymnasium for at least an hour long work out. He would occasionally challenge other crew members to a tennis match, a sport which Anderson had been playing since his youth.

Anderson was considered an all-around individual as he was smart, strong, talented, and sharp and a soldier with high personal standards. But all his training and experience had not prepared him for what he was about to experience.

Anderson was relaxing in *Take Ten*, one of the restaurants on the Pegasus, when the order came over the ship's communication system for him to report to the Docking Bay seven. He heard Mary Lincoln's name mentioned as well. He had grown closer to Lincoln ever since their meeting on the Blood Moon. Both had almost died and they each lost some close friends on that chlorine gas covered moon. During the months of their deep space flight they had spent time together socially. He genuinely liked her and admired her quick wit and perky personality. They had not been sent out on patrol together before so this assignment, whatever it was, would be enjoyable. Or so Anderson had thought.

Anderson had been enjoying his after work out breakfast with some of the other officers when his name was called. He quickly finished his coffee and told his ship mates that he would see them when he returned. Anderson was already in his long sleeved dark blue Space Command Class C uniform. His Lieutenant bars were on each of the collars. The center of his uniform had a gold zipper that ran from his mid-section to his neck. On each shoulder was a gold patch that had the U.N.S.C.

*Pegasus* logo inscribed on it. On the sleeves, just above his wrists, were dark red stripes to signify him as a member of Search and Rescue. He had his Spetsnaz issued burgundy beret in his belt.

Anderson walked to the metal corridors and directly to the stairwell that he would descend to the lower level of the *Pegasus* and to the Docking Bay. When he descended the wide staircase from the docking bay entrance to the lower level, he observed several computer and engineering technicians working on two of the Allen Type Fighter ships near the protective outer hull of the Battle Cruiser. There were hundreds of other similar ships that were not being attended to and their landing ramps were secured to the floor of the docking bay with metal clamps.

Anderson noticed that Lieutenant Junior Grade Mary Lincoln was already standing in front of the small life sciences supply room on the east side of the lower level. She was being issued a navy-blue enviro-suit and a web belt with some of the standard issued weapons for any pilot that was going out on patrol. The laser pistol was the most noticeable of the weapons along with a few knives, stun darts and two hyper dermic needles one filled with anti-venom and the second with a powerful mixture of vitamins and minerals to help with fatigue related to lack of sleep.

Lincoln had also survived the conflict on the Blood Moon but suffered the loss of her left leg. She now had a metal prosthetic leg that looked, worked and was an exact replica of the leg she had lost. In fact, the leg gave her more strength than the average human limb would provide her. Even though the skin on the leg was artificial, it looked exactly like human skin and she could feel the sensations of touch, heat, cold, wind and pain on the limb as if it were her natural leg. It took her a few months to get used to controlling the limb.

As she learned of the increased strength that the leg provided her, she had accidentally kicked in a metal door once and on another occasion, stomped her foot on a tiled floor, crushing it. The leg had been designed, built and patented by the Allen Corporation and was widely used by medical professionals as a replacement limb.

Lincoln had volunteered for the mission to search for the *Bismark*. When she took the challenge to join the mission she rejected her father's requests that she start her career as a pilot on his Battle Cruiser. She had not turned down her father due to any ill will toward him but rather because she knew that Yuri Gorski was going to be on the same crew. Her strongest desire was to find a way to have the feelings in her heart for Gorski to end. She loved him and no longer wanted to have those lingering feelings. Their relationship had been a stormy one and when things were good they were the best. But his carousing was not conducive to her mindset or the goals she had set out for herself.

She broke off the long-term relationship with Gorski and hoped that one day she would find love again with another man.

But Gorski was not the only reason she joined the search. Lincoln had spent four years as one of the best cadets learning under Admiral Seward. He had told her once in a private conversation that he had lost one of his sons on the *Bismark*. She hoped to discover the final fate of Seward's son as a gift to the man that had taught her so much about being an officer and a pilot.

Lincoln smiled when she saw that Anderson was approaching her. She hugged him and gave him a kiss on the cheek. "Alan, so good to see you."

"You, too, Mary," Anderson embraced her. "Looks like you and I have been selected for a little adventure."

Lincoln laughed as she began to pull the enviro-suit on. "You think that it might be one of the Raumschiffs from the Bismark?"

"What else could it be?" Anderson proposed in question form as he accepted his enviro-suit from a life sciences technician.

"No other human made ship has ever traveled out this far before," Lincoln said while was checking her helmet over. "This could be our first real clue as to what happened to the crew of the Bismark. You and I could be about to solve this mission all on our own."

"If we do, you buy the first round."

Lincoln laughed as she affixed her helmet over her head, "All right, Lieutenant Anderson. You're on. So, did you score with that nurse you were hitting on last night?"

Anderson slid his legs into his enviro-suit and shook his head side to side. "No. I wasn't her type."

Lincoln laughed at that, "What? She doesn't like athletic and handsome white men with thick blonde hair and an adorable Australian accent?"

"She might like some of those qualities. But I wasn't her type."

"Did she say what her type was?"

"I think she would have preferred that you were the one trying to take her to bed," Anderson said and laughed.

Lincoln began walking toward her space craft as she was now fully covered by the protective enviro-suit. "You remind me of my friend Les. He had terrible luck with women."

Anderson followed her toward the two Allen Type Fighter space crafts that were waiting for them. "I thought Les married that pretty girl from the Bordeaux area."

"He did. I am referring to his luck before he met Sophia." Lincoln stopped in front of her space craft and put her left foot up on the small indentations on the side of the ship that were used to make climbing into the cockpit easier for the pilot.

"My offer still stands, Alan. My friend Vanessa likes white men and she is exotic looking with dark hair and eyes. I promise that you will really like her. Let me set you two up."

Anderson began climbing up the side of his small space craft, "You keep saying that. After all these months, why haven't I met her yet?"

"She always works different shifts than you. I still haven't met half the skeleton crew. There's almost two thousand of us on board and only a handful of us are awake. You would think we would have met everyone by now."

Anderson sat down in his seat and began his security checks, "But there's only about a hundred or so of us awake. Everyone else is in cryo-sleep. After all this time in deep space, I agree with you. We should have at least met each other. The ship is big but not that big."

"My father told me that his biggest chore as a commanding officer is to meet each crew member." Lincoln also started her safety protocols that were required before she would be cleared to depart the docking bay and take the ship out for the mission. She received her computer reports that the oxygen regeneration apparatus was functional. "My father takes pride in knowing all of his officers by a first name basis. He spends hours studying the personnel files on all of his crew so that he will know their names, talents, weaknesses and just how much he can ask of them."

Anderson informed Major Idris that his ship was cleared and ready for takeoff. "Mary, it sounds like your father is a good commander. May I ask why you are here and not with him?"

Lincoln pressed the controls on her computer panel before her and smiled as her transparent metal canopy began to seal shut over her head. "I wanted to prove I can be a good officer and a pilot without my father. Plus, a man I respect told me that one of his sons was a member of the Bismark crew. I wanted to be a part of bringing his son home, if he is still alive. What about you, Alan? You could have taken any assignment in the eight solar systems. Why this one? We have no clue what is out there."

"That is the reason, to see the unknown. That's why I got into this line of work in the first place." Anderson secured his over the shoulder safety harnesses. "Plus, one of my uncles was a Marine on the Bismark. I thought I would try and find out where he had gone off to."

With both ships cleared for space travel, the secondary metal bulkhead began to seal shut behind their ships, separating them from the rest of the docking bay and protecting those behind the wall when the outer partitions opened and exposed the docking bay to outer space. Flashing green and red lights illuminated the docking bay with loud warnings from the ship computer stating: "Warning! Warning! Outer hull will be open in sixty seconds! Warning! All personnel are advised to seek cover behind the secondary docking bay hull! Warning!"

Anderson already had his engines on and placed the visor of his enviro-suit helmet down so that it was secure. His canopy had already sealed shut and the interior of his ship was protected from the dangers of the space vacuum. "Ready for duty, Lieutenant Lincoln?"

"Ready sir," she responded. Anderson outranked her by one officer grade so all the decisions would be his. Lincoln was glad that Anderson was with her. He was always calm and steady in his approach.

They both watched from their individual space craft as the outer hull began to open. They observed the darkness before them and a few stars in the far distance. They waited for the Major to give them clearance to launch. They did not have long to wait. The order to proceed was given to them less than five seconds after the outer hull had opened.

Lincoln took hold of her half-moon steering mechanism and lifted it up just slightly to guide her space craft up a few feet above the docking bay metal floor before she pushed the accelerator control to begin the flight. Her ship slowly flew out of the docking area and was soon surrounded by space. She had her computer display four views so that she could monitor her north, south, east and west as she flew. Her southern screen showed the Battle Cruiser growing smaller as she increased her speed. She could see that Anderson's ship was right behind hers and gaining.

"Command Station, this is Lincoln. Please forward the coordinates of the abandoned ship to my computer."

"Mary, this is Ginger. I am sending you the coordinates. Happy hunting!" Lincoln recognized the voice of Ginger Collins.

"Thank you Ginger," Lincoln responded as she pushed the accelerator with her right hand to increase her speed while keeping her left hand firmly on the steering mechanism.

"You in a hurry?" Anderson asked her.

"Aren't you? Think about it, Alan. If this ship is from the *Bismark* then we can down load the computer information and solve the mystery of her disappearance."

"Could be wishful thinking there, Mary. The ship is in bad shape and that might mean the computers are damaged as well. If this ship is one of the *Bismark* ships, then it just means we are heading into some danger that has not yet revealed itself to us. We need to be careful."

"Is that what they taught you at Spetsnaz?"

Anderson laughed, "They taught us not to rush to our own death and right now you are flying faster than necessary. But since you are closer to the ship, why don't you scan her for life forms or any power sources on board."

"Fine," Lincoln decreased the speed of her ship and then requested that her computer initiate scans on the ship that she could now see to her north-east.

"I am detecting a slight power source in the bottom level of the Raumschiff," the computer reported. "And I am also detecting life forms. There are ten humans on board and they are alive."

"Come again?" Lincoln felt her heart beating faster.

"There are ten life forms on the ship."

"Alan, did you hear that?"

"Yes, I sure did. I suppose that means I should go in for a closer look."

Lincoln frowned as his words sunk in, "You mean you plan on boarding her?"

"Yes, that is exactly what I am going to do. Keep trying to contact the crew and let them know that I am coming."

Lincoln was soon within two hundred feet of the listing Raumschiff. She slowed her speed and began to fly in circles around the ship. She could see that Anderson's ship was doing the same. They both observed several holes in the hull of the Raumschiff as well as burn marks on the metal.

"Were they in the middle of a laser battle?" Lincoln wondered out loud as she inspected the hull damage.

"Or something worse," Anderson said softly as he studied the damaged ship. "Looks like some of that hull damage might have been caused by some rocket explosions or floating debris. Well, if there are ten survivors of the Bismark waiting to be rescued then we may very well solve the mystery as to what happened to her."

Anderson slowly guided his space craft closer to the larger vessel. His first thought was to attach to the Raumschiff by using her docking mechanism. He pursed his lips when he was close enough to observe that the docking mechanism had been damaged. It looked as if it had been torn off the side of the Raumschiff.

"Mary?"

"Yes, Alan?"

"I am going to have to enter the ship by spacewalk. There is no way for me to dock to her. This ship is far too damaged to make such an attempt."

Anderson put his space craft in full stop and unbuckled his safety harness. He reached behind his pilot seat and found his white and red search and rescue back pack. He affixed the strap of the pack over his left shoulder and instructed his computer to depressurize so that he would not flung out of his seat when the canopy opened. Anderson had trained for space walks on numerous occasions at the Academy. This would be his first time to float out into space for real. He ordered his computer to open the canopy and looked up.

The canopy opened upward and Anderson pushed himself out of his seat. Using his small jet functions on his enviro-suit boots, he slowly flew in the direction of the damaged ship. It took him approximately ten minutes to make contact with the outer hull of the Raumschiff. He grabbed the left corner of the rear of the space craft with his hands. He directed the computer of his enviro-suit to activate the magnetic gloves so that he could hold on to the hull. He looked over his shoulder and could see his stationary ship and Lincoln's ship circling around his position.

Anderson turned his attention to his mission and began crawling over the hull to get to the rear loading area which would be the best location for him to gain entry. He heard Lincoln urging him to be careful as he moved. His biggest fear was tearing his enviro-suit on one of the jagged hull breaches as he crawled past them. He remembered his training that had taught him to breathe slowly. Several cadets at his Academy had been flunked out due to their sheer panic at being in zero gravity and surrounded by the darkness of the simulated space environment. It was not a natural act for humans to undertake.

Anderson finally made it to the rear entrance of the Raumschiff and activated the lights on the top of his helmet and on his shoulders. He pulled his back pack from his shoulder and slowly unzipped it from the top. He fished around and found the small computer inside. He pulled it out in his right hand and placed it next to the keypad on the side of the rear entrance. Each Raumschiff had a thirty-digit security code of letters, numbers and symbols that would allow a Space Command employee to enter the craft from the outside. Anderson ordered his enviro-suit computer to link with the hand-held computer device and he smiled when the small screen lit up with a light green color.

"Computer, I know it is very badly damaged in there. Can you link with the on-board computer and ascertain her security entry code?" Anderson asked and knew he was hoping for the impossible. He waited for the small computer to attempt to hack into the side entry control and open the back hatch. Anderson was ready if the attempt to link his small computer with the security hatch computer failed, he would have to cut his way through the hull.

"Alan, I have scanned the entire craft. The identification numbers were burned and melted from the hull. No way to tell which ship this was," Lincoln reported with a bit of disappointment in her voice.

"We'll know what we are dealing with soon enough," Anderson told her. He smiled when the small green screen of his hand-held computer changed from green to yellow. "We are in."

Anderson crawled away from the rear exit as he knew that it would soon slid open outward and then down. He heard

Lincoln tell him congratulations as she watched the back door begin to slowly open.

"Mary, report to the Command Station that I have gained entry to the ship. I am going to go in and locate those ten life forms. Stand ready. We may need a Medical Raumschiff out here soon to transport the survivors."

"I will alert Major Idris," Lincoln responded.

Anderson watched as the rear entrance ramp lowered and the hatch opened upward. He could hear the strain of the metal as it slid open. He heard a clanking noise as the old ship had been forced open. He pulled out five one-foot long and one-inch-thick plastic rods from his back pack and twisted them one at a time. As he did so, the plastic rods began to glow with a bright, white light. He tossed one of the rods inside the Raumschiff and stepped inside. He tossed in a second light rod and waited for the rear loading area of the space craft to light up from the temporary lights. Anderson slowly walked in with his enviro-suit boots now using their gravitation function. He scanned the area around him. He saw floating weapons and computers all around him. His small computer began to shine a light forward in the direction of the detected life forms. Anderson knew that the life forms had to be in the storage room in the bottom level.

"Mary, there are clothes, loose metal, food containers, laser rifles and laser pistols floating inside here. I can see a few computers that were either not secured or they were blown loose from the battle. My search and rescue computer is directing me to the belly of the ship."

"Be careful," Lincoln called out.

Anderson slowly walked toward the hallway that connected the rear loading area with the lower level and the ladder that would lead upward to the command room, computer control room and weapons room. The upper level was the pilots section. The underbelly was the normal location of the kitchen, medical area, the engine room, living areas and the storage area. He tossed another of his light rods down the hallway and followed it. He found the ladder leading upward and he threw one of the light rods upward to illuminate the area, just in case he needed to inspect it later, and kept walking to the ramp leading downstairs. He found the slight drop of the stairs and dropped the fifth light rod down.

"Crikey!" Anderson sucked in his breath.

"What is it, Alan?" Lincoln called out.

"Lined up against the walls are a bunch of cryo-sleep tubes," Anderson reported. "I bet they have our ten life forms inside."

Anderson walked down the steps and pulled out two more light rods from his back pack and twisted them. He tossed one down the end of the hallway. He kept the other in his left hand as he kept walking. He counted twelve cryo-sleep tubes and stopped in front of the first one. He held the light close to the tube and could not see inside due to it being covered with dust. With his right hand, he began to wipe the dust from the tube. He noticed that it had a crack on the thick glass casing. He finally got a look at what was inside, and saw a human body that had some decaying flesh covering about fifty percent of the skeleton.

"Shit!" Anderson jumped backward.

"Alan! Are you okay?" Lincoln was alarmed by the obvious fear she heard in his voice.

Anderson cursed at himself for letting the sight of the dead body get to him. "Yes, Mary. I just got startled, I'm fine."

Anderson regained his composure and moved to the second tube. He began wiping the dust aside and was surprised again by what he saw. Except this time, it was not by a dead body. He whistled. "She's beautiful."

Anderson inspected the face of a lovely blonde haired woman. She was asleep and seemed very much at peace. He looked down toward her shoulders and noticed that she was wearing a military uniform. It was an older version of the Space Command uniforms that consisted of a turtle neck sweater and long sleeves. The woman had a set of gold bars on her sweater that signified that she was a Second Lieutenant. "Now what is a pretty girl like you doing in a place like this? Computer, is she alive?"

"Yes," the small computer responded.

"I'll be. Mary. Get that Medical Raumschiff over here. We have ten cryo-sleep tubes that need to be moved to our medical area."

"It's on the way," Lincoln told him. She began to communicate his orders to Ginger Collins. Both women secretly hoped that this discovery would lend a clue as to the cause of the loss of the *Bismark.*

Anderson moved to the second tube and wiped the dust away and saw a man with dark skin sound asleep. He had a similar uniform as the woman to his right and had enlisted bars on his collar. "Mary, these uniforms are around the right time period of the Bismark. I got a Second Lieutenant and a Lance Corporal. When we thaw them out they may be able to tell us what happened to their mother ship."

"Medical team is on the way Alan," Lincoln confirmed. "Everything looks good from up here, no debris or dangers. You can go ahead and start bringing out the cryo-sleep tubes."

"Copy that," Anderson said as he lifted the tube of the Lance Corporal inside. He began to carry the entire tube in his arms back to the rear loading bay of the ship. The normal standard procedure was for the medical team to have a few doctors and explorations officers in enviro-suits to take each of the cryo-sleep tubes on board. Fortunately, each of the ten cryo-sleep tubes had not been connected to the ship's power source. Had they been so connected then the tubes would have been dependent on that sole power source and the ten humans would have died. But these tubes had individual solar cell batteries attached to the back to keep the humans in cryogenic freeze. He checked the levels of the solar cells of the Lance Corporal and determined that the man could have lived another sixty or seventy years.

Lieutenant Junior Grade Vanessa Blair received her orders from the Command Station to take command of an emergency medical rescue operation about fifteen kilometers from the current position of the Battle Cruiser.

Blair was fresh out of Sikorsky's Academy where she had received her degree in Astral Navigation. She had been proud to graduate and then be selected to serve in the historic mission to find the lost *Bismark*. Blair was a striking young woman with blonde and brown streaks in her mostly dark hair. Her mocha colored skin was smooth and she had never had any issues with skin blemishes in her youth. She had light brown eyes that sparkled and her perfect teeth melted any person that saw her smile. She had a curvaceous body that turned heads while she wore her skin tight dark blue flight suit.

Blair had performed masterfully at the Academy with high marks. She loved to fly space craft and was excited when she received the order to report to Docking Bay Two. She ran quickly down the stairs and met the Chief Medical Officer, Doctor Kim Jeongjo and the resident psychiatric Doctor named Mozgov at the lower level. There were three other nurses, two exploration officers and a weapons officer present. Each of the medical staff were dressed in their solid white two piece uniforms which consisted of short sleeved tunic and slacks. All the doctors and nurses had belts around their waists that was utilized to carry their compact medical packets filled with medicines, hyper dermic needles, scanners, bandages and other items for emergencies.

Jeongjo had been born on Sikorsky's Planet and spent her entire life there through her graduation from medical school. She was a few inches over six feet tall with dark hair and eyes. She had spent the last twenty-one years of her life in the service as a surgeon on several battlefields until finally receiving her appointment as a chief medical officer on a science vessel named the *Arizona*. Soon after she learned of the mission to locate the *Bismark* and volunteered to serve on that quest. She had two adult children that were studying at the university on Sikorsky's Planet. Her husband had died years ago and she never remarried.

Mozgov had claimed her roots to Eastern Europe on old Earth and had earned her doctorate in psychiatric medicine at Moscow University. She had practiced in several hospitals located in the Ukraine, Latvia, Poland and Bulgaria before accepting an offer to serve as chief resident of psychiatry at the main hospital in Clovis City, planet New Edinburgh. While she served at that hospital she had become close friends with Doctor Freya Cardenas and retired Admiral Seward.

When she learned of the three-yearlong mission to search for the *Bismark*, Mozgov submitted her volunteer application to the Admiral of the fleet to serve. She had been named chief psychiatrist for the mission. Mozgov was fluent in several Eastern European languages and the official Space Command languages of English and Chinese. She was five feet three inches tall and had dark brown hair with light blue eyes.

She had never married, mainly due to the huge gap in the population percentage between men and women. Without a love in her life, Mozgov wrapped herself in her career and became one of the most widely published authors on the issue of psychiatric brain disorders from long term exposure to cryogenic sleep. In her research on the many patients she worked with she found that many space travelers claimed that after some time in cryo-sleep they had out of body experiences. Mozgov learned that some claimed to meet other people and interact with them in their subconscious. Mozgov interviewed individuals that her patients had claimed to speak to in their sleep. She could find no witnesses to corroborate the claims made by her patients. She concluded that those that were in cryo-sleep for periods exceeding five years would have dreams, hallucinations or fantasies that they could reach out to others and have conversations with them. It was a dilemma that warranted more research.

Blair had not met the three female nurses that had opted to assist Jeongjo and Mozgov with the ten cryo-sleep tubes. That led her to conclude that the nurses worked different shifts than she did.

Blair noticed that they were each quickly dressing into their enviro-suits in anticipation of their approaching spacewalk to recover the ten cryo-sleep tubes.

Blair only knew two of the others present. One was Ensign Edward McCluskey from the Explorations Section. Blair had observed that the man had an explosive temper as he was known to get into too many fights in the bars. But he was an above average officer with a good working knowledge of weapons, physics and geology. McCluskey had been involved with one of the computer technician girls ever since the voyage of their ship began. Blair recalled that McCluskey was from planet Athena and had graduated from one of the Academies on that planet. He was short in stature, had thick dark hair and eyes. He kept himself physically fit, as required by the military regulations, and liked to read books on physics in his spare time. He had an accent that was common among the people that were born and raised on Athena. His uniform was a one piece, light brown long sleeved Class C that was standard issue to all the Explorations Team.

The second officer that Blair personally knew was Lieutenant Eamon O'Grady from the weapons section. She had met him and his wife through Mary Lincoln after one week out into space. All the single women, and a few of those that were married, lusted for O'Grady given his tall, muscular body, green eyes and light hair color. He had handsome features and was extremely intelligent. He was a doctorate recipient from Clovis Academy. He had attained some fame when he survived being stabbed by a poisonous Saharakaree on the Blood Moon. O'Grady was a by the book type of officer and he had little use for service men and women that showed up for work in uniforms that were not up to standards. O'Grady's uniform was a deep purple and he had a hand laser attached to his utility belt.

The other explorations officer was a female with blonde hair and blue eyes that had the rank of Lieutenant on her brown collar. She was slender and medium height. Her name tag read Iavarone.

Blair took possession of an enviro-suit and quickly began to pull it over her uniform. She said nothing as she made certain that the protective clothing was properly secured. In the distance, she saw the solid white medical Raumschiff that was assigned to the mission. Each Battle Cruiser had five medical Raumschiffs that were fully stocked to operate as a floating hospital in space. The color of white was used to make sure that even the dimmest witted of technicians could not mistake them from the black or blue Raumschiffs. After she had finished zipping up her enviro-suit and inspecting the helmet, Blair walked quickly to the space craft and onto the back receiving ramp. The nurses and doctors were close behind her. Iavarone, McCluskey and O'Grady boarded last.

Within seconds, Blair had climbed the ladders of the Raumschiff up to the pilot section and sat in one of the two seats there. She had no co-pilot assigned to assist her as the plan was for Lincoln to dock with the medical space craft and serve as her co-pilot on the return trip. Blair reached up to the computer panel above her head and began flipping switches to begin her safety checks. She could hear the engines rumbling to life as she kept up the ritual of preparing for lift off.

"Computer, check oxygen regeneration capability," Blair instructed.

"Operational," the voice of the computer responded.

"Dark matter converter?"

"Operational."

"Solar energy cells?"

"All fully charged."

"Hull integrity?"

"No breached detected."

"Rear thrusters?"

"Operational."

"Gravity controls."

"Operational."

And so it went, through another thirty systems checks. Blair reported to the Command Station that her ship was checked and safe for space travel. She received the order to proceed. Blair asked her computer to patch her into the rest of the crew.

"This is your pilot speaking. The secondary hull is closing behind us. We will soon be separating from the Battle Cruiser and entering deep space. Please fasten your safety harnesses and prepare for a short flight. There will be no movie or popcorn service today as the trip is far too short. It is my pleasure to serve you on this flight. We hope that you chose to fly United Nations Space Command in the future."

Iavarone laughed from her seat. O'Grady checked his safety harness and leaned back in his seat. The medical staff were in the lower level preparing to receive potentially injured patients. Iavarone, O'Grady and McCluskey were sitting in the second level of the medical ship in the area known as the command level.

"Everyone wants to be a comedian," McCluskey mumbled to himself.

Blair smiled as the outer hull of the Battle Cruiser began to open. She took hold of the steering column with her left hand

and reached over to the accelerator lever with her right hand. As soon as the hull was open she lifted the ship upward and slowly guided her out of the docking area and into space.

Anderson had slowly moved the cryo-sleep tube with the Lance Corporal out of the damaged ship. He used his thrusters on his enviro-suit boots to propel him out into space as he held the tube in his hands. Lincoln watched as Anderson carried the cryo-sleep tube out into space.

"Looking good there, Alan." Lincoln told him.

"You too," Anderson said as he looked up at her circling space craft. "Where's our medical team?"

"Look to your south-west," Lincoln answered. "They are just about here."

Anderson smiled as he saw the white Raumschiff approaching. He released the cryo-sleep tube that had the Lance Corporal inside and he returned inside the damaged Raumschiff to retrieve another tube.

Blair observed the activity before her as she began to slow the speed of her ship. "Folks, we have one patient in space and our S and R officer has returned inside the ship to recover another patient. We are less than two minutes away. Everyone ready for a spacewalk?"

O'Grady, Iavarone, McCluskey and the three nurses were already at the rear of the ship and watching the secondary bulkhead closing to ensure the occupants of the space craft would be sealed off when the rear loading ramp doors opened. All six of the crew had attached cables to the space craft and their enviro-suits in case their jet packs failed. They were going to recover all ten tubes by passing them down to each other like the old firemen used to pass buckets of water to put out a fire. It would take at least an hour to get them all inside.

The back door opened and McCluskey leaped out into deep space first, followed by Iavarone, O'Grady and each of the nurses brought up the rear.

McCluskey slowly flew toward the first cryo-sleep tube and ordered his enviro-suit computer to stop the jet pack power and glided into the tube. The Ensign took hold of the tube by using his hand-held Magnetizer. The Magnetizer was critical in every day space travel, especially in construction as it would attach to metal objects, even those that weighed about a ton, and allow a human to move the object while at a distance. McCluskey slowly turned around and saw Iavarone about fifteen feet behind him. She motioned to him that she was ready. She also had a Magnetizer in her hand. McCluskey used his jet pack to fly toward her and he handed her the tube. Once Iavarone had hold of the cylinder, McCluskey released his hold on it and he turned to see Anderson coming out of the damaged space craft with another tube. McCluskey urged his suit computer to take him in that direction to assist the other officer.

Iavarone took the first tube to O'Grady and in turn he took it to the closest nurse named Clark. And the process continued ten times until all the tubes had been recovered and safely placed on board the medical space craft. The three nurses returned on board their ship and waited as O'Grady, Iavarone, McCluskey and Anderson joined them on the back-loading ramp. The seven reported in to Blair that they were all safely on board as the back ramp began to close and the hull slid shut. The secondary hull opened after the area had been flooded with oxygen.

Anderson was the first to remove his helmet. He stood over the ten cryo-sleep tubes and smiled, "Got them all in safely."

O'Grady put his long arm around Anderson's shoulder. "Good job out there, Alan."

Anderson smiled at the compliment from the man that had become one of his best friends. "I wonder where these folks were headed. I tried to check the memory banks on their ship and it was completely damaged. There were no stored flight plans at all. I couldn't download any information as to the identity of these ten passengers. Looks like they were on a one-way trip to an indefinite shore."

By then Doctor Jeongjo had entered the room. She had on a medical outfit that was normally used for surgery. "Carry the ten tubes to the medical area. We are going to scan them for viruses and bacteria. If they clear, then we will wake them all up."

Her order was easier said than done. Moving the cryo-sleep tubes in space where there was no gravity to work against was easy. Now, on board the ship and with full artificial gravity, the full weight of the tube and the human sleeping inside demanded more of the person carrying it. Each of the tubes weighed about three hundred pounds. Iavarone smiled and showed everyone her Magnetizer.

"These will work inside the ship as well as outside," she told them.

"You heard the doctor," O'Grady said to the others and pointed to the tube closest to him. "Ed, give me a hand with this one here."

McCluskey and O'Grady lifted the tube up using their Magnetizer devices and slowly carried it up the ramp and down toward the medical area.

Iavarone and Anderson lifted the tube with the woman inside and walked slowly as they slowly brought her to the large medical area. Anderson noticed that the area that Jeongjo and Mozgov were waiting was about fifty yards long and thirty yards wide. There were fifteen beds for patients in the middle of the room. Anderson observed several computers mounted on the metal walls and rows of tables below them with numerous medical instruments, towels, gauzes, needles, and scanners.

As Anderson and Iavarone carried in the second tube they saw that the first one had been placed on the floor. Jeongjo was scanning the tube with a small hand held computer device. Mozgov directed for Anderson to set the second tube on the floor as O'Grady and McCluskey walked out of the room to retrieve the next tube.

Two of the three nurses carried in the third tube and set it next to the others. Once they did so Jeongjo ordered them to get out of their enviro-suits and assist with the medical portion of the mission. The third nurse received a similar order.

That left Anderson, Iavarone, McCluskey and O'Grady to bring in the other seven tubes. As the transfer of the tubes from the receiving area to the medical section continued, Lincoln docked her ship to the medical ship. She waited for the docking tube from the medical Raumschiff to attach to her smaller space craft on the bottom. Lincoln opened the bottom of her space craft and crawled into the docking tube and found herself in an airlock to the Raumschiff. She saw the smiling face of Blair on the other side waiting for her. After the airlock had been pressurized, Blair ordered the computer to open the interior airlock doors so that Lincoln could join them on board.

"Welcome aboard," Blair greeted her friend.

Lincoln hugged her, "Thanks. Did all of the tubes make it?"

Blair nodded, "As far as I know all ten are alive. The medical staff are scanning them for dangerous bacteria or viruses. So far so good. They are about to wake them all up."

Lincoln smiled, thinking that the mission that led them into deep space would soon be solved. "And soon they can tell us what happened to the Bismark."

"Come on, let's go join the others." Blair pointed to the ladder leading downward. She had placed the ship on full stop and had the computer auto-pilot initiated to react in case of any emergency. Blair led Lincoln down to the large medical area.

Lincoln whistled as she saw the ten tubes on the floor. Everyone had shed their enviro-suits except for Anderson. Lincoln noticed that when Blair and Anderson looked at each other for the first time they both smiled. Lincoln could see the look in Blair's eyes that indicated that she was immediately attracted to Anderson. Lincoln walked over to Anderson and stood next to him.

"And it didn't cost anything," Lincoln whispered to Anderson.

"What?" Anderson whispered back to her.

"Her smile at you. It was free. That is the best kind."

"She is really pretty," Anderson said softly.

"Glad you think so. That's my friend, Vanessa. The one I have been trying to introduce you to. You like?"

"I like," Anderson affirmed as he saw Blair smiling at him again.

"Listen up," Doctor Mozgov said to the group. "We are going to start waking them all up. When we do, there is no telling how they will react. I have considerable experience with people that have spent a decade or longer under cryo-sleep. Many of them will have delusions that they have been in contact with others by way of out of body experiences. We believe that is an unintended consequence of the mind being dormant for such a long period. There is also a huge danger that the patient will be suffering from vitamin deficiencies. They may also have issues with reality. They will believe that they are in the presence of their former planet or shipmates from the Bismark. With that having been said, when they become verbal, let me do the talking. I might need you to help restrain one or more of them as some patients similarly situated have been known to panic and begin to run, fight or become a danger to themselves or others. Everyone ready?"

"Ready," O'Grady nodded.

Jeongjo and her nurses opened the tube containing the woman with the Lieutenant bars on her collar. They had decided that since she was the only officer in the ten tubes that they would learn more from her about the mystery of the Bismark. The other nine tubes had enlisted men except one of them seemed to have a civilian man. They had assumed that he was civilian since he was not in any military uniform that was recognized by their computer scans.

Anderson and the others watched in silence as the woman was lifted by the three nurses from her tube and placed on one of the hospital beds. Her uniform was a two piece with a turtle neck sweater and dark pants. The uniform had some tears and burn marks on it. She had a web belt around her mid-section that had a few knives, a laser pistol and what looked like a beret.

Nurse Clark removed the web belt with the weapons attached. None of the assembled rescuers wanted the woman to wake up from years of cryo-sleep and see them all as the enemy.

The burgundy colored beret fell to the floor.

"Hey, doc." Anderson approached and picked the beret up from the floor. "Her beret. Look at the color, it's just like mine. She's a member of Spetsnaz."

O'Grady nodded when he heard that comment, "Computer, give us all names of the female crew members of the *Bismark* that were graduates of the Spetsnaz training course."

They all waited for a few moments as the computer analyzed the request.

"There were no females on the Bismark that had graduated from the Spetsnaz training," the computer responded.

Jeongjo inspected the woman on the bed, "She had a name tag that looks like it was burned off except the last letter. It looks like an 'I'."

"There was a female Professor named Bellinski on the Bismark," O'Grady commented. "But I don't think she was military."

"Maybe the situation was one that left her in the position that she had to grab whatever clothing she could get a hold of," Blair commented.

Mozgov suddenly made a noise to get the others to be quiet. "Her eyes are fluttering. She's waking up."

One of the nurses gave the patient an injection of vitamins and minerals in the neck to help boost her energy.

The woman opened her eyes slowly and closed them due to the brightness of the lights. She took in a deep breath and then sat up rapidly, gasping for air.

Two of the nurses, Betances and Jebali, stood on either side of the woman and held her arms so that she would not fall backward. The woman was breathing heavily for air and began looking around wildly. She was trying to focus on the doctors and nurses before her. She was stunned to be alive. She began to recall the last few seconds before she desperately ordered her Marines to lock themselves into the cryo-sleep tubes. Her mind was still stuck on the last few seconds of events that had occurred almost seventeen years earlier. To the patient, the stress of the moment seemed like it had just happened.

"Lieutenant, I am Doctor Mozgov. Can you tell me your name?"

The woman began sputtering something that was in a language that none of them understood. To the shock of all witnessing the event, the patient flipped nurse Betances who had been holding her right arm. Betances screamed as she flew several feet and then crashed onto the floor. The patient leaped to her feet and pulled free of the other nurse. She was screaming hysterically in the unknown language. She could not understand why no one would respond to her questions.

O'Grady and McCluskey instinctively moved in to restrain the woman. They never stood a chance. She kicked McCluskey in the chest and sent him flailing backward into O'Grady.

"What language is she speaking?" Blair wondered out loud as she ran to help Betances back on her feet.

"It's some form of old Earth Baltic language," Mozgov said as she reached for a hyper dermic needle to stun the patient before she hurt anyone else.

Lincoln moved in with Blair as the patient shoved one of the nurses into Jeongjo. She kept screaming something in the unknown language repeatedly. Lincoln reached her first and put her hands on the woman's arms.

"Miss, please calm down. We are trying to help you. Please." Lincoln looked into her grey-blue eyes that were flashing with a mixture of fear and desperation.

The woman considered her eyes for a few seconds. Lincoln believed she had seen those eyes before. She listened to the woman as she gasped for air.

"English," the woman said. "You speak English."

"Yes. Yes, please tell us in English what happened?" Lincoln urged her.

"My husband. I must get to my husband. My sons." The woman now was holding Lincoln's arms with her hands. She was staring into Lincoln's eyes as if she were pleading with her through her stare. "They fired on the ship! My men! Hilts! Spiller! Where are they? They made it to the cryo-sleep tubes with me!"

"Your men are here and they are alive. We want to help you," Lincoln assured her. She could not get over why the woman's eyes looked so familiar to her. She had seen those eyes, those piercing grey eyes somewhere before. "Tell me your husband's name."

"Nikolai. I must find him. The fire in the sky is coming. Everyone is in danger. I must go to him." The woman said and then repeated it over and over.

O'Grady whispered to Mozgov, "I have memorized the names of all the officers on the *Bismark*. There was no officer named Nikolai on her."

"A scientist or civilian?" Mozgov whispered back. "She keeps mentioning a fire in the sky. Did the *Bismark* encounter and exploding star or some other phenomena?"

Lincoln continued to prod the strange woman as the others were speculating as to the meaning of the phrases the woman kept repeating to them. "Ma'am. What section did Nikolai work under on the *Bismark*?"

The woman looked at Lincoln as if she were crazy.

"Bismark? No. Nyet. Nikolai and my sons were going to the other place."

"What place?" Lincoln asked.

"The purple planet," the woman said. "My sons! I must get to them. I must see Piotr and Yuri. Why aren't they here?"

At that moment, Lincoln felt as if someone had poured ice in her blood. She knew who the woman was. "Oh my God."

"What?" Blair asked as she noticed the look on Lincoln's face.

"She isn't from the *Bismark*," Lincoln said to the others with certainty in her voice. She knew who the woman was because her first love had been her oldest son. Lincoln had heard the story from Yuri Gorski several times about how the military establishment fired on her ship when he was just a few years old.

It had been an event that had defined Gorski as he developed into a man. "This is Yuri Gorski's mother."

"Yes," Melita Gorski nodded. Her heart was pounding in her chest in that one of the strangers before her knew who she was. "Take me to my husband. My sons. Please. Please."

Mozgov had heard the tragic tale of how the wife of Colonel Nikolai Gorski had died. She dropped the hyper dermic she had been holding in her hand, stunned by the events unfolding before her. "Impossible."

"Please help me," Melita Gorski repeated desperately. "I have to get to my family!"

Her last sentence was a loud scream and it echoed throughout the space craft. Lincoln held the mother of her former lover close as she begged for help. The rest of the rescue crew were too shocked to say a word.

After the rescue team calmed Melita Gorski down, they listened to her story from over sixteen years ago about the Derelict ship she had boarded. She told them in painful detail how most of her team died and the last-ditch efforts made by her to survive.

"When I realized that we had been fired upon, I directed my Marines and Doctor Shaw to get back into our Marines Raumschiff. I knew our only chance was to disconnect from the docking portal of the alien ship and put some distance between us before the rockets exploded. We did not get very far. The explosion rocked our ship, a few of my Marines were swept out into space when the hull breached. Eleven of us made it to the lower level and secured cryo-sleep tubes so that we could hide and wait for a rescue attempt.  I remember the feeling of being frozen and falling asleep."

"And did you dream?" Mozgov asked.

"I not only dreamed, I saw things. Many things. I could visit people I knew in my sleep. It was as if my soul was able to travel through the world of dreams. I could communicate with some of those I met." Melita was rubbing her temples and smiled when Iavarone entered the room with a fresh cup of coffee for her. She took the cup and sipped from it, savoring the flavor. "How long have we been in the stasis sleep?"

Jeongjo looked around at the others and took Melita's free hand in hers. "You have been in that tube for almost seventeen years. So much has happened since then."

Melita looked at each of the faces with desperation in her eyes. A lone tear ran down her left cheek as she dared to ask the next question. "My husband and my sons? Are they still alive? Are they here?"

"They are all alive and well, at least they were when our mission began a few months ago. We have been out of communication range with the rest of humanity for quite some time. But I can assure you that all three of them were alive and healthy when I graduated from the Military Academy with Yuri," Lincoln told her with sympathy in her voice. "Piotr grew into a very handsome young man and had lots of ladies after him."

Melita laughed as she wiped the tear from her face, "He must look like his father. And Yuri? Is he married? How is he?"

"Well, I have to say that it is the greatest honor to know that I was a part of finding you." Anderson spoke up. "Yuri is like a hero to some of us. Mary, Eamon and I were with your son on a place called the Blood Moon. We were ambushed by some very bad people. Your son led us and we fought them. I am alive today because Yuri is the man that he is. I feel like I owe him my life."

"As do I," O'Grady added.

"Yuri is a Second Lieutenant in the Military Intelligence section of the Space Command. He is serving on a Battle Cruiser back in the Eight Solar Systems. He is not married, at least he wasn't when I last saw him," Lincoln informed her.

"And Nikolai? Where is he? Did he find another woman when he thought I was dead?"

Lincoln smiled and shook her head side to side, "Nikolai never tried to meet another woman. I overheard him once tell one of his closest friends that no woman would ever be able to compete with your memory. He really loved you. He still does."

Melita sighed and sipped from the coffee cup some more, "How far away are we from my boys and Nikolai?"

"A few months' flight," Anderson answered her.

"I need to get to them. In my sleep, I saw a brilliant explosion. It was like a fire in space. Not a supernova, but like a massive eruption of energy like I have never seen before. In my dreams, it was the signal of the beginning of an all-out war. We must go back to civilization and warn the people. I must find my sons and warn them. I have to find Nikolai. Please, can you help me get to them?"

"Lieutenant, we are in the middle of a very important mission and we cannot turn around. I think that you are going to be stuck with us for several months until we find the Bismark. I am very sorry that we cannot help you," Jeongjo told her softly.

"Doctor, what if we let Lieutenant Gorski and her Marines take this Medical Raumschiff and fly back to planet New Edinburgh?" Blair snapped her fingers as she spoke. "We have five Battle Cruisers, over one hundred Raumschiffs and thousands of Allen fighters. We could spare this one ship to get these ten home. I am sure that the other nine have loved ones that will want to see them."

Jeongjo leaned back in her chair and thought for a moment, "That would be up to the officers in command. Let me consult Major Idris and I will get back to you.

Idris took in the information regarding the discovery of the survivors that were recovered. She listened to the idea from Blair and decided to consult with Captain Yuschenko. As was his normal pattern, Yuschenko waved at the camera in his quarters and told Idris to use her best judgment and leave him alone. Idris decided that the humane thing to do was to give the ship to the ten people so that they could return home.

Idris directed Ginger Collins to connect a direct line of communication with the Medical Raumschiff and informed them that they were to give the space craft to Lieutenant Gorski and her men so that they could return to humanity. Idris requested of the pilots that were on the Medical Raumschiff if any of them would volunteer to pilot the ship for the Marines.

Lincoln quickly volunteered to do so. She owed Yuri so much. His actions on the Blood Moon had been decisive and saved several lives. If anyone present should be the one to return his long-lost mother to him, Lincoln felt that she was the one that should do it. Idris thanked her for volunteering and asked for one of the nurses to volunteer to go, just in case one of the Marines suffered from some unforeseen medical condition due to the lengthy cryo-sleep. When the communication with Idris ended, Lincoln began to say her farewells to O'Grady, Anderson, Blair, Iavarone and Mozgov. Although Lincoln regretted that she would not be able to complete the mission to find the *Bismark*, she was elated that she had been a part of finding the mother of the man she loved alive and well.

# CHAPTER TWO

The Glorious Leader had sent in enough soldiers, human slaves, alien slaves and weaponry to bring all of the population of Clovis City, planet New Edinburgh to its' knees.  First the moon base was overrun and the long-time commander and her family were forced into air locks and released into space without a space suit. Then they invaded the planet surface and began a campaign of barbaric proportions. Decent and good men and women were slaughtered. Well respected servants of the public were shot dead; some were ripped to pieces. Marine Corps Colonel Nikolai Gorski was arrested and Major Sigebert Evart was murdered. Most of the incarcerated vile criminals were released from prison.

The lawyer that had led the prosecutions of those criminals had been targeted for execution. Sean Collins, his two sons and a trained assassin named Mary Sierra destroyed a Raumschiff full of soldiers that had been sent to kill them.  They fought off a superior number of soldiers and in the aftermath of the battle Collins directed Sierra to take his sons and his daughters away to a safe place.

The subdivision had been damaged during the melee. While the medical staff arrived to assist the injured, Collins had one last duty to perform. For two centuries, his family had been the guardians of twenty cryo-sleep tubes from the planet formerly known as Akarzdamedia. In eighteen of those large metallic and glass tubes slept Queen Danu of the Akarzdamedians and seventeen of her closest family members. The last two tubes had the humans named Diarmuid and Keira Brey that history had recorded died during the war against Akarzdamedians. But they had not perished as all school children were taught by the state-run education system. They lived and rescued the Queen of the alien enemy.

Collins' home had two underground levels. The lowest level was a vast wine cellar that he would occasionally partake on an older bottle of spirits to entertain guests or to wind down after completing a long week before a judge or jury on a difficult case. The level above the wine cellar had been off limits to everyone, even his own children, due to what was inside. It was sealed off by thick metal doors and only he could gain access to the chamber hidden behind the steel casings. Inside the chamber was a room that was long in width and had a ceiling of just under twenty feet high. There were numerous desks built into the metal walls that had several computers, refrigeration and freezer units for food storage, three weapons lockers with laser rifles, laser pistols, scatter shot laser pump rifles, knives, flame throwers, thermite grenades, spears, throwing stars, swords and other military paraphernalia from history. The ceiling had numerous cooling tubes made of metals that were glowing a bright silver color and were known to be found only on Akarzdamedia.

Collins wore a bloodstained dark set of sweats and tennis shoes when he entered the chamber. There were twenty beings resting in ten-foot-long cryo-sleep tubes. Two were humans from two centuries past. They had been born and raised in Ireland and took part in the invasion of planet Akarzdamedia alongside Vladimir Sikorsky and the other conquerors of that alien race. They were Diarmuid and Keira Brey. History had recorded that they both died soon after the war against the Akarzdamedians ended. But they cheated history and Sikorsky by devising a clandestine scheme to help the Queen of the aliens and many of her family to escape certain death. They stowed them all away on their space craft and hid them from the human occupation until it was safe to transport them off the planet. The Brey family had been their guardians ever since, passing the responsibility of watching over the Queen from generation to generation.

Collins had been appointed to be their caretaker pending the time to revive them arrived or when he passed the torch of responsibility to one of his children. He had waited for many years for a sign that the Queen of Akarzdamedia should be revealed to the world. Her people had called her the Queen of Hearts due to her charity and even handed treatment. Collins had met many from her home world and all spoke of her with reverence and love.

Collins had been watching the current events in the world. The Sikorsky family, also known as the Royal Family, had committed planetacide against the Chronosians, which was the term to describe the humans that had settled the lunar body called Chronos. Eight hundred thousand men, women and children were murdered by one weapon of mass destruction. Other worlds followed suit and began to rebel against the tyrannical rule of the Sikorsky's. And now, Sikorsky had responded with an iron hand and declared that he would massacre billions to maintain his power.

The time had finally come to bring the Queen of Hearts back to her people.

Collins ordered his underground computer system to revive the twenty sleeping beings inside the tubes. The lawyer sealed the doors behind him just in case more of the MI soldiers were sent to finish what the first group had failed to do. He walked to the corner of the chamber, rubbing his palms together nervously. He had no clue what to expect when the leader of the alien race woke up. Humanity had dropped nuclear warheads on her planet and vaporized millions of her people. Her husband had been publicly executed by Huang Tan on the steps of the Akarzdamedian capital building.

Collins watched as the glass coverings on the top of the tubes began to slide open. There was a hissing noise like the sound of steam releasing. The smell was something that Collins had never experienced in his life. He covered his face as the grey smoke rose to the ceiling. He could hear his computer system warning that the aliens were waking. Collins boldly walked through the smoke and stood over the tube that contained Queen Danu. He was naturally curious and had a million questions to ask her. He stood silently and looked down at her.

He took in a deep breath when her eyes began to flutter.

Collins took several steps backwards when Queen Danu suddenly rose upward. Her entire body shot straight up, her arms were crossed across her chest. Her eyes were still closed as she was on her feet, standing on the cryo-sleep tube that held her in a suspended state for two hundred years. Her skin was black. She was about eight feet tall, slim and had a head like the Anubis of ancient Egypt. She wore a one-piece green and yellow robe that was wrapped around her body. Collins held his breath in anticipation. He smiled as her eyes slowly fluttered open. Danu looked down at Collins with yellow eyes that seemed to glow.

She moved her head from side to side as she inspected the room and noticed the other nineteen tubes around her. She slowly looked over at Collins and her eyes locked with his.

"I have slept long," Danu spoke the first words she could muster. "I am the Queen of the Akarzdamedians. You are a man from Earth. What are you called?"

"Sean Collins."

"Sean Collins of Earth." She looked over at the two humans in their tubes and she pointed in their direction. "You are of their seed?"

"So I have been told, Queen Danu."

"You are the one that woke me from my sleep?"

"Yes."

"Has the fire in the sky occurred?"

Collins frowned at that question, "I don't know what you mean. A fire in the sky?"

"Then it has not happened yet," Danu said as she stepped down from her tube and onto the floor. She stood in front of Collins and gazed into his eyes. Collins felt as though she were looking into his very soul. "I see the heart of a man of honor before me. You have suffered because of the Sikorsky regime as I and my people have. How many years have passed since I was placed in the sleeping tube?"

"Two hundred years."

Danu began walking around the room, inspecting the tubes of the other seventeen sleeping Akarzdamedians. "They murdered my husband. I am certain that the Council of Nine were also annihilated. But you knew that already, do you not? They dropped weapons of terrifying power on my people. I begged for a truce. We could not understand the reason for the attack as we went to Earth as a peaceful people. It was not the first time we were treated so by humans."

"You visited Earth before then?" Collins now had the chance to ask his questions.

"Yes we did. The early humans considered us as Gods and built statues in our honor, carved our likenesses into stone. The Pharaohs worshiped us. We had rivers and nations named after us. Many of your ancient tales or mythology were based on our ancestors. Manannan Mac Lir, Cuchulain, Donar, Wotan, Tyr, Freya, Balder, Sif, Zues, Hera, Athena, Pluto and other names were from our people. We were written about in your Bible, first as angels that took human females as mates and later when the one named Joshua attacked us and killed an entire settlement of our people. We had visited your planet in the hopes that we could develop an understanding between us. We came for peace but instead we found death."

"I am sorry," Collins felt ashamed of his humanity at that moment.

"It was not of your doing, Sean Collins, so you have no reason to feel guilt. My only question of you is whether the people of Earth are ready to live in peace with us?"

"Most of us are ready," Collins said. "There are others that are only concerned with their own power. They are fighting us now. Your people need you to lead them in the fighting that will soon be upon us."

Danu stopped in front of the tubes of Keira and Diarmuid Brey and looked down at them. She touched the tubes with her long fingers and ran them across the glass. "These two sacrificed everything to save me. They demonstrated that there is hope that our people can co-exist and work together for the common good. While I slept I often dreamed. My ancestors came to me and showed me the fire in the sky. They showed me your Queen who will stand by my side in battle. I am called back to join with your Queen to bring back peace to both our peoples."

Collins shook his head slowly with confusion at her comment, "We have no Queen."

"Yes, you do. She is on this world and I have seen her face in my dreams. She will lead your people against the evil that is here. I must join her."

"I am sorry, but I know of no such person."

Danu watched as two other Akarzdamedians were jolted upright and stood over their cryo-sleep tubes. She smiled as they slowly opened their eyes. The aliens began to converse in their native tongue and Collins was not able to understand their conversation. By their body language, he deduced that Danu was their leader. Each of the Akarzdamedians would bow to her and stood behind her.

Danu looked back at Collins, "If you have no Queen then all will be lost. I have seen her in her black regal clothing, her dark hair flowing as she rides her chariot into battle. She will lead thousands. She is here. She must be here."

Collins looked on in awe as other Akarzdamedians were waking from their slumber. He listened as the Queen was speaking in words that made sense in her native language but did not translate well to English. She kept going on and on about the human queen and Collins patiently related that there was no such person. Perhaps there was such a person that she eluded to but the idea of a queen or a warrior queen might be different between the cultures. Collins was also not a believer in the occult or other superstitions and the statements by Queen Danu regarding the future were difficult for him to accept.

"You do not believe me, Sean Collins?" Danu asked as if reading his mind.

"No, it is not that I do not believe. It is just that we have no queens or kings. Those titles were abolished in our culture centuries ago. If there is a warrior out there, she must be going by another title. I am sorry that I cannot pinpoint her for you."

"You seem to doubt that which you cannot see," Danu observed of the man. "Humans seem to have that in common. I once told the Brey's of the existence of the Layers of Realities and they did not believe me."

"What are you referring to?"

Danu held out her hand and many bright colors began to appear and were creating several circular patterns. She smiled as the colors slowly grew in size and became a scaled down version of her home world's binary sun system. The eight planets were orbiting the large sun and the much smaller one next to it.

"You see before you the planetary system of Akarzdamedia," Danu explained. "This is the system as it exists in this Layer of Reality. There are countless other realities hidden in the unseen layers. You might call them planes of existence or alternative realities. In many, I never was born. In others, I am not the Queen of my people. In others, your Vladimir Sikorsky never lived and never invaded my planet.

"There are numerous versions of you, Sean Collins. Many never pursued the same career that you did. Some married different women and had children that you will never have. In between the Layers of Realities are the buffer zones where the Astral Angels live. They watch over us and guard against any that attempt to breach the buffers and cross over to another

Layer. The Angels are all knowing and they are resolute in their pursuit for order in the multiple Layers. They rarely intervene in any one Layer. But they have injected themselves into our Layer due to the barbaric past of humanity. You see, the Angels are both concerned and hopeful that we can right the ship in this level of reality. They believe that the family members of Vladimir Sikorsky will attempt to cross over to another Layer and begin to subjugate those species."

"Are you saying that these... Angels...are watching us to see how this all turns out?" Collins was not convinced as he had never seen any proof of such concepts. He had heard stories of astronauts that had been on long voyages into deep space that claimed to see glowing beings or apparitions that they could not explain. Some of the astronauts would relate that these life forms would speak to them and ask them to do things. Collins had never seen these Angels and therefore he did not buy into their existence. He lived a life of proving things to judges and juries. Since he saw no evidence to support their existence, Collins could not conclude that they did indeed live.

Danu smiled at Collins for a moment and saw that many of her people were waking from their sleep. "Sean Collins, the Angels do exist. I will give you an example from your history. There was a man, similar to Sikorsky, that brought your planet to war. There was a nation on your planet that was called the

United States. The warriors of that nation were on the brink of entering the capital city of the evil leader. They had to cross a bridge into a city that I recall was called Remagen. The bridge was ready to collapse at any moment. The warriors of the United States sent their best engineers to try and support the bridge as their tanks and troops crossed to enter the city and hopefully end the war. After the last warrior and vehicle crossed, the bridge collapsed. You see, Sean Collins, the Astral Angels were there, holding the bridge upright so that the warriors of good could end the reign of evil."

"And they are going to help us in this war?" Collins was skeptical of her version of the history of Earth.

"The truth is, Sean Collins, they already have. In my dreams, I have seen that the Angels allowed some humans to enter the buffer zones between the Layers of Existence. The Angels have selected many humans that have hearts of honor and revealed themselves to them. Many of those selected humans have made a difference already. Some will do so in the future. Do not doubt what you cannot see. There are powers greater than ourselves. You are a good man, Sean Collins. You raised you children to be good. There are many others such as you that strive to do the good and noble thing when the time comes."

Collins watched as the Queen turned away from his so that she could greet her waking family members. Collins pondered her words and hoped that the Queen had not slipped into some form of mental health problem in her long slumber and become psychotic. Either she was wise and well informed or she was hallucinating and hearing voices.

Danu and some of the Akarzdamedians were embracing and speaking their native language together. Collins felt left out as one by one they seemingly expressed joy at being reunited with each other. Collins walked over to the tubes with the two humans and watched them. To his shock, the man named Diarmuid Brey began to arch his back as if in pain. A sound of agony was coming from deep in his throat and his eyes began to flutter. Collins realized the man was fighting for oxygen.

"I need help!" Collins cried out as he pulled the heavy man from the cryo-sleep tube. Collins was quickly assisted by two male Akarzdamedians as they laid Brey on the blue metal floor.

One of the aliens inspected the man and looked at the Queen. "His physiology could not take the two centuries of cryogenic sleep. He has suffered a stroke. He is dying."

"We need to do something!" Collins had wondered what he would learn from the Brey couple on the day he revived them. They could not just die like this. There was too much knowledge in their heads about the past and especially regarding their interactions with Vladimir Sikorsky. They could tell the world the historical truth so that the Sikorsky propaganda machine would be put on the defensive.

"Humans do not have our life span, Sean Collins." Danu put a hand on his shoulder. "You are not as able to withstand some of the realities of space travel. Our kind can sleep for thousands of your years. Only one that is in spectacular health may attempt such a feat and even that person would only have an eighty percent chance of surviving when revived. I am sorry for this. Diarmuid Brey was warned by us that he was not physically fit enough to attempt what we refer to as The Long Slumber. He elected to try so that he could be with his wife."

Collins watched as the elderly Brey died on the floor. His heart had ruptured due to the strain of the revival process from the cryogenic sleep. Collins looked over at the tube that contained Keira Brey and feared that she would suffer the same fate. She was much younger than her husband and had a slender build as she had been a marathon runner when she was on Earth. Collins prayed that she would survive the process. He could see that her eyes were fluttering.

"Will she make it?" Collins wondered out loud.

"She has a better chance due to her physique and her youthful appearance," Danu told him. "I believe she will survive the process of revival. Do not despair, Protector Sean Collins. Diarmuid Brey is with the Astral Angels now. He will suffer no more."

Collins pulled out a blanket from one of his closets and covered the body. He had hoped to spend time with the Brey's to learn about what happened two hundred years ago when they had betrayed Sikorsky. Collins wanted to know why they made the choices that led them to this moment. What had Sikorsky done that led them to become the protectors of Danu? Now the reasons of one of the two would probably never be known. If the other survived she would have a grand tale to tell.

Danu continued to usher in her family members as one by one they rose from their tubes. All eighteen survived the two-century slumber and were stretching their long arms, some doing jumping jacks to get their blood flowing. They were communicating in their ancient tongue, a language that Collins did not understand. The word he heard most when they referred to him was "Prazhoriuos" which Collins would later learn meant protector.

Collins watched as Keira Brey slowly opened her eyes. She tried to say something but no sound came from her voice. She looked over the features of the man standing over her with an inquisitive expression on her face. She realized that she had been brought out of her long sleep. She smiled at Collins. She moved her right hand and pointed to her throat in hopes that the man would realize that she was thirsty. Collins nodded that he understood her non-verbal request and he walked over to one of his large refrigeration units to retrieve a sixteen-ounce glass bottle of filtered water. He quickly opened the cap and handed it to Brey. She smiled and slowly sat up to take a drink. The cool water felt wonderful as it entered her mouth and she let it slide down her throat. She drank it slowly as she had recalled warnings that many humans that went through cryo-sleep would wake up vomiting or suffer nausea.

Danu and two of her male Akarzdamedians were now standing next to Brey.

"You are alive. We are elated," Danu said without any detectible emotion in her voice. "The day has finally come, Keira Brey, to rise up against the mass murderer Sikorsky. We must find sustenance and then begin our part in this war."

Collins looked over the eighteen aliens that were standing before him. "Well, I know a good restaurant."

Danu frowned, "What is a restaurant?"

"Trust me. You all will love it," Collins told them.

Danu did not seem to understand the term. She walked around the chamber and finally stopped next to Keira Brey and helped her out of her cryogenic tube. Danu placed her hand on Brey's forehead and began channeling some of her energy into her. Brey stiffened as she felt a strange increase in body energy flow through her. It was as if she had electricity flowing through her veins. Her eyes were wide with a wild look in them as Danu smiled down at her. Brey's red hair began to rise and soon she was floating a foot off the ground. "What are you doing to her?" Collins was alarmed as he watched the scene.

"She is giving her energy, Prazhoriuos," a female Akarzdamedian answered for the Queen. "Do not disturb her. She must concentrate to transfer energy sufficient to help Keira Brey to match our levels. Danger is all around us and we all must be prepared to relocate and defend ourselves from the evil ones."

Collins remained quiet as he waited for Danu to complete the act. Brey slowly lowered back onto her feet. The color was back in her cheeks. She smiled at the Akarzdamedians and Collins.

"I feel much better," Brey said. She was surprised that she could suddenly speak. "Where is my husband?"

There was silence in the room. Collins assumed that the Akarzdamedians did not know how to express condolences for the loss of a loved one. He decided to speak up. "I am very sorry, but your husband did not survive the process of Reawakening. We are all deeply sorry for your loss."

Brey looked at Collins, her bottom lip was quivering. "Where is he?"

"Over here," Collins took her by the arm and led her to where Diarmuid's corpse was located. He knelt and slowly removed the blanket that was covering the man.

Keira Brey kneeled over him and touched his face with both of her hands. Her tears of grief were dripping down on his forehead. "I pushed him into this. He wanted to save all of you and then return to our home in Ireland to live out our lives. He wanted to help our children with their children. I insisted that we enter the cryo-sleep with you. I caused his death." She fell on his chest and began crying hysterically. "My dear sweet husband. I am so sorry I did this to you."

Collins, Danu and the others watched in silence as Brey grieved over her loss.

After several minutes, Brey stood up and pulled the blanket back over the face of her lost husband. She faced the others and wiped the tears from her cheeks. Her eyes settled Collins. "You woke us up? Have things gotten worse? Why did you decided to wake us now?"

Collins nodded, "A war has started. It is two centuries since you went into cryo-sleep. Vladimir Sikorsky has now lived for two hundred forty-one years and he has led the expansion of human dominion to eight solar systems. What he did to the Akarzdamedians he did to the predominant species that were on nine different earth-like planets. There are other planets and moons that we, I should say that humans, have colonized through the stolen technology from your people." Collins motioned to Danu when he spoke his last sentence.

"You said a war?" Brey prompted him to continue.

"Yes, there is a war. Some of our citizens have finally woke up and come to the realization that Sikorsky and his family must be ousted from power. As we speak, there are many rebellions on many different planets. The ones that have not stood up are experiencing military style crack downs of epic proportions. The Sikorsky's have sent in elite soldiers and alien slaves here on this planet and are killing any that they perceive as disloyal."

"What planet is this?" Brey asked as she sat down on one of the metal chairs as she was feeling dizzy from her long sleep. Her legs were aching from the short time she had been standing, her head was pounding and she had a low ringing noise in her ears.

"This is planet New Edinburgh. While you were in cryo-sleep, Sikorsky has moved the central government of humanity from Earth to Akarzdamedia. He controls everything from there. His children, grandchildren and great grandchildren are the ones that hold most of the powerful positions in the government and military. Due to current events, there are many of those people called commoners and the Sikorsky's refer to as sheeple that have determined it is far past the time for a change in leadership. The people are ready to fight back." Collins walked around the room as he spoke. "Several of the military leaders already have begun a civil war against the Sikorsky's. There have been many casualties. Sikorsky also has a terrifying weapon of mass destruction. He used the weapon on a moon that had a human population of over eight hundred thousand men, women and children. Everyone died. Sikorsky must be stopped."

Brey nodded and looked up at Danu, "My husband and I believed in peace. We also concluded, quite correctly, that Sikorsky was not interested in peaceful co-existence. If what this man is saying is accurate, then the people of both our worlds need to hear from us. They need to know that there are others that desire a change as they do. The question is how do we do it? How do we communicate to what has grown to populations on many different planets and moons?"

"We use the government controlled news media," Collins told them.

"And why would the news media government employees of Vladimir Sikorsky help us?" Danu wanted to know.

"They won't help us," Collins said. "We have to take their facilities by force. Once we do that we can broadcast your message to all the corners of the eight solar systems. All the humans, Akarzdamedians and other species will hear our words and they will all make their own decisions. I believe that the vast majority of them will decide to fight."

"And there are such facilities on this planet that we can take?" Brey leaned her head back in hopes that it would relieve her of the discomfort from her throbbing head.

"There are many of them," Collins walked over to one of the refrigeration units and found a bottled water for Brey. He opened a drawer near the unit and found some aspirin. He approached Brey and handed them to her.

She smiled with a look of relief as she opened the aspirin bottle. "Then what are we waiting on?"

Collins pointed in the direction of the weapons lockers, "First we arm ourselves. Then we borrow or steal a space craft. Once we take those steps, we go to the area that has the largest news reporting building on the planet."

"And where would that be?" Brey asked as she swallowed four aspirin and took several gulps of water.

"Lynott's Land. I know some powerful people there that might be willing to help us out." Collins said with a bit of dread in his voice. "It will be very dangerous as General Leta Tan runs everything there. She is a tyrant. If she suspects our true intentions she might kill us all. Even my friends would not be able to protect us from her if she gets it in her head that we are some sort of a threat. We have to be careful and keep a low profile."

Brey laughed, "And here I thought you were waking us up for chat over some pretzels, shepherd pie and draught beer. Let's get on with it then."

# CHAPTER THREE

Jorge Calderon had trouble sleeping. He had tossed and turned the entire night in his guest suite in the eastern mansion located on the property owned by Patrick Doyle Lynott. He asked the computer timer in the room for the time. It was five thirty-two in the morning. The fifteen-year-old stared at the ceiling of his room and missed his bed at his home in Clovis City. He missed his mother, father and abuelita. He missed his pets and the brothers, sisters and cousins that did not make the journey that led to a crash landing in the Forbidden Region and finally to the current location he and five of his brothers found themselves in. His brothers and other shipmates of the Raumschiff named *Clovis 21* survived attacks from sand spiders, Dozals and Verburgt. They lost three ship members in the attacks.

He finally sat up in the bed and stared at the window. He wondered how his sisters were doing. He stood up on his feet and found a pair of beige pajamas in one of the desk drawers and slipped them on. He slid on some black slippers and decided that he wanted breakfast. He walked to his door and asked the mansion central computer to open it. The door slid open and young Jorge walked out into the wide hallway that led to his right many suites and to his left a long, winding staircase that would take him to the lower floors and the kitchens and dining rooms below.

The mansion was dark and there was silence all around him. He walked as quietly as he could down the stairs. He saw a few domestic cats on the stairs and they stared at him as he passed by them. He made it to the ground floor and noticed that all evidence of the night long party had been cleaned up. The dirty plates, glasses, steins, banquet tables, chairs and carving stations were all gone. The wooden and tiled floors were all cleaned. It was as if there had not been over one hundred individuals dining and drinking excessively in the vast area a few hours earlier.

He noticed that the several fire places were still lit and the flames were about a foot high in each. He was about to conclude that he was all alone when he heard some voices in the kitchen. He walked toward the dark red double sliding doors that led to the large area where the food had been prepared the previous evening. He paused at the doors and listened to the conversation on the other side. He did not recognize the voices.

"So now that we have one of the cadets married into the family, we need to start pressuring the others. I want to have more of the girls brought over to spend time with the three single Calderon boys." It was a male voice with a deep baritone sound.

"You mean Juanito, Xavier and Jose?" A female voice responded.

"I like Gauthier. He looks like a movie star." Another female voice stated.

Jorge began to back away from the doorway when a third female voice echoed in his ears. "Wait. Someone is outside spying on us."

The red doors slid open and Jorge froze in place. He tried to move his feet to run, but felt as if some invisible force was prohibiting him from moving. The first person to approach him was a woman with milky white skin, dark hair and eyes that were glowing as if they were on fire. It was a Child of Athena, one of the Harcourt's, which explained why Jorge could not move. She was using her mind control powers to hold him in place. Two attractive women that Jorge had seen at the side of Jason Ward and Patrick Boyle Lynott walked toward him next. The fourth person to exit the kitchen area and confront him was the Lynott patriarch himself.

"How much did he hear?" Saia Lynott demanded.

The woman with the glowing red eyes was not walking, she was hovering around the frozen Calderon boy. It was as if she were a witch from the old scary bed time stories that Jorge heard from his mother when he was much younger. Her arms were outstretched and her long dark hair seemed to be moving upward as if she were touching an electrical source. She shook her head as she slowly descended to the tiled floor and faced him. She was only a foot away from Jorge and was floating around him. He could see that her eyes were all red, there was no white, no pupils or other colors. Jorge could feel his mind being probed by some unseen force. His inner most thoughts were being read like an open book and he could not stop the intrusion as much as he tried.

"He heard nothing important," the levitating woman said to the others.

"Then release him, Zauriba," Patrick Doyle Lynott commanded her.

Jorge fell to his knees when the white Harcourt woman named Zauriba withdrew her mind control over him. He placed his hands on the floor and looked up at the man and the three women. "I wasn't doing anything wrong. I just came downstairs to find something to eat."

Lesa Lynott knelt next to him and helped him to his feet. "It is okay. Jorge, right?"

"Yes ma'am," he responded as he stood to up on his feet. His knees were still shaking from the feeling of losing all control due to the Harcourt woman using her powers on him. He felt as if he wanted to vomit.

"Are you hungry, Jorge? We have plenty of food in the kitchen," Lesa offered.

"Yes, ma'am. I couldn't sleep. I really would like something to eat." He was terrified being surrounded by the four adults, especially the Harcourt with the blazing eyes. He felt as if she could see through his very soul.

Patrick Doyle Lynott put his arms around Jorge's shoulders to comfort him. "Saia, take the young lad and fix him something to eat. Remember what I said when your first arrived, son. My home is your home. Do not be afraid. Zauriba is my daughter from my wife that I met on planet Athena. Zauriba is a fourth-generation Harcourt. Her powers are much more enhanced than those of the others of her kind. Do not be alarmed by her. She only wanted to protect her foolish old father."

"I understand, sir. I would have done the same for my mother." Jorge said as Saia took his hand and led him toward the kitchen. The truth was he was ready to leave with anyone if it meant that he did not have to be in the same room with the woman with blazing red eyes. "Thank you for the hospitality, sir."

"Carry on, lad." Lynott waited for Saia to take the teenage boy to the kitchen and seal the door shut behind her. He led Zauriba and Lesa to the far end of the large banquet room and found a table in the western corner, near a fire place. He sat down and watched as Zauriba used her telekinesis powers to cause a chair to pull out from the table so she could sit down.

"You want me to obliterate him, father?" Zauriba asked, looking back at the closed kitchen doors.

Lynott glared angrily at his daughter. He had witnessed her kill a man once before. It had been one of the most horrifying things he had ever seen. She had caused the victim to explode from the inside out simply by using her mental powers. "No, I do not. You read his mind?"

"Yes, father."

"And he heard nothing of our plans?"

"Nothing."

"Then let it be. He is an innocent kid. He is harmless. Besides, his brothers would be all over us if he were to disappear. We do not need that kind of scrutiny right now."

Zauriba used her mind to cause a large carafe of red wine to float across the room along with several crystal drinking glasses. The items settled on the table top in front of her half-sister and grandfather. Lesa Lynott always found Zauriba's use of her telekinesis power unsettling.

"He is not harmless," Zauriba told them as the wine was landing on the table. "When I was in his mind I learned all about him. For a young teen, he is quite brave. He fought off several Dozal all by himself, using only a piece of six-foot-long metal that had been sharpened into a spear. He did it to help his brothers while they were all fighting for their lives."

"Why does that make him potentially harmful?" Lesa wanted to know.

Zauriba looked upon her with her solid red colored eyes, "He is a danger because of his loyalty to his brothers. If I do as you want, dear grandfather, and take the minds of Xavier, Jose and Juanito, manipulate them to follow you, that boy that is eating some hard boiled Cawler eggs as we speak could be a problem. If he learns that we are using his family, he will fight for his brothers. He is not afraid like others his age might be."

"So then we can do the same mental, how did you phrase it, mental reprogramming? We do it too little Jorge, too." Lesa waived her hand in a dismissive manner as she accepted a full glass of red wine from her grandfather. "Or we can bribe the kid with some of our other sisters like we did Cobb. I saw the way he was staring at my chest. He would love to have a woman in his bed, just like any other man."

"He is only fifteen," Zauriba told them. "We would have to get some of our teenage half-sisters to service him. Frankly, that might prove to be difficult since most of them turned out to be homely looking. I was in his head and I saw what he likes. He has a crush on one of the cadets that was on the ship he arrived in, the one named Nikki. He likes the blonde girls and yes, Lesa, he likes a nice rack as well. Do we have any cousins or half-sisters that are fourteen to eighteen that might fit that description that do not have unfortunate facial features?"

"All of my children and grandchildren are lovely, Zauriba." Lynott growled.

"Yes, father. Yes. All parents think that of their offspring." Zauriba sighed and drank from one of the glasses. "I told you years ago that over half of them should have been thrown into the ocean as the garbage that they are so that the Britva could have a taste of human flesh. They are not pretty enough to use to get men of power to join you, father. All they do is take up space in the other mansions and breathe precious air that the rest of us need."

"You are speaking of your own sisters! How dare you!" Lynott was getting angry at Zauriba's attitude toward her siblings. It was not the first time that she was so blunt in her opinion regarding the other siblings and grandchildren.

Zauriba knew that she could kill Lynott with just one thought. She could cause his brain to implode, or tear his heart in half. But he had always been decent to her and never treated her as different as others in the family had done.

"Please do not misunderstand my words, father. I say them not to insult but to prove a point. Your daughters are all pretty much married off. The ones that stayed here in the mansions with their husbands produced some lovely girls. However, the majority were not so lovely. Saia and Lesa are very attractive. Last night you gave away the five prettiest of my half-sisters to Jason Ward as wives. Then you married off three more of our best bargaining chips to that slob named James Cobb. You are slipping, father. Those three should have been used for politicians in power or captains of industry. I can understand giving some of them to Mister Ward as he may obtain power again. But to a mere cadet pilot? Why?"

"Because those cadets will prove useful. Cobb is now loyal to the family thanks to your half-sisters doing their duty and marrying him. Plus, Cobb comes from one of the largest families on the planet. That means votes at the ballot box during election season. Would you have married him had I decreed it, Zauriba? If I had directed you to marry Cobb, would you have dared to defy me?"

Zauriba's eyes looked as if they were ready to burn holes into Lynott. She was silent for a few moments as she considered her answer. "First, you would never waste me on a peon such as Cobb. You have always been saving Saia, Lesa and me for something special. Secondly, you know very well that I would always do my duty for this family. Now, back to the issue at hand, how do we keep the boy Jorge in line? His snooping around late at night is not a good thing."

Lesa snapped her fingers and pointed at the others, "Our cousin Numina, she looks like the Nikki girl. She is sixteen, I think. She is well endowed and she is not, as you say, homely looking. I will bring her from the main mansion and instruct her as to the arts of seduction. It is time for her to learn, anyway. Now, Zauriba, are you able to take control of the minds of the Calderon boys as you claim?"

Zauriba glared at her half-sister, "I am a fourth-generation Child of Athena. I could move an entire mountain with my mind and crush you to death with it without lifting a finger. How dare you question me?"

"Enough bickering!" The elder Lynott slammed his fist down onto the table. Lesa and Zauriba had an ongoing sibling rivalry that would show itself every now and then. Lynott detested being caught in the middle of their personal spats.

"Lesa, bring Numina over to lure the boy Jorge into her good graces. Zauriba, get into the heads of those other cadets and do as we agreed. Jason will be waking up soon and we need everything to be in order. The news from Clovis City has not gotten any better for our position. I need men and women that are willing to fight and die for us. Do it, Zauriba. Do it now."

"Yes, father."

Lynott stood and stormed away from the table in the direction of the kitchens.

"Just because you have all your awesome powers does not mean you will inherit all of this when he is finally gone. There are more Harcourt's out there that could be far more advanced than you. What will you do when one of them confronts you? You keep alienating the rest of us, you will fight alone." Lesa warned Zauriba.

"The secret here is simple, dear Lesa. I do not give a damn about you. I do not need you or Saia or any of the others. I am all powerful. I can make you jump into the swimming pool outside and drown yourself. But I keep you alive to amuse father. When he dies, your death will follow and you will not die easily. On that day, I will become the sole leader, owner and matriarch of Lynott's Land."

"I'm not feeling the love here, sister."

"That is because there is none."

James Cobb woke up expecting to find that the previous evening had been nothing more than a dream. He slowly opened his eyes and looked around the suite he was sleeping in at the Lynott Mansion East. He soon found that he had not dreamed at all. It had been real. Lying naked in the bed with him were the three Lynott granddaughters that he had been paid a handsome dowry to marry. He tried to contain himself and avoid waking the sleeping beauties by making some loud outburst.

He recalled that after being paid by the owner of Lynott's Land, Cobb married the three women and took them to bed. He had the wildest night of sex in his life. Having three women at once was more than just a fantasy, it had been a dream come true. Cobb maneuvered himself out of the bed, being careful not to wake his new brides. He wanted to find his friends Manuel Calderon, Gauthier and Varek to brag to them about his sexual exploits with the three women.

After slipping out of bed, Cobb slowly walked to the large bathroom, slid the door shut behind him and quickly brushed his teeth. After he finished he crept around the room, looking for his discarded clothing. He found his underwear handing over an antique lamp and his socks on opposite sides of the room from each other. It felt like forever to him, but he finally had on his clothing. He moved to the door and whispered to the room computer to open the doors. He stepped out into the hallway after the mansion computer system complied and opened the doors. They closed behind him.

Cobb noted that it was silent throughout the large castle like dwelling. He had thought that he would have been the last in the location to wake up. He was the only cadet that had the smarts to take Lynott up on his generous offer of marrying into the family. Three beautiful wives and a big paycheck on top of that was more than he had ever hoped for in life. He walked down the long hallway and found the room of Basil Varek. He knocked on the door.

The door slid open and Cobb was not surprised to see that Varek was not alone. In bed with his friend was Wanda Essex. The two cadets had grown closer over the short time they spent in the Forbidden Region rescuing others. Essex was asleep in Varek's arms. Varek put his index finger to his lips so that Cobb would know to be quiet. The door slid shut behind Cobb as Varek slowly moved himself away from Essex and sat up in the bed. He found his boxer shorts and pulled them on. There was a gold bathrobe on the floor that Varek threw over his shoulders. He motioned for Cobb to step out into the hallway so that their discussion would not wake Essex.

As the door closed, Cobb faced Varek in the hall. "Dude! It was so killer, man. Killer. Three women at once. Basil, you need to get Lynott to give you three of his girls, no, make it five or six! I think I am going to go ask him for a few more. Last night was the most amazing sexual experience of my life! Even better than when I did the corpse in the mortuary! Ditch the Essex woman. Do it Basil!"

"Well, James, I am happy that your wedding night and honeymoon went so well for you. But I am very happy with Wanda," Varek chose his words carefully due to his fear that the

Lynott's were spying on them. Ever since they arrived, Varek has felt uncomfortable and he was certain that Patrick Doyle Lynott was hiding something from them all. The lack of any Lynott sons or grandsons was troubling to Varek and the disappearance of Kia Marble only enhanced his suspicions.

"Basil, do not be a fool. Do you know how much money Lynott paid me to marry them?" Cobb was waving his hands around as he spoke. "Man, you know that I was ready to die out there with John and Tara. We were going to blow ourselves up, man. Go out in a pyre of glory, you know? We would have been immortalized in the history annals. I was ready to die, man. I decided that it would have been killer, man. But then I wake up here. It's like the Gods wanted me to be here, you know? Like I was meant to be here. And you too, Basil. You too. I was meant to marry those girls and I think that you were meant to be here, too. Man, Basil. You should take some of the Lynott girls and the money and then live like a king."

Each of the Bragg Gang members were accustomed to Cobb's rants. Varek ran his fingers through his hair as he decided that it was too early in the morning to listen to Cobb, much less debate him. In addition, Varek needed some coffee to wake up. The more that Cobb spoke, the more Varek's head pounded.

"James, I need some coffee and aspirin," Varek told his friend. "And I need some more sleep. Can we discuss this further over lunch?"

"Yeah, man. It's all groovy man. I will see you at lunch time. I am gonna take some naked pictures of my wives to show you and the guys. Man, there were tits and ass everywhere last night, all in my face man. I can't wait to tell my brothers when I get home. My father will be so proud of me when he sees that I married three hotties. Man, I am so stoked that I think I could have sex twenty-four seven, man. You know they say that Red Dust increases the sex drive. Maybe I should go buy some. What do you think, man? I'm gonna go talk to John and Manuel. They need to think about this, man. Really, you know? Basil? Basil?"

Cobb had been so busy speaking that he failed to notice that Varek had already returned to his room to go back to sleep with Essex. He looked up and down the hallway and realized that he was alone. "Okay, what room was John in?"

Manuel Calderon had missed out on most the previous night's festivities as well as the attack from the sand spiders.

He had gone to bed early with his new girlfriend, LaTania Serpas, while his friends and brothers drank and ate. At twenty-one years of age, Manuel had not considered settling down with a woman. He had been more focused on his studies and building motorcycles with his father and siblings. In fact, Serpas had been the only woman he had slept with more than once. All his previous sexual experiences were one night propositions. He slid out of the bed and made sure that he did not wake Serpas. He studied her lovely face, she seemed at peace while she was sound asleep. He covered her upper back with the sheets so that she would keep warm.

He located his gold bathrobe that was part of the vast treasure trove of clothing that the Lynott family had given to each cadet. He wrapped the sash around his waist and proceeded toward the door. He looked over his shoulder to make certain that Serpas was still asleep before departing the room and entering the long hallway. He checked the timer on his holographic-communication device It was six a.m. The large mansion was eerily quiet. He wondered if her were the only one awake.

As he descended the stairs, he checked his messages on the communication apparatus. There were several from his sister Reynita, one from Bret Bragg, and one from his father and three from his friend Derek Regehr. He commanded the mechanism to display the messages one at a time. Regehr informed him that they had been arrested and later escaped. The second one from Regehr was demanding to know where all the Calderon's had gone to. The third was a demand for a return call. All the messages from Reynita centered on her concern for him and her other five brothers. Manuel knew he had to go outside to a private location to call them both back due to his suspicions that they were being watched. His father's message echoed Reynita's concerns for his safety. Bragg's message was the longest. He went on and on about how the cadet dormitories had been surrounded by the MI soldiers and had been quarantined. He referred Manuel to some satellite chat rooms that had videos posted of female cadets being raped by the soldiers and some being killed.  Bragg ended the message by indicating that he was on his way to the hospital with one of the injured cadets.

Manuel stepped onto the first floor and saw that a Harcourt woman and one of the Lynott women were in the far corner near a fireplace, drinking wine and speaking in hushed tones. The Lynott woman, that Manuel recalled was named Lesa, stood up abruptly and stormed out of the room and outside to the swimming pool area. The Harcourt woman turned her head to Manuel and he immediately noticed that she was very different in her appearance than the other Harcourt's at the Academy. She had fiery eyes, all red, and dark hair that seemed to be filled with electrical energy.  Her skin was white as snow, just like the others, but the eyes and hair startled him. She smiled at Manuel.

"Good morning. My name is Zauriba Harcourt Mallory Poston Lynott. And you are Manuel Calderon, oldest brother of the clan that is sleeping in our mansion.  How do you like our hospitality, Manuel?"

He swallowed and approached the woman to shake her hand. "Well, everything is just wonderful. I am grateful to you and your family. Has anyone else gotten up, yet?"

Zauriba shook Manuel's hand even though she seemed a bit uncomfortable with the act. She began staring at the ceiling and seemed to be concentrating as if she could see through the walls. "Your youngest sibling, Jorge, is in the back kitchen eating pancakes and poggie bacon with my half-sister Saia. Your friend James Cobb is on the upper floor, waking people up. Nikki Blomquist and Nina Eklund are upstairs playing with some of the house cats with balls of yarn. Ah, Cobb just found the room where John Gauthier and Tara Haddad are sleeping. He just woke them up."

Manuel took in the words of the woman and deduced that she was reading minds. He had met Harcourt's in the past. There had been Jack who was a rival of the Bragg Gang. Melissa, Ann and Brandon had been the others. Each of them were students at the Academy, but none of them had solid red eyes and none of them had exhibited such a willingness to use their powers to spy one others. At least not in Manuel's presence. Melissa had developed quite the reputation as a vixen, using her skills of mind control to take things that she wanted.

The fire red eyes were new. None of the others had that physical appearance.

"You do not approve?" She asked Manuel.

"Approve of what?"

"Of my using my Athenian powers to read minds. I assure you it is not by choice; it is like instinct. Just like your ability to breathe air without thinking about it. My mind is so far advanced that I just do it. Right now, Cobb is telling Gauthier to leave the Haddad woman and marry into my family, not in those exact words mind you. But you get the point?"

Manuel could feel that she was reading his mind as well. He had wondered why there seemed to be little in the way of security measures in the Lynott mansions. Now he understood. The family had at least two Harcourt's that he had seen since arriving. Most likely there would be many more to keep the family safe by reading the minds of any visitors to the property.

"I don't judge others," Manuel finally told her truthfully. "Just as I hope no one else judges me."

"Very fair answer," she smiled and pointed at the north wall of the mansion, looking up at the ceiling as if she could see something that Manuel could not. "You should wake all of your friends and get them under into the basements. They are onto you. The satellites watched your ships land here. They are coming. They will be here soon. I can see their Raumschiffs leaving the MI Command Post and General Tan has been given orders to either arrest you or kill you all."

"How do you know this?"

"I heard the conversation between Tan and General Kimberly Sikorsky. Since then, I have been concentrating my powers on Tan since the moment you brought danger to my family by being here. Go and round up the others. My father will handle Tan. If her soldiers see any of you here, it will go very badly. You know how sadistic Tan can be."

Manuel swallowed and began to operate his communication device to contact Gauthier and Varek. She put her hand over his hand-held machine and shook her head. "No, sir. They are scanning us for any satellite communication attempts. If you use that device, they will know it. Get them all down here now. Wake them if you must, but get them below."

"Fine, we do it your way," Manuel walked quickly toward the stair case and placed his machine back into his belt attachment. "And thank you. I don't know how we will be able to repay you for your kind acts."

She was still smiling at him, her red eyes seemed to be changing to differing shades of color. "My father will certainly have demands to make later. Everything has its' price."

As Manuel ran up the stairs he recalled that his father would always tell them TANSTAFL which stood for the phrase: there ain't no such thing as a free lunch. Based on her assertions, the Lynott family expected something in return from the cadets. Manuel shuddered as to what that something might be.

Tara Haddad had a white bathrobe covering her as she tried to keep her temper under control. Her arms were crossed over her chest as she listened to Cobb go on and on about his sexual experience with his three new wives. She gave her boyfriend, John Gauthier, a look of disapproval. Gauthier shrugged at her to communicate that he could not do a thing to shut Cobb up. Mercifully, Manuel could be heard down the hall, banging on doors and yelling for everyone to wake up and get down to the basement. Cobb ceased his ranting and stepped out into the hallway to see what the excitement was about.

"And he had a crush on me?" Haddad whispered to Gauthier. "Unbelievable."

Gauthier laughed, "Babe, he once taped a long sausage link to his leg under a tight pair of orange leather pants because he thought he could get women if they were led to believe he was hung over ten inches. Clearly it was false advertising, but he did get a woman that night. We were at O'Malley's and she was a pilot from the Athenian system and into some wicked S and M. The next day, Cobb showed us burns where she put out her cigarettes on his back."

"And he is your friend?" Haddad looked for some shorts to throw on before Cobb returned. "You know why I never slept with him?"

"No, why?"

Haddad pulled a blue t-shirt over her head and straightened out her hair, "I heard that he had worked for the coroner and was caught screwing a dead woman. So when he started pursuing me, I turned him down. Was that rumor true? Did he screw a dead body?"

Gauthier nodded as he dressed, "Yes. He bragged about that one, too. James is my friend and my friend is into some freaky stuff."

"Glad I didn't let him bed me."

"Me too," Gauthier kissed her.

"Guys! We gotta go!" Manuel was now at their door, his voice sounded desperate and his face was expressing an urgency that Gauthier had only seen once before from Manuel and that was while they were trying to survive in the Forbidden Region. "General Tan was sent to arrest us all. There is a basement area where we will all be safe! Leave everything and get down stairs, now!"

Haddad took Gauthier's hand in hers, "And we thought the worst was over."

Gauthier looked out the window of their suite and noticed that there were some space craft from the north, heading in their direction. He could hear the approaching Raumschiffs. Tan was infamous to all the citizens of planet New Edinburgh. She hated men and reveled in killing them. As the ranking MI officer for the entire planet, she generally operated with impunity. Nobody crossed General Leta Tan and lived to tell about it. Gauthier had no desire to suffer her cruelty. "The worst is coming."

The Ward family had already assembled below as the cadets joined them. Patrick Lynott was there giving instructions that everyone was to remain in the basement area until he or one of his family came for them. Jessica Ward seemed content as she was cuddled in the arms of cadet Franco Vezpucci. Blomquist and Eklund had dragged Truang out of bed and were holding her upright, with her arms over their shoulders. Truang was still drunk from the previous evening and she was not able to stand up on her own. The Calderon brothers were arriving one by one, running down the stairs at full speed as the distant roar of the space craft engines were growing louder. Raklitz was present, with her eight inch by four-inch all-purpose scanner hidden under a dark sweater. She was concerned that Yung Tao's security was watching her every move.

Pepito was the last to descend the stairs, holding hands with Barbara Villandiego as she ran by his side. The couple were dressed in black shorts and blue t-shirts, compliments of the Lynott family.

"They are landing," Zauriba warned the group, never looking in their direction as she stared at the ceiling. Her face was contorted with concentration. "Tan is on board, but I am reading two General Tan's. I am confused. There are two of them. How can that be?"

"We'll worry about that later," Jason Ward responded. "Everyone, get down to the basement." He led the others to the back of the mansion and they found a portion of the tiled floor had slid open revealing a long staircase. Ward was the first to begin the long walk downward, followed closely by his daughter Klara. Varek and Wanda were the next two to step onto the basement stairwell. One by one and two by two, the Wards and the cadets rapidly ran downward as they each had one common fear.

Five solid black Super Raumschiffs landed on the private landing strip of the private Lynott family property. The two other space craft that the cadets had stolen were gone, thanks to the intrepid efforts of Yung Tao and his daughters. The Lynott family security had lowered both craft underground to avoid detection by Tan and her soldiers.

As the ships descended, each coded named *Sapho*, General Leta Tan was salivating at the news that there might be some men that were wanted for committing treason hiding out at the Lynott Mansions. She sat in the command section of *Sapho 1* and was looking at several scans of the property. She saw no evidence of the space craft that General Kimberly Sikorsky had ordered her to investigate.

The Battle Cruiser *Lysander* had tapped into the planetary satellite system and was monitoring the activity on the planet surface in addition to all holographic-communication transmissions. The ship detected the actions of Varek and the other cadets over the Forbidden Region and followed their activity for some time. When Varek landed the ships in the Lynott's Land territory, Tan was selected to investigate. She ordered that five of her *Sapho* Raumschiffs be sent in and visit the Lynott family, unannounced, so that the criminals, if any existed, would not have time to cover their tracks.

In each of the five ships were fifty of Tan's MI female army along with two pilots per ship. Although an army of two hundred fifty might be overkill to perform a simple arrest, she did not want to take any chances of losing the opportunity to take some men back to her military compound for an enjoyable session of torture and butchery.

Sitting next to Tan was her new weapon. It was a green skinned clone of the deceased super assassin Junior Ragnarsson. But he had a major alteration that had been performed by Tan's prisoner, Doctor Matthew Rosenburg. This clone had the entire memories and brain patterns of Tan as opposed to Ragnarsson. The clone knew everything that Tan knew and had her personality traits and shared all her values. It was her double except for the fact that it had a different body. The green skin pigmentation took some getting used to, but Tan was elated to have him along. She had named him Junior Ragnarsson Tan. The clone asked, no, he demanded, that he be referred to as J.R. He seemed to like that name above all others.

As the ships touched ground, Tan stood to her feet, grabbed hold of a laser rifle that was lying at her feet on the metal floor of the ship and barked orders for her female soldiers to surround the Lynott building.

"What would you like for me to do?" J.R. Tan asked.

"Search the mansions," she told the clone. "See if there is any sign of them. Kill all the female cadets that resist. Give them a chance to surrender first. Some of them might be quite lovely and I might fancy getting to know them much better. Stun the men. I want some new meat for the orgy tonight."

"I want to have some of the women," J.R. told her. "I am fully functional. I lust, Leta. I desire. Give me at least one."

Tan smiled at the clone. She had always wanted to have a man's sex organ, if only for one night, to see what it would be like to rape a woman. She wanted to experience that power, the feeling of complete sexual domination. Now she could do so in the cloned body that Matthew had fixed for her. Tan was glad she had kept Matthew alive as opposed to killing him as she had first wanted to do. He had been more than useful after she was given the fifty Ragnarsson clones that had been found in the belly of the *Blitzkrieg*. Now she had a double. Soon she would have forty-eight more just like J.R. and as Matthew had promised her, she would soon have her immortality.

The five ships landed in unison. The female soldiers in solid black uniforms were leaping from the rear exit ramps onto the ground, each with a laser rifle in her arms. They began to surround the mansions and waited for Tan to give them further instructions through their microchip receivers that were implanted in their ears.

Tan and J.R. walked down the exit ramp of their Raumschiff with confidence. In the distance, Tan could see that Patrick Lynott and several of his Tao security soldiers, daughters and granddaughters were around him.

Tan smiled at Lynott and he returned the gesture. They had known each other for more than a decade. Tan had supplied Lynott with several wives and Lynott had been generous enough to give her men to satisfy her sadistic urges. Lynott detested the settlers living on his land mass that failed to pay their debts to him. When it would become clear to Lynott that a man was about to default on a loan, he would have the man apprehended and sent to Tan for execution. In return, Tan would send over one of her enlisted ranked soldiers to marry Lynott or one of his sons. It was a good relationship. Each of them received benefits from the trades.

"Leta, you look quite well!" Lynott said as he greeted her. They hugged for a moment. "To what do we owe this visit?"

"I am here on business, Doyle." Tan said as J.R. Tan was catching several odd stares from the Lynott women and guards. The green skin certainly attracted attention from everyone. Tan knew that the entire Lynott family had a reputation of keeping themselves informed as to all current events. It was likely that several of the Lynott clan recognized the features as Junior Ragnarsson. At some point during her meeting with Lynott, Tan would have to explain the origin of the green Ragnarsson.

"Obviously," Lynott responded and motioned toward her ships. "What kind of business are you here on? Nothing illegal is occurring here, I can assure you."

"Of that I am certain, Doyle. You have always followed the directives of the Glorious Leader. I am here searching for some fugitives from justice. There are those that would oppose the new military command in Clovis City. Many were cadets and they stole several space craft to escape. The satellite system tracked two of those ships here, to your property."

"I detect uncertainty in your voice, Leta." Lynott said.

"Yes, well I know of your scan blocker that you utilize on your personal property. The two stolen ships were lost by the satellites shortly after they entered the Lynott Land Territory. The trajectory of the ships would have led them either to your property or they would have flown over. The ships were never detected again and the only landing strip that they would have approached based on their flight path would have been right here, where we are standing."

"I assure you that no criminals landed here," Lynott lied to her, looking right into her eyes. "We have been feasting, as normal. No one has molested me or my family."

"I am glad to hear that, Doyle. But General Sikorsky asked me to personally search the premises." Tan nodded toward one of her Colonel's. "We need access to all of your mansions to make sure no one has hidden themselves from us. This is as much for your protection as it is for planetary security. You do understand?"

The Colonel motioned for the platoons to move toward the five mansions.

"Naturally," Lynott responded.

"Then you will give us complete access to your five mansions?"

Lynott hated the fact that the government soldiers could search private property without a court order. It had been the law for almost two centuries under Vladimir Sikorsky. The right to privacy had been eliminated for all of humanity by the stroke of a pen after Sikorsky consolidated his power. Lynott could not protest. It would be futile and most likely would land him in prison if he tried.

He watched in silence as the soldiers began to enter the mansions and search each one, top to bottom. The entire exercise took three hours. As the search went on, Lynott invited Tan, her Colonel, the green clone and her pilots to join him at the main mansion for brunch. The clone politely refused and assisted the soldiers in the search.

Fortunately, the government never got their hands on the original blueprints of the Lynott mansions. The fact that each of the large dwellings had basements was never known and went undetected in the search. The Ward family and the cadets were not found. Even the green skinned J.R. found nothing to indicate anything out of the ordinary.

The bedrooms in the eastern mansion looked cleaned and the bed sheets were made. J.R. Tan concluded that it was too perfect. They were seeing exactly what Lynott wished for them to see. Tan was partially correct in her assessment. Zauriba used her powers of mind control to manipulate the soldiers that searched the eastern mansion. Although the soldiers saw some scant evidence that the guest rooms had been occupied, Zauriba could wipe those mental images from each of them.

Tan and her soldiers eventually departed. The General thanked Lynott for the food and hospitality and made every apology if her short intervention on his property brought about any inconvenience for him or his family. They hugged before she boarded her ship.

The intrusion by Tan took approximately three hours. As the black MI Raumschiffs lifted off, Lynott waved at them as he returned to his mansions. He did not see that General Tan was not willing to give in so easily.

She had directed J.R. Tan and three of her non-commissioned officers to repel from their ships before they crossed the boundary of the property. Tan's ship flew close to the ground so that none of the three would be injured in the effort. They lowered the towing cable and the three slid down the length of it by using specially designed gloves to protect their hands from the metal as they rapidly descended.

J.R. Tan let go of the cable when he was fifteen feet from the ground. He landed on his hands and feet in a crouching position. Before the green skinned clone was a thick tree line with branches of green, red, brown, yellow and orange leaves of varying shapes and sizes. He ran for it to find cover, his eyes darted left and right as he moved, looking for any security guards or civilians. The two MI soldiers were close behind Tan and all three made it behind the thick trees. All three were wearing black

Class C uniforms and had burned wine corks to paint their faces with black streaks to break up the contours of their faces. Each had a web belt around their waist and shoulders that held knives, laser pistols and black packs filled with grenades, stun darts and other weapons. Likewise, the three had a laser rifle slung over their shoulders.

J.R. watched as the space craft carrying General Tan and the others in their party back to the MI Headquarters. In his brain, he had all Tan's knowledge, memory and experiences. But he had many additional areas of expertise that had been programmed into his once blank mind. He was filled with the ability to use martial arts, boxing and knives better than most humans. His body had been reinforced by his original creators with metallic bone structure, enhanced sense of smell, long range vision, infrared vision, the ability to detect body heat behind walls or other structures and an ability to hear at a rate ten times the average person. He knew that his skin pigmentation was not the only thing that made his different. He was special. He was Leta Tan with the exception that he was superior to what she was.

Before being dispatched from the scientific chambers of Doctor Rosenburg, J.R. Tan learned that there were another forty-eight clones just like him with the exception that they had not been given any memories. Accordingly, they would not be able to be activated until that moment when they are blessed with the memories of another. Tan had not yet determined how he would be able to co-exist with the real Leta Tan. She seemed to give him autonomy to do as he wanted within certain parameters. She had not shown herself to be a threat to his existence. But if she did, he was prepared to cut her throat and take his rightful position as the commander of the MI soldiers at her palaces and headquarters.

Tan looked at the two MI women with him. Both wore Staff Sergeant Stripes on their collars that were painted grey so that they would not call attention to the as a pair of gold or silver ranks would. The women were brunettes, one shorter than the other and each with average features. Their bodies were toned and adequate to him. He could feel the lust in him that was ready to drive him wild and smiled at the women.

"Strip off you clothes," J.R. Tan ordered them.

"What? Why?" One of the women asked, startled by his order. The other laughed, thinking that the demand was a joke.

"Because I do not want to tear your uniforms from you. You will need them after we finish. I want sex with both of you, right here, behind that tree over there."

The women exchanged concerned looks which caused a delay that was not acceptable to J.R. He walked over to the shortest soldier and took her into his arms and kissed her lips. Her eyes were wide with surprise and she looked over at her fellow soldier, who was watching with interest. J.R.'s hands began roaming all over the woman's body which caused his manhood to stiffen.

He quickly unzipped the front of the woman's uniform and kissed her neck and shoulders. The woman did not resist, knowing that the green skinned man was her commander, or rather had the mind of her commander, and that all the soldiers that served under General Tan were required to submit to her sexual demands at one time or another. The soldier wondered if she was to be the first for the clone to have sex with as she allowed him to pull her uniform off.

She willingly pulled off her bra and panties and found a comfortable spot on the grass to lie down on. The clone was on top of her quickly, kissing her naked body all over before thrusting his erection inside of her. After he climaxed, he turned his attention to the taller soldier, who had removed her clothes while he was having sex. J.R. mounted the second woman and could not believe the pleasure he obtained from the two women. After he finished, he ordered them both to dress so that they could finish their mission. J.R. concluded that he wanted more women, hundreds of them, so that he could use them for his pleasure.

After they were all fully clothed, he pointed in the direction of the northern mansion. J.R. wanted to search that location first and then move on to the next until they found the traitors that were most certainly in hiding. The two soldiers began moving slowly through the tree line toward the mansion to begin their covert operation.

During the time that General Tan searched the mansions, the cadets and the Ward family members impatiently waited underground. The Lynott family had spared no expense in stocking the basement with the finest and most up to date appliances and comforts. There were fifty bedrooms with king size beds, all made with red satin sheets and expensive black comforters. There was a communal shower at the far east side of the basement. The large kitchen was located on the west side and in the center, was a large entertainment area. Blomquist, Eklund, Juanito and Jason Ward took control of the kitchen and began searching the pantries, freezers and refrigeration units for food to cook the others. The rest were either hoping for some aspirin to soothe a hangover or a cup of strong coffee to wake them up.

Villandiego and Raklitz had quickly accessed the computers and began pulling up news of the current events around the eight solar system realm of humanity. A female reporter was on and she was confirming that the Second Fleet had been wiped out. As she reported that there were no survivors, Essex was overcome with grief from the loss of her older sister. She found the closest bedroom and sat on the bed. As she wept, Varek joined her and held her close in his arms.

The rest watched in silence as the Glorious Leader warned the rest of humanity that treason would be punished swiftly.

Other planetary news stations reported other rebellions. They listened intently to the news of planet New Berlin. The citizens on that lovely paradise of a planet joined with a few battalions of soldiers to rebel. The live images of the bloodshed on the streets caused many of the Ward's to turn their heads away. Similar news came in from planet New Sao Paulo.

There was an interview with a Doctor named William Wakefield on planet Cootron in which he claimed the planet to have achieved independence from the Sikorsky regime. As the Doctor spoke, his resume of accomplishments ran across the bottom of the computer screens. Each of those watching the broadcast were impressed with both his scholastic achievements and his calm demeanor as he spoke. He claimed that all of the Royal Family that had been ruling Cootron were dead. Wakefield pointed at the cameras of the news reporters and issued a threat to the Glorious Leader to stay away from Cootron.

"Stay away from this solar system. We are a free planet and we will defend our territorial integrity with force," Wakefield said with conviction. "If any UN ship, Battle Cruiser, Science Cruiser, Transport or any other form of space craft enters this area of space, we will destroy it. We will show the soldiers of the Glorious Leader the same mercy given to the

Second Fleet. We will kill all who dare to intrude upon our sovereignty."

As the hours passed, they waited for the Lynott's to notify them that they were free to return to the upper floors of the mansion. The news continued to trickle in and the reporters finally produced a list of the dead or missing from the First Fleet and the members of the Sikorsky's Planet Defense System. Varek, Cobb, Gauthier and the Calderon brothers took hard the news that one of their number, Renee Starr had died along with her older sister, Jayne. Renee had been one of the original Bragg Gang members.

The Starr family was one of the many that had first settled planet New Edinburgh, leaving Old Earth in search for a new life and the opportunity to find land and wealth on the new world. Cobb took the news worse than the others as he had grown up with the Starr siblings. For most of his life, he had been their next-door neighbor.

"Their family is going to be crushed," Cobb muttered to the others as he rubbed his hands together. "Last year Roy died and now this. How much tragedy can one family take?"

Gauthier sat next to Haddad on a black leather couch. They held hands as the news reports continued. Admiral Perdicas of the First Fleet gave an impromptu press conference about the sacrifices made by the service men and women of the fleet. He urged the rest of humanity to mourn the sacrifice made by the men and women of the First Fleet that perished in the battle against the traitors Khan and Allen.

Gauthier gripped Haddad's hand tightly, "That son of a bitch got those girls killed. I bet he used them as pawns to test the weaknesses of the enemy. Remember how Admiral Seward used to tell us about Perdicas and his tactical ideas? He would send in the drones and then lesser members of his crew to die so that he could observe the fighting patterns of his opponent. I bet he did the same to the Second Fleet, probed for their weaknesses before unleashing his main assault on them."

"I am so sorry, John," Haddad whispered to him. "You knew them well?"

"Only Renee. Jayne did not go to the Academy here. She went elsewhere. I knew Renee for about two years. She was a good person."

"And Wanda lost her sister on the other side of the ledger," Haddad pointed out. "This is shaping into a true civil war. Friends and neighbors killing each other. Brother versus brother and sister versus sister and for men like Sikorsky and Perdicas? You know what I am most afraid of, John?"

"No, what is that?"

"I am afraid that with all of the top-ranking men and women that seek freedom dying off, there will be no one left to lead the rest of us." She moved up closer to him. "Khan, Allen,

Seward, Hibbert, Warren, Weems and all of those other ranking officers are dead. We may have to find some fossilized commander from the past to rise up to lead us."

Gauthier nodded as she spoke, "Even if we found such a person, would they be willing to take the risk?  Sikorsky is cruel an uncompromising. He and Perdicas would not allow any of the Second Fleet to surrender. I doubt that any man or woman enjoying their retirement would place themselves or their families at Sikorsky's version of mercy."

From behind them, Gauthier and Haddad heard the question that everyone wanted to ask. Gauthier turned to see that Eklund was repeating it again and again. "What kind of world will we be going back to?"

The question was answered with an uncomfortable silence as each of them dared not contemplate the future that waited for them all.

# CHAPTER FOUR

The Orka Raumschiff shot up out of the ocean and was flying low, just twenty feet over the water. Cadet Derek Regehr handled the half-moon steering mechanism with ease. He flew the ship like a professional.

Sanjeeta Nehwal was next to him as his co-pilot. She smiled when she saw that they were no longer surrounded by the deep blue waters of planet New Edinburgh. Although she was studying to become a pilot, she had found the time under the water stressful. She had experienced what she believed to be claustrophobia. She kept the others in the dark regarding her sweaty palms and dry mouth and her lingering desire to hide against a wall and cover her eyes. She forced herself to fight through her fears. As an orphan, she had to become a survivor and overcome obstacles more challenging than this. She would persevere.

Elektra proved to be a fast learner, operating the tactical screen at Nehwal's left hand side as if she had been handling those duties for years. Using her index fingers, she expanded some three-dimensional computer screens and retracted others. She had a tear drop microphone and headset over her long dark hair and occasionally issued a firm, yet polite, command to the Mikec sisters. Nehwal studied Elektra's face and saw that there was still some residue of the tracks of the tears that she had shed when her uncle Drimios died to save them all. Despite the grief from her personal loss, the look in her eyes was one of focus and determination. The cadet from Corinth, old Earth, was resolute to complete one last task. She was going to strike back at the enemy invaders and blow up their Battle Cruiser that was in orbit around the planet.

"Weapons section, are we ready?" Elektra spoke into her tear drop microphone. There was no emotion in her voice. If they succeeded in destroying the *Lysander*, thousands would most likely perish. But the move would damage the morale of the Sikorsky forces in ways they could only imagine. The Battle Cruiser protected their dominion over the air space of the planet. Without her, the rebellion would have a chance.

"Ready to fire on your command, Elektra," Jasna Mikec responded from the second level of the space craft.

"We have two nuclear warheads that are hot. Repeat, they are hot," Jasna's older sister, Zorana, stated.

Arch Frazier said nothing, staring at a blue and gold three-dimensional view of the *Lysander* from the computer station. He had several screens up, all of them of varying sizes that seemed to surround him. He was watching the views of the ship from top to bottom, east and west, to ensure that no enemy ships were coming in to intercept them. He also watched the targeting grid for the nuclear missiles. They were on target with the *Lysander*. Even of the Battle Cruiser could use counter-measures to cause both missiles to detonate early, the magnetic pulse and the shock wave from the explosion would cause damage to the large war ship.

"Fire!" Elektra ordered.

"Firing Missile One!" Jasna said as she pressed the red button before her on the computer console.

"Firing Missile Two!" Zorana announced seconds after her sister and pressed the firing mechanism.

"Missiles launched," Regehr announced as he felt the Orka shake slightly with the projectiles shooting out of their launch tubes and into the sky.

"That is a big affirmative," Arch Frazier reported. "I am tracking the two missiles that are armed and ready. They are on their way to the *Lysander*. At the present rate of speed, they should impact in about one hour."

"And if they try to outrun them?" Nehwal asked.

Elektra and Regehr glanced at her over their shoulders.

"The missiles will follow the target; they each have sensor devices that control their trajectory and direction. It is like the old heat seeking missiles that have been slowly phased out of use over the last few years," Regehr told her. "They are smaller so they can maneuver and they are ten times faster than the Lysander. Now, we need to make ourselves scarce, otherwise, the Lysander will fire on us. How about hiding in Clovis City?"

Elektra nodded in the affirmative to Regehr's selection of destination. The military wanted to occupy and control the city, not destroy it, which would allow the crew of the Orka ship to hide among the population there. "Clovis City."

"And what will we do when we arrive there?" Nehwal wanted to know.

"Then we attack the soldiers that are holding all of the students' hostage in the dormitories. We free them and then lead them into war." Elektra was cracking her knuckles as she spoke. "We get those MI soldiers to realize that their days of raping and killing are finished. Since Sikorsky killed everyone on the Second Fleet, then we should do the same to his people."

"Kill them all?" Jasna spoke into her tear drop microphone.

"Only those that refuse to join us," Elektra smiled and winked at Nehwal.

Nehwal smiled back at her, "Join us or die? I can live with that. And while we free the cadets, we need to free the orphans in those homes. They will join us, I guarantee it."

Regehr began typing commands onto the computer console before him to change the course of the ship. As he typed he had to ask the questions that had been nagging at him for the past several hours. "Elektra, I have to ask you something. If it is too personal or if you do not want to answer, just tell me to shut up. But I must ask, your family names intrigue me. You and your aunt are named after characters from the Greek Mythology. But your cousin Drimios, where did that name come from?"

Elektra pursed her lips as she thought about her cousin whose body was lying in the lower level. "First, it is not mythology. It is all true. My family rejects the Gods that are in the Bible or the Koran. We see those books as false and petty attempts by those in power to control men and women. I pray to Hera. She is real and sits in Olympus, watching over us. My cousin Drimios worshiped Poseidon. His name was from another God. Drimios was a son of Zeus, at least there were some ancient writings that were discovered to suggest that. He had been a forgotten God for centuries until the famous archaeological digs in the ruins of Northern Africa two hundred years ago. The tablets there had numerous stories about Drimios and his courage. Many of the stories that had been attributed to Perseus and Hercules had been stolen from the word of mouth legends of Drimios. My aunt Themis was named by her mother who had been a judge in the Corinthian Courts for many years. She was supposed to stand for justice."

"There was nothing just about what your aunt did to us," Nehwal commented.

"No, there was not anything just about it," Elektra agreed. "I dread her reaction when she learns that her son is dead and that we have escaped. She can be a very vengeful person."

"But we did not kill her son," Regehr reminded her.

"We will never get the opportunity to tell her our side," Elektra said solemnly. "She will blame us and come for us."

"Then we need to disappear quickly. Hang on, I am going to get us close to a private landing strip in Clovis City I know about. I doubt that the military knows that it exists." Regehr told them as he cut hard right on the steering column.

The Orka moved to the right and Regehr increased the speed. He was aware of the satellite system in space and that their ship had most likely been detected by their monitors. The operatives at the MI stations would be collating the data and would put together that the Orka ship was responsible for the nuclear attack on the *Lysander*. Regehr speculated that they would have about a twelve-hour window to land, leave the ship and then attempt to blend into the rest of the population before the MI soldiers would close in on them. He disagreed with

Elektra's views on religion. Regehr had been raised by his parents to be a Christian. He silently prayed to God that twelve hours would be enough time to get away.

# CHAPTER FIVE

Colonel Nikolai Gorski was a prisoner. He had been arrested by the top-ranking officers that had arrived aboard a Battle Cruiser and took total control of the planet New Edinburgh. He had been shackled while standing in his former office as the usurpers took over. He was forced to watch them murder his best friend, Major Sigebert Evart, before being dragged down the hallway of the United Nations building and locked into a conference room with his subordinate officer and fellow prisoner, Captain Rafer Tierney. The two men sat in silence as they heard explosions around them, the space craft passing overhead and the sounds of laser fire.

Down the hallways they could hear the screams of their co-workers being arrested or shot if they resisted. Gorski wished he could order all the employees of the building to capitulate and avoid being killed. He stared at the floor in silence and wanted to pray for his children and the children of Sigebert Evart, but he believed in no Gods. He had never been brought to any church as a child, nor had he ever read the religious propaganda that was sometimes broadcasted on the viewing screens or disseminated on the streets. He wanted whatever god or power or supreme being that existed out there would find a way to protect his sons and the daughters of Evart who were now being hunted for execution. He had never felt so helpless in his life.

He looked up when he heard the door to the conference room slide open. He saw the sexy and treacherous Rebecca Rosenburg walk into the room and sit down at the farthest side of the conference room table from them. She was smiling and licked her full lips as she observed the despair on the faces of the two men. The animosity between her and Gorski had built up over the short time she had worked in the UN building. She despised him due to her inability to corrupt the man, despite her best efforts.

"Your son caused the death of my father and two of my brothers," she began in a mocking tone of voice. During her incarceration, she had speculated in her mind what she would say to Gorski if she ever faced him again. "You, Evart and Collins then prosecute me and my other siblings, lock us away, get death sentences on some of us, and you thought you could get away with all of that? We are Royals! Today is a day of reckoning. My entire family is resolute in taking this planet back for good. Right now, our soldiers and alien slaves are tracking down all that were loyal to you and your friends. Hell, we even decapitated all the jurors that found us all guilty and posted their heads on pikes all around the city. Look outside the windows and see for your selves. Go ahead. Look."

"I would rather not," Gorski mumbled.

"You remember, Colonel, all the times I threw myself at you?  All you had to do was fuck me. I was all yours. You could have married me and then you would have been one with us. You should have taken me when you had the opportunity."

"I would rather make love to a Poggie," Gorski hissed at her.

Her smile faded into a contorted look of anger. "That can be arranged, you're an arrogant bastard. I now have the power of the United Nations Security Council, at least I will after Lyss resigns. He was a useless and pathetic wimp anyway.  He and his family will be killed in due time after the power had been passed over to me. We sent out a hit team to kill Collins and his family. We lost contact with that team several minutes ago. You wouldn't know anything about that, would you?"

"Even if I did, I wouldn't tell you." Gorski's voice was even. He was doing his level best to avoid showing any emotion. He did not want to give her the satisfaction.

Rebecca was silent for a moment as she moved her gaze from Gorski to Tierney. "You should know that it is only a matter of time before we apprehend the Collins family and your son, Piotr. We will give each of you a fair trial, at least fair per our standards, and then promptly execute each of you before the sheeple. I can't wait to see each of your heads on display for all of those sniveling people out there to cry over."

Gorski looked away from her. He wondered how such a beautiful woman could become such a heartless person. He considered his next words to the woman carefully. "History is full of tyrants that over played their hands. Eventually even the people that you have such low regard for will have enough of your mistreatment. You and your brothers and sisters will push the masses too far. In my country, the czars made that fatal error and then the communists made the same mistakes. History will not remember you well, Rebecca. The good news for you is that it is not too late to change direction. You could release the Captain and I and help us protect the people from any further harm. You are a smart woman. Look around you. Look at the suffering of the victims from what is happening out there. Look into the eyes of the people then consider your own heart and ask yourself why you are doing these things. Ask whether your actions will put you in the category of the evil leaders of history or with those that strived to bring peace to the people."

Rebecca laughed at what she concluded was Gorski's naiveté. "Fuck the people. All of you exist to serve me and my family. You are all toys, play things. Pets. We do with each of you as we will. You, Evart. Collins, Goldsmith, Li, Wyclyffe,

Rice, Ward and all the others that had made the error in judgment to support you, will all die badly. We already killed some and we are hunting the rest down. You will all die."

"Then I guess it is too late for you," Gorski looked away from her again. He realized that Rebecca was a lost cause. He had nothing further to say to her.

"Despite my feelings in the matter, my sister Juliana wanted to speak with the two of you before you are taken away to your 'trial' for treason. You will be found guilty and immediately executed here on the court yard of the U.N. Building. Everyone will watch you both die and after we apprehend Collins, he will die and all your bodies will be hung on display for all to see. I will leave you now, Nikolai. Sadly, had you done the right thing and played along with me, you would be a General now. And you would have been allowed to live."

Rebecca slowly stood up and smoothed the bottom of her blue dress over her shapely legs. She walked toward the door and waited until it opened for her. She walked out of the room without looking back. The door remained open.

"You should have screwed her sir," Tierney tried and failed to make a joke out of the situation. Gorski did not laugh.

Juliana Rosenburg walked into the room next and she closed the sliding doors behind her. She was wearing a black skirt and white button up top. She had black slippers on her feet. Her obsidian earrings and matching necklace looked lovely on her soft skin. She sat down in the same chair that her sister Rebecca had used. She was silent for a few moments as she tried to muster the right words. Gorski noticed that her hands were shaking.

"I wanted to tell you both that I am sorry," she started off. Her voice was wavering from emotion. "I don't blame any of you, or Mister Collins, for arresting us all. I was raped several times while in the prison you put me in. Those men were brutal, cruel and had no remorse for the harm they did to me, my siblings and the other prisoners. But it made me understand what my family has been doing to others for years. Decades. Centuries. I am sorry about the Major. He was a good man and did not deserve that. My family is cruel, but we all are not like the rest. I had a brother named Cush that stood up to my father and Uncle John. It was many years ago. They killed him in front of us all. Tortured him, cut him to pieces and we all had to endure his screams of pain. We all learned that day the price of not doing as father told us. I wish I was as brave as Cush. He would have liked both of you and most likely would have been your friend as he shared your values and your commitment to others."

"We are both sorry about the attacks on you in the jails. We had no idea those things were occurring. Why are you here?"

Tierney asked as he realized most of what she said was directed at him.

She leaned forward with tears in her eyes. "When I first met you, I saw a dashing and handsome man. As a young girl, I always dreamed that one day, a man like you, a knight, a hero, would come and take me away from all of this death. Take me away from my cruel father and the rest of my family. But it never happened. Cush rebelled and died horribly. Penelope is now out there somewhere, gathering forces to fight against the Glorious Leader. Kristin and Nicolette are helping her. They were the brave ones. But me? I am nothing but a coward. I stand by and do nothing while people suffer."

Gorski could hear the torture in her voice, almost as if it were from self-loathing. "You still have time to be brave. You still have time to help the people. This is not over by any stretch of the imagination. You can still be like Cush and Penelope. You can make a difference. You just have to decide to do so."

"How?" She was in tears now. "I don't know how."

"In Russia, we had a saying, that if you had to be someplace you would be there," Gorski told her softly. "It simply meant that if you have to do something or be somewhere, you will find a way to do it. Nothing would stand in your way."

Juliana wiped the tears from her beautiful face and took in a few deep breaths as she tried to compose herself. "I suppose you have not been told. The Second Fleet was wiped out. Admiral Khan and all his troops are dead, which means the rebellion is essentially over. So whatever happens might be academic anyway."

"You don't believe that," Tierney stood tall. "If you did you would not be here."

She stood and walked toward him, "I came here because I wanted to find out what it was like to be kissed by a hero, by a knight. Do you mind if I kiss you good-bye Captain?"

She had a suspicious look on her face as she walked toward Tierney.

"Why not?" He responded to her. If he was going to die at least he could go to his grave knowing, he was kissed by one of the loveliest women he had ever seen.

Juliana wrapped her hands around Tierney's neck and leaned up to kiss his lips. He responded and pressed his lips against hers. As they kissed, he felt her tongue move into his mouth and she maneuvered a small metal object into his mouth. She pulled away quickly and was smiling at him.

"Thank you my knight," she said as she walked toward the door.

Tierney was rubbing the metal object with his tongue. It felt like a key of some sort.

"It isn't too late," Gorski stood up in a last effort to convince the woman to help them.

She smiled, opened the doors and walked out without saying another word. She left the doors open behind her.

Tierney held his hands under his chin and spit the metal object out. It was indeed a key. He realized that it was the key to their handcuffs and leg irons. He immediately used it to remove his cuffs and then his leg irons. He ran over to Gorski and did the same.

"Heroic after all," Tierney said as Gorski gave him an astonished look.

Once both men were freed from their shackles they looked over at the open doorway.

"Looks like she left the door open on purpose," Gorski concluded.

"The stairwell is just thirty feet away," Tierney whispered. "I say we make a break for it. If we make it to the large court yard below we would have a slight chance to steal a vehicle and get away before the guards realize we escaped."

"Let's do this," Gorski said softly. He was certain that he could find troops that would be loyal to him and follow a counter-assault against the Rosenburg occupation.

The two Marines moved to the doorway and Gorski peered out and looked up and down the long hallway. There were a few soldiers in solid black Military Intelligence uniforms walking about. None of them were facing the conference room.

Gorski could see the stairwell entrance in the distance, a mere thirty paces away. He nodded to Tierney and the two men moved into the hallway and walked rapidly to the door to the stairs. They were in the stairwell quickly and fortunately no one saw them.

Without any words, the two men ran down the stairs as fast as they could. Gorski and Tierney knew that it was a Thursday and that all the major governmental agencies held their weekly general meetings to vote on new laws and resolutions. If what Rebecca said was true, that Lyss was resigning, then there would be a full house of assemblymen and women, reporters, concerned citizens and security to witness the event. Their descent down the stairs was over eighty floors. Since most of the activity was presumably occurring in the major committees, Security Council and General Assembly chambers, they had a better than average chance of getting out of the building unseen. Both men stepped lightly from metal stair to metal stair to not make too much noise from the heels of their boots banging.

The two men made it, undetected, to the emergency exit at the first-floor level. They looked at each other and nodded. Gorski pushed open the door and they expected to hear alarms screaming. But there was only silence.

They stepped out onto the massive courtyard and saw that Rebecca had not been lying. There were numerous poles that were about twenty feet high with human heads on them. Many civilians were in awe of the sight; most were looking away with disgust. They noticed that in the distance there were thousands of alien slaves including Saharakaree, Babbcottiatta, Akarzdamedians and others. There were some pink and light blue skinned humans with antennae's above their eyes. Gorski had never seen such skin pigmentation on a human before but had head news reports that some of the third-generation humans from Cootron and Athena had developed different skin tones due to the minerals in the food and water. There were a few hundred MI soldiers on patrol as well as a few brigades of Marines.

Behind the rows of slave aliens and soldiers were hundreds of Raumschiffs and small fighter space craft. Gorski concluded that if anyone attacked the capital, they would be in for one hell of a fight. The two men began to run for the south part of the courtyard when a dark blue hover van pulled in front of them. It was a double deck ship that was cruising two feet off the ground and had sliding doors on either side. Any occupants on the inside of the van were obscured by the tinted windows and thick outer metal shell of the vehicle. Gorski was certain that their escape attempt had come to an end. The only reason a hover vehicle would stop at that moment and location would be because the pilot recognized him and Tierney. Gorski watched silently as the dark tinted window of the driver side slid down to reveal Juliana Rosenburg.

"Get in," she directed them.

Without question, Tierney and Gorski opened the side sliding door and jumped into the floating vehicle. They had not sat down before Juliana began steering the hover van upward about five feet from the ground and gunned it forward at a speed of two hundred kilometers an hour. Gorski looked around and found weapons in the back seat with them and noticed that they were the only people in the vehicle.

"Get some weapons and prepare to get out," Juliana said softly. She had planned on helping the two men get to safety, even at the risk of her own life. For the first time, she felt as if she was doing something that actually mattered.

"Brave after all," Tierney said to her. "Thank you for helping us."

"You are welcome. Now you two need to get off of New Edinburgh. I have a pilot friend that will fly you to another planet, no questions asked. Once they realize you are gone, this whole solar system will go into lock down. The Sikorsky's will send out assassins and promises to reward anyone that brings you both in. So much has happened before and since you were both arrested. They killed almost all the planetary leaders that were friends of yours. The lawyer that oversaw prosecuting me, Mister Goldsmith? They killed him and most of his family. Even his little children. Those that were not found are hiding and being hunted by hired assassins. The kids might be hidden well, but that won't last long. They will all be found and will die, most likely as horribly as their father did. I cannot and will not be a part of killing innocent people, which is why I am doing this."

"What will you do?" Gorski asked her.

"Stay here, I suppose," she shrugged as she responded. Her eyes were moving from her three-dimensional computer guidance system screen and her one-way observation window before her. She held the steering column tightly in both of her hands as she navigated the ship past other flying craft. "I have no choice. If I leave, my family will come after me, too."

"Yes, you do have a choice. You can help us fight back," Tierney urged. "You have just proven that you are ready for the challenge. What you just did by freeing us took nerves of steel. Help us take back the planet."

"Nerves of steel? I am ready to crap my pants I am so scared. You two need to leave and go hide somewhere safe. That is the end of the discussion."

"And how do I leave my son Piotr behind?" Gorski asked her as he was inspecting a laser rifle that she had in the back of the van. "The Evart family? Sean Collins? All the other assembly members that supported us over the years? The major families here like the Glenn's, the Cobb's, the Calderon's, the remaining Goldsmith's, the Essex's, the Kander's, the Rice's, the Ward's, the Li's, and the Starr's. Not to mention the Andolini family that has been close to me and my sons for about seventeen years now. I cannot abandon them."

Juliana pulled into the main landing strip of Clovis City and brought the hover van to a stop. She lowered the vehicle to the transparent pavement. In the distance were hundreds of private and military transport space craft. She ordered her computer to turn off the engine and she swiveled her chair around so the she could face the two men behind her. She had a look of desperation in her eyes.

"I know that you love these people, and I am sorry. But there is nothing you can do for any of them. They already wiped out almost the entire Goldsmith family. They are dead. The entire Rice family is in custody already. You know what they did to them? Do you? They raped the women, even the little girls. One of them was ten years old and they had a large slave Babbcottiatta rape her. She was dead after enduring a few minutes of it. It ripped her vaginal sex organs in pieces. They did it on live broadcast so the rest of New Edinburgh could see the price for not following the Royal Family. The other young Rice girls are being torn open for their body parts. Those that are over the age of twenty-five are being sent to the arena in Rosenburg Ranch to be eaten by giant reptiles. Do you understand me?"

Gorski was gritting his teeth when he heard the news of the Goldsmith and Rice families. He recalled his interactions with them fondly. They had been good and decent citizens. He leaned forward and took her hands in his. "You risked everything by helping us. I intend to die for these people here and I will not leave my son behind."

"Juliana, you have come this far," Tierney added softly. "We have people loyal to us here on the planet. We can mount a challenge."

She laughed out loud and then smiled at Tierney. "You really are a knight. I did this for you, Captain. I know this may sound crazy but I am in love with you. I fell for you that day you came marching into my father's mansion at the Rosenburg Ranch. You were the most gorgeous and debonair man I had ever seen. You were so handsome in your uniform. I would have left with you without a second thought if you would have just asked me. But you never did."

Tierney sighed, "I am asking now."

She laughed again for a few seconds and then pointed in the direction of a black Super Raumschiff in the distance. It had some red trim around the sides and on the back-docking entrance. "That's my ship. She is all yours. And, dear Captain, I am all yours, too."

Gorski gave Tierney a look before he jumped out of the hover van. Tierney followed his commanding officer. Both men had laser rifles slung over their shoulders with laser pistols in hand. They thanked Juliana for rescuing them before jogging toward the space craft she had pointed out. They now had weapons and a space craft. All they needed now was a plan of action and more soldiers to implement it.

Juliana parked the hover van in a lot nearby and sat in silence as she mulled over her next move. She would most certainly be fingered by her half-sister Rebecca as the most likely culprit in assisting the two men in their escape. Her siblings would kill her, probably in a similar manner that their father killed Cush. Or, she could take her chances and follow Gorski and Tierney on their mad plan to fight back. She had a small brown back pack sitting in the passenger seat that was full of weapons she had accumulated in case of confrontation. She ordered the hover van computer to turn off the engine and she grabbed the back pack with her right hand. She decided she would join the handsome men in uniform. If she was going to die, she would rather do so next to them.

Gorski and Tierney ran to the open rear loading entrance of the space craft. The loading ramp was resting on the transparent metal pavement and that the doors were wide open. The two marines walked quickly up the ramp and were met by a man wearing a dark blue, one piece, collared flight suit that had no patches or rank on it. The man looked to be in his late twenties or early thirties. He was tall, slender, had dirty blonde hair, a long beard and his skin looked to be tanned. He had gold loop earrings in each ear lobe and a tattoo of a black scorpion on the right side of his neck. He heard the clanging of the boots on the metal ramp and turned his attention to Gorski and Tierney.

"So you both made it out alive. That's good." The man gave Gorski a longer look as if he knew who he was.

"You knew we were coming?" Tierney extended his hand to the stranger.

"Yes, welcome aboard the Roadrunner 3. I am her new Captain." He shook Tierney's hand. "My name is Jericho Griffin."

Gorski shook the man's hand and began looking over the rear of the space craft. There were three walls that were filled with scatter shot laser rifles, laser rifles, advanced sighting sniper laser rifles, laser pistols of all kinds of makes and models and knives. Gorski noticed that there were mounted on the metal mesh wall several jet packs on the east wall to assist a single person in an enviro-suit for flying through space. The jet packs were a design the Gorski did not recognize and he assumed that they came from the Rosenburg Corporation.

On the floor below the jet packs were several white one-man flying wheel-less solar powered hover motorcycle machines. Gorski had ridden in them in the past. They can reach speeds of three hundred fifty kilometers an hour and would fly about fifteen feet from the ground. They were great for maneuvering through tight spots such a jungles or mountains and caverns.

"So, Mister Griffin, are you with the Space Command?" Gorski asked to learn about the man. He was far too young to have reached retirement eligibility yet his uniform had no rank insignias or patches indicating what ship or unit he was from.

"No Colonel," Griffin said as he moved boxes of supplies to the west wall and securing them with clamps so that they would not move or shift during flight. "I was. I was chaptered out and lost my commission because I was stupid enough to disrespect my uniform and my unit. I got what I deserved."

Griffin wanted to keep the conversation from getting into the details of what had led to him losing his rank as the event had involved Gorski's oldest son. Over one year ago, Griffin had been a pilot and an officer on the science cruiser called the Colorado. While on a routine supply requisition, Griffin followed his friend Heinrich Jahn and their squadron commander, Boris Ilyasova, into a bar called Tinkerbelle's that was on Space Station Cy-7. While there they met a very attractive cadet from Clovis Academy named April Mejia. The three men were so used to doing as they wished with women as they were officers and pilots that they were incensed when Mejia was not amenable to their public advances which included fondling her and attempting to have forcible sex with her on one of the tables. She had been rescued by cadet Klaus Rhinehard.

Griffin and his friends assaulted Klaus which caused a full-scale brawl in the bar against Mejia's friends. Those colleagues were the other members of Gorski's Gang. Everyone ended up arrested and taken to the Tank. The result was that Griffin's Captain fired him and filed criminal charges. Griffin resigned his officer's commission in disgrace. While he was interacting with Gorski, he hoped that if those facts were ever revealed it would not be held against him.

"But you can fly this space craft?" Tierney asked as he was inspecting the weapons.

"Yes, Captain," Griffin lifted another crate and carried it toward the west wall. "I can fly her. After I was chaptered out I did some illegal weapons smuggling for the Rosenburg family. That's how I got to meet Juliana and the rest of their family. I guess you could say that she and I were never on the same page as the rest of her kin. I got away from them after I saw just how cruel the others could be."

"What did you see, Mister Griffin?" Gorski was curious.

"I watched a hired killer for the Rosenburg family, a lady named Ulla Ragnarsson, murder a pretty young girl named Lupita for no reason. It made me sick and I was ashamed of myself that I failed to stop it. The girl did nothing to deserve losing her life." Griffin paused from his work and stood up straight. "I went into hiding after that. I did not want anything to do with the Rosenburg's anymore."

"You witnessed the murder of Lupita Calderon?" Tierney blurted out. He had assisted in the early stages of the investigation as several high-ranking officers had been left stunned on the floor when the Fenster siblings had been kidnaped and the Calderon girl was found dead on the floor of the ballroom. The crimes had never been solved.

"Yes sir. I did. I found her older sister, Reynita, and told her what I saw and who did it. She was very emotional. I guess the two girls were very close. I hope that the killer gets brought to justice someday.  I thought of a girl that I had used to think of as my little sister. We were in an orphanage together. I was always protecting her from the bullies in the facility. One day they got to her when I was not around, they killed her. Watching what Ulla did to Lupita reminded me of the girl in the orphanage. It is so senseless to kill so many innocents."

Gorski heard footsteps coming up the metal ramp and he glanced over his shoulder to see that Juliana was joining them. Gorski smiled as that her inclusion gave their small army a troop of four soldiers. Or four fools.

"I once commanded Lupita and Reynita's father," Gorski told them in a continuation of his conversation with Griffin. "He was a Lance Corporal in my platoon during the

Dinosaur Wars. When I was promoted to Captain he rose in rank as well. He made it all the way to First Sergeant. He is a good soldier, at least he was. He retired a few years ago with his full pension. He still lives here on Clovis City. He has more children than I ever dreamed of having. I hope that the killing of Lupita doesn't mean that the Calderon family is being targeted as well."

"Are we ready for lift off, Jericho?" Juliana asked as she felt saddened by the open discussion of the murder of the young girl. Griffin had already told her of the tale and that the Royal Family had been behind the kidnaping of the Fenster kids.

"Yes ma'am," Griffin responded and directed his attention at Gorski. "Where are we going, Colonel?"

Gorski looked at Tierney and paused. "When you went to help with the repairs of Space Station Cy-7, do you recall who the officers and engineers were that were left to staff it?"

"Yes sir. Doctor Gia Terajima was left in command of the station. Lieutenant Darby O'Neal is still there, so were Officers Dante Friedmann and Anna Tatum. They are all good friends of mine."

"Can we rely on them?" Gorski asked carefully.

"Depends on what we are asking from them," Tierney responded. Out of the corner of his eye he could see Griffin and Rosenburg listening to their conversation.

"I want to go on the offensive," Gorski informed him. "We are losing too many good people and far too many of our friends have been killed. I think it is time for a little pay back. If we were to look at what has happened as a game of chess, then we would want to first move to take their queen. I want to take away their most important chess piece."

"Which is what?" Griffin was intrigued.

"Their Battle Cruiser. I want to put together a team to infiltrate the Lysander and take her away from the new military leaders." Gorski pointed to the ceiling, "She is in orbit over the planet as we speak. We take her out of the equation and they will no longer be able to have the threat of dropping nuclear missiles on us if we later repel them from the U.N. headquarters. Will O'Neal, Friedmann, Tatum and Doctor Terajima help us?"

Tierney rubbed his jaw with his hand as he pondered that question. None of the four that Gorski mentioned had any love for the Sikorsky's. "They just might, sir. They just might."

Gorski turned toward Griffin, "How quickly can you get us to Space Station Cy-7?"

"About two hours," Griffin responded. He wanted to warn the Colonel that Dante Friedman and Darby O'Neal were two men that were on the under the table payroll of the Rosenburg clan. But to do so, he would have to implicate himself as a co-conspirator in numerous felonies. That was not something he was willing to do at this point. "But their security is heightened. They are checking flight permissions and identification codes closely. Even if I get you there, we might not be able to dock and if we dock, we might not be allowed to leave. Your plan is very risky."

Juliana cleared her throat, "You forget, Jericho, that this ship was constructed by my uncle and his engineers. We have state of the art computer systems that have access to all the security codes in this ship's computer system. We can use those codes to tell the station security that we are making a delivery of food to one of the Hotels. We make up any cover story and we can land on their docking area. We can do what the Colonel said. It will be easy."

"It would be easy if we had someone on board that knew how to operate the computer systems." Griffin shrugged, "I can fly this ship. But I have a limited knowledge of computers."

"Then you men are in luck," Juliana smiled as she walked toward the hallway that led to the ladders to the command area, weapons section and computer room. "I know all about those computer codes. You fly us, I will get us in and we let the Colonel and the Captain do their thing when we get there."

The three men watched as she began climbing the ladder to the second floor of the space craft.

"I think I like her," Tierney said to Gorski.

Griffin laughed, "Well, she is single and available, Captain. Let's close the rear entrance and get our security checks done so we can get this little rebellion off the ground."

Gorski walked back to the rear of the ship and pressed the red button on the wall to seal the rear of the Raumschiff. He had no illusions about the odds they faced. He calculated their chances of success were probably less than ten percent. But from his perspective he had to make the attempt. Piotr was in danger as were others. He had to protect his son as best he could.

Tierney had already joined Juliana on the second level of the space craft in the large computer room. From that control area, Tierney could operate the weapons systems on the large ship. He sat down in the square shaped room on a leather cushioned swivel chair behind the computer section for weapons command. He smiled at her as she took a seat across the room at the ten-foot-long row of computers. She was typing on holographic keypads commands to gain access to the space station. She had a headphone set over her ears that had a tear drop microphone on her left cheek. She smiled back at Tierney when she realized he was in the room with her.

Gorski climbed up the ladder to the third level which was the pilot section. Most of the Raumschiffs that Gorski had been on had seats for two pilots only. On this space craft, there were five seats facing the computer panel and the transparent metal view window. He chose the seat next to Griffin. He had two hours to get to know this self-confessed rogue pilot. Gorski found the man to be an interesting dichotomy. He had a history of being willingly involved in some bad events but he was striving to change his ways. Gorski decided to trust the man as long as he never gave him a reason not to. But just to be safe, Gorski resolved to keep a fully charged laser pistol attached to his belt.

After five minutes of safety checks, Griffin had the Raumschiff airborne and flying in the direction of Space Station Cy-7. Griffin was enjoying the flight to the station, playing some heavy metal music in the flight cabin. He began to mull over in his mind how he could warn Gorski and Tierney against landing on the space station. Griffin had been present when Friedman and O'Neal accepted pay offs from Ulla Ragnarsson and on earlier occasions when one of the Rosenburg family would bribe them. The two men could not be trusted. They would stab Gorski and Tierney in the back without a second thought.

Griffin had been lost in his own thoughts as he flew the Raumschiff. He snapped out of his silence when the ships security alarm systems began to ring out loud.

"What the hell?" Griffin yelled out as the loud sirens were echoing throughout the ship. "Did they already find us?"

"No," Juliana answered through the ship communication system. "Our scanners detected two nuclear warheads that passed by us. Thankfully we are not the intended target of the nukes. They came with a quarter of a kilometer of our position."

Gorski pumped his right fist, "Where are they headed?"

Juliana and Tierney both frantically looked over several tactical three-dimensional screens and looked at each other with confusion. One view displayed the missiles bursting out of the New Edinburgh ocean, sending a large cascade of blue water and foam into the air as the missiles rose into the sky.

"Sir, it looks like there are others fighting back," Tierney responded. "Those two nukes were launched from the ocean by an unknown ship. They are on a collision course with the Battle Cruiser Lysander. Does this mean what I think it does?"

Gorski nodded, "It means that we are not alone. We have some pretty crafty allies that just sent a serious message to our enemies. If those missiles hit the target it will be a huge blow against the Sikorsky's. The Lysander is a historic ship and the favorite of the Glorious Leader."

"How many crew members are on the Lysander?" Tierney asked.

"The ship computer scan indicates that there are about three hundred left on the ship," Juliana told them. "All of the rest of her crew that arrived here are on the planet surface. If those missiles take out the Lysander, then the advantage of the MI on the planet surface will be damaged. I can guarantee you that my family will retaliate."

"Will the nuclear blast effect the space station?" Gorski asked as he was now looking at a tactical screen tracking the trajectory of the missiles.

"No sir," Tierney assured him. "The station and the Lysander are currently on opposite sides of the planet. There are several military Raumschiffs around the Lysander that will most likely be vaporized in the explosion. Sir, this is huge. Whoever launched those missiles has balls of iron."

"I hope we get to thank him, her or them very soon," Gorski said softly. His thoughts were mixed. He wanted to take the Battle Cruiser to use for himself in the war. But this was far more effective. The warship would soon be a nuclear cloud and the soldiers in Clovis City would no longer have that big stick to threaten the people with. "I would bet that my son and his friends had something to do with this. Those cadets are fearless."

"If the Lysander goes, the invasion force will react." Griffin stated the obvious. He noticed that Gorski was rubbing his jaw with his right hand. "They have many prisoners that they will torture and execute for what they will call the insolence displayed by attacking their Battle Cruiser."

"They are torturing and killing prisoners anyway. At least now they will know that they are facing a population that is willing to stand up to them. Juliana, do you have communication triangulation ability on this ship?" Gorski continued to rub his chin as he spoke.

Squinting her eyes, Juliana looked at Tierney and finally responded to Gorski with a question. "Why would you want to know that, Colonel?"

"Whoever launched those nukes are going to be aligned with us. We need to speak with them. Can you use the triangulation programming to chart where their ship might be and open an encrypted communication channel with them? I do not want any eavesdroppers hearing our discussions. We need allies and in my book, anyone that shares our goals and his willing to fight back like that is someone I want on my side."

Tierney stood over Juliana's left shoulder, "I know what he wants us to do. We need to use the computer to estimate the location where the nukes were launched from. From that grid point, we can estimate the possible location of the ship now. We then use our communication system to send an encrypted message to the ship that we thing launched the missiles. If they respond to our requests, we can determine who they are and attempt to negotiate an alliance."

Juliana was still looking at her computer panels with a furrowed brow. She had never attempted such a task before. "Perhaps you should do it. I don't understand what you are asking of me."

Tierney took her seat after she stood up. He began typing commands on his holographic keypad. "We are simply going to triangulate the location of the missiles with the possible launching point to the possible locations of the ship that launched them. It will give us a radius of possible locations of the ship. Our scanners will be able to detect all of the ships inside that radius and then we can make an educated guess as to which ship would carry that kind of weaponry."

She smiled at him as she put her left hand on his shoulder. She began running her hand over his back and neck. "I will take your word for it, Captain."

Tierney liked how her hand felt as she continued running it up and down his back. After just forty seconds, the computer indicated that it had located three possible ships within the possible distance. "Colonel, we have three ships that might be the one that fired on the Lysander. I am sending the specs up to you on the tactical section in the pilots' section. My money would be on the Orka ship headed for Clovis City."

Gorski trusted Tierney's judgment. An Orka would carry many nuclear weapons as part of its' arsenal. "Contact that ship. Let them know that I wish to speak with them."

"Yes, Colonel." Tierney responded as he began accessing the communication system. He typed out an encrypted message to the Orka and signed the message as Colonel Nikolai

Gorski. He looked over his shoulder at Julianna. "Now we wait for a response."

Julianna slid into his lap and wrapped her hands around his neck. "And what should we do while we wait, Captain?"

Tierney gazed into her fetching eyes and ran his right hand into her long hair. He leaned into her and they locked lips. As they were kissing each other, their message arrived at the Orka space ship.

Elektra Frazier had been concerned that their firing on the Battle Cruiser would be detected by the enemy on the planet surface. She looked at the screen to her left in the pilot section of the Orka and swallowed. Nehwal stared at the red blinking light that signified that they were being sought out to communicate with another ship. Regehr shook his head from side to side. He did not trust it. Most likely it would be Admiral Zachariades demanding to know what was going on, or a pesky MI soldier on some watch tower demanding why they had not yet arrived with the promised prisoners. Either way, talking with them would be a bad move.

"Computer, can you identify the origin of the communication request?" Elektra crossed her arms and began pacing, waiting for the response.

"Yes. It is from a Super Raumschiff that is currently on a flight plan to Space Station Cy-7. My computer memory program has insufficient data to determine the ownership of the space craft." The computer voice responded. "But there is an encrypted message. You would need a voice activated password to open it."

"Who would send us an encrypted message?" Regehr was confused. Zachariades would not do such a thing. She would come right out and demand the information she sought. The same would be true for any MI operative.  This was a message from another source.

"Reynita or one of the others on our side," Elektra concluded after some thought. "But what is the password to open the message?"

The message then opened and was displayed on all the screens on the ship.

"Well I'll be. It was opened just by your voice." Nehwal said. "If this is the enemy, then they are being far too covert about this. They would just shoot us out of the sky."

Arch Frazier and the Mikec sisters read the message from Colonel Gorski as did the three cadets in the pilot section. There was silence among all of them for a few moments.

"Colonel Gorski is alive and wants to work with us," Regehr broke the silence.

"Or it could be a trap. This might be from the Sikorsky's and they want to get a fix on us by using their advanced communication systems," Nehwal countered.

"Arch, what do you think?" Elektra called out loudly.

"I think we have nothing to lose by responding," Arch told the others. "Think about it. We all have seen the wanted ads for Gorski. He is worth a million dollars to whoever turns him in. He must know he is taking a huge risk by reaching out to us. Over these past three years, I have gotten to know the man and one thing he does not do often is take risks. He is deliberate in his decision making and considers every angle of a problem while developing a solution. If that message is from him, he must know that we fired on the Lysander."

"How would he know that?" Nehwal cut in.

"I don't know how, he just does. Perhaps he saw us do it or he used some geometric formula to track us to our likely location. I cannot be sure. But I am sure of one thing. We need allies. If this message is from Colonel Gorski, then we cannot afford to ignore it." Arch paced back and forth as he spoke. "If we are still running this little troop as a democracy then I vote that we respond to him. If it is not him, we will know it quickly and can shut off the communication in time to avoid any viruses being downloaded onto our main frame and causing us to crash. We have little to lose and everything to gain here."

"I agree with my husband," Elektra added. "We should respond and see if it is the Colonel. With Seward, Hibbert, Warren, Rice and Evart dead, we are short of experienced military leaders. Reynita is smart, but she lacks the combat experience that Gorski would give us. Jasna?  Zorana? What do you say?"

The sisters listened to the couple as they had presented their case. Neither of them could recall ever meeting Colonel Gorski and therefore had little to add.

Jasna shrugged at her sister, "You're the oldest.  What do you think?"

"I say we respond. We have nothing to lose but our lives and right now we are all living on borrowed time anyway," Zorana said to the group.

Regehr and Nehwal had been inclined to vote no.  But they were clearly outnumbered. Instead of making an issue of the situation, they both voted to contact the messenger.

"So, who does the talking?" Regehr asked them.

"Right. Who will speak for us?" Nehwal nodded her head.

"I will," Arch announced. He recalled how he had been complimented by the Colonel over a year ago when he had chartered a Raumschiff to go to Space Station Cy-7 and rescue Elektra, Yuri, Staszko, Gillis and Evart. "The Colonel and I know each other. Not well, mind you, but he will remember me."

"All right lover. I am opening the communication channel now," Elektra announced.

Arch stood in front of the small communication camera on the second level. He cleared his throat, with the understanding that his three-dimensional image would be revealed to the person on the other end of the communication. "Colonel Gorski, can you read me? Colonel? This is cadet Arch Frazier. You remember me from the Blue's City over a year ago? Sir? Are you there?"

Nikolai Gorski pumped his fist when the three-dimensional image of Arch Frazier appeared on the communication screens. He had been correct; it had been a friend of Yuri's that had launched those missiles. The Colonel had fond memories of Frazier. When Yuri and his band of carousers had been in danger on Space Station Cy-7, it was Frazier that had chartered a ship to go to rescue them. He was a brave kid and loyal to his friends.

"Arch, yes I am here." Gorski responded quickly. "I have escaped and am on the run. What is your status?"

"About the same, sir. We are on a stolen ship and trying to find a neutral place to land."

"Son, I saw what you did. Launching those missiles was the right thing to do. You will get their attention and level the playing field in the upcoming battles. You wouldn't happen to have Piotr on board with you? Or any of Evart's wives or daughters? The Sikorsky's and Rosenburg's have offered rewards for their heads. I need to make sure that they are all safe."

Arch shook his head in the negative, "Sir, they were taken somewhere else by Stella and Paolo Andolini. Stella said that they would be safe with them. They took Piotr and all the Evart girls. Every one of them, sir. I have not heard any news of them being captured, so I must assume that they made it out of the City safely."

Gorski smiled with relief that his son was in good hands. Piotr was in danger and would be killed on sight by the MI soldiers under the command of General Sikorsky if found. Gorski always believed that his two sons could handle themselves in any situation, but a trained sniper would be able to kill from a safe distance and no amount of training or preparation could protect an individual from that form of ambush. "Good, son. Good. Who is leading your rebellion?"

"Reynita Calderon and some other officers. They are all off rounding up weapons, ships and numbers. We have already lost several of the cadets loyal to our side. Most of our losses were some of the upper-class cadet pilots. They tried to get to Admiral Seward, but after Seward was killed we lost touch with those cadets and we believe they were all shot down over the Forbidden Region. The Academy Dormitory buildings have been quarantined and are currently surrounded by several hundred soldiers loyal to General Sikorsky and Secretary General Rosenburg."

"I understand, son. What were you planning on doing next?"

"Sir, we were hoping to get the twenty thousand cadets out of the dormitories and charge the capital buildings," Arch told him slowly, his voice indicated a lack of confidence in the plan. "What about you?"

"I am trying to obtain more allies. Look, Arch. You are a brave young man, even though you refused to join up with the Marines. Your wife, Elektra, is tough as nails and I imagine she is there with you listening to our conversation. I need you to stand down for a day or two. Land somewhere safe and hide. I will contact you in about forty-eight hours with a plan to make those bastards pay for the pain and death they have inflicted. But for now, go underground and hide. You and your wife are smart kids. Keep your holographic-communication devices charged so that I can find you. Any questions?"

"Yes, I have a question. What if you fail to contact us in that time period?"

Gorski sighed and crossed his arms over his chest. Although the kid was a geology student, he certainly knew how to look ahead at the potential for failure and what to do in the event the unthinkable occurred. "Then you need to assume that I am dead or captured. At that time, I recommend you go forward with your plan to free the cadets from their dormitories. Arch, I need to stress to you and your friends just how dangerous the situation is. The Sikorsky's sent in one of their best Generals to get control of this planet. She is a sadistic woman and does not believe in taking prisoners. The new Secretary General, Rebecca Rosenburg? She is a sociopath. I worked with her when she was an assistant under Lyss. Never trust that woman. If you get captured they will kill you and your death will not be quick, especially if they learn you were responsible for blowing up their prized Battle Cruiser. Lay low and hide. I will be in touch with a plan of action. And whatever you do, if you come in to contact with Alexander Lyss, do not trust that man. They may have forced him from power, but he is not the sort of man that you can rely on. He is motivated by money and the Rosenburg's will always be the ones that can pay the best."

"Thank you, sir," Arch said as Gorski's three-dimensional image faded away.

Elektra was still standing in the pilot section and she had watched the entire conversation between her husband and Gorski on the screens. Nehwal and Regehr looked at her with the expectation that she would give them more orders.

"Derek, can you get us to that private landing strip without being detected?" Elektra asked him.

"Yes I can."

"So we are going to do what Gorski ordered?" Nehwal asked.

"Then let's go and find one close to the best hospital. My husband needs to have his arm treated."

# CHAPTER SIX

Cadet Astronaut Dino Black felt fortunate in that he had cleared the airspace of Clovis City. His stolen Raumschiff was towing four Allen Type Fighter space ships below it by use of enhanced cables. He had only a few cadets that were on board with him and only one of them, Brandon Harcourt, knew of his plans. Black throttled the Raumschiff to full speed as time was not a luxury to be wasted. He was mindful that Reynita, Elektra, Mia Nguyen and other cadets were placing themselves in harm's way to build an army to fight the Rosenburg occupation army. Black had grown to love planet New Edinburgh and had dreams of one day retiring in a nice home on the purple planet and live out his days. But with the arrival of the Sikorsky led soldiers from the Lysander, Black witnessed the mass murders of several prominent families. He had felt he needed to act.

So Black stole a fully operational Raumschiff from the cadet engineering depot as well as four Allen Type ships so that he could do his part. He flew to the land called Ferro's Province that was mostly owned by the Nour family. It was an area on the northern continent of the planet that was rich in diamonds, gold, silver, platinum, bauxite, cobalt, titanium, tungsten, iron, nickel, natural gas and free running streams of fresh water. Ferro's Province had a population of just under two hundred thousand men, women and children as well as several hundred aliens from the planet Akarzdamedia that had been forcefully moved from their home world to assist in the mining process.

Black took the ships to a military outpost in the southern part of Ferro's Province that was operated by his cousin, Leandrianna Black. She was an engineer with several advanced degrees from Sikorsky's Planet and she had no love of the Glorious Leader or his family. She was a civilian that contracted with the military and was well compensated for her knowledge and experience. One of her degrees was a doctorate in advanced weapons with a concentration on explosives. Dino planned on filling the four Allen Type Fighters with enough firepower to disable certain locations in Clovis City when the final battle began. Leandrianna was much older than Dino and she was the reason he decided to attend Clovis Academy. She had told him that Admiral Seward was the best pilot instructor in the Eight Solar Systems. She had been right. Seward was the best until the bastards working for the Rosenburg's murdered him.

Black whistled to himself and smiled at Brandon Harcourt and Trey Glenn who were sitting next to him in the pilot section of the ship. They were closing in on their destination and had made excellent timing.

Black and Glenn did not question the fact that their ship was not contacted by the MI. Nor did they think to question the reason that the Space Command fighter pilots in Clovis City failed to pursue them. Black believed that he was lucky. The reality was that his friend Brandon Harcourt had used his powers to make their Raumschiff and the four Allen Fighters in tow underneath them invisible to radar, heat sensors and the naked eye. Brandon had always passed himself off as the average Child of Athena, one that possessed mind control, pleasant scents that assisted him in attracting a mate or the ability to read a person's mind. But Brandon was much more than that, a secret he shared with only one other classmate at the Academy. He said nothing to his friend Dino Black of his covering their ships from detection. He smiled and acted as if he were enjoying the ride, all the while using his powers to obscure them from all manner of scanning devices.

Unbeknownst to the three men, cadet Lu Wang was pacing back and forth in the lower level of the Raumschiff, trying to find out what Black and his group were up to. Wang had previously betrayed Dirk and Therese Fenster to the Rosenburg's for a healthy pay day. He hoped that he would be able to use the information he would gather by pretending to be Black's friend as another nice cash pay off.

The sun set as General Kimberly Sikorsky watched the red-orange hue turn to darkness. She was uneasy given the number of cadets and military service men and women that had defected or fled. Her biggest fear was that they would attempt to rebel against their newly formed military structure. Although she was concerned, she was pragmatic and never was one to sit back and allow events to occur which caused her to react. She decided to be proactive and prepare for the inevitable war.

One of her many moves was to kill the top leaders on the planet that were not related to the Rosenburg's. Her secondary moves were to ensure the loyalty of those that had displayed competence in the past and would ably replace those that were eliminated. The General had been successful in convincing Professor Rand to take over the Academy as the new Dean. Although there were many students that had accused Rand of sexual harassment, there seemed to be no other issues with her background check.

Former Secretary General to the Security Council, Alexander Lyss, was assigned to become the manager of domestic affairs in Clovis City. He would take charge of the mundane chores of assuring competent administration of the orphan homes, garbage collection and disposal, immigration and visitation management and street cleaning. Lyss was livid when he was told of his demotion but calmed down when the subject of his family and their well-being was mentioned. Lyss was smart enough to comprehend the veiled threat from the General. Either do as he was told or watch his children die.

She had also bribed Space Command Captain Karl Schneller, the former personal pilot to Lyss, to lead the Clovis City fighter pilots in case of confrontation. Although Schneller had been difficult to recruit, he became very reasonable when his children and wives were arrested and sent to one of the several temporary prison camps that had been built throughout Clovis City. Sikorsky gave Schneller an ultimatum, either join the new military leaders or watch as his children were beheaded. Schneller, being the astute man that he was, agreed to Sikorsky's terms.

"Ah God!" Rebecca Rosenburg yelled out as she shook with orgasmic rapture. She had consummated her new relationship with Angus McWilliams several times and she found that each sexual encounter with the man was more pleasurable than the previous. She was lying on her back, on top of her large desk in her sound proof office located on the eightieth floor of the United Nations Building. Her naked body was covered in sweat, her breathing was deep and her heart rate was increased due to the animal magnetism she felt for McWilliams. He was on top of her, naked as well, with his erection still inside of her. He was also breathing heavily and kissing her lips and breasts as he reveled in the moment of pleasure. Before they had started making love, Rebecca had McWilliams take an extra dose of drugs that enhanced the sexual experience and increased his stamina.

"I have some sisters and cousins," Rebecca told him in between breaths.

"For a threesome?" McWilliams asked hopefully.

"No. No. I want you to get some of your friends for them," Rebecca paused and moaned as he kissed her breasts. "One of my cousins, she is really hot. She needs a man."

"And you want me to set her up?"

Rebecca nodded and smiled as he continued to thrust himself inside of her, slowly, with a rhythm that sent chills throughout her. "Yes. She likes pilots."

McWilliams kissed her lips softly and continued his thrusts into her. "I have a friend from the Bragg Gang, he is stationed in the ice caps science station. He just got his commission. He would be good."

"Name? Ah, Angus, that feels so good!"

"Johann. Johann LeSkaysner."

"Good," Rebecca said as she wrapped her legs around McWilliams. "I will have him transferred here. Don't stop!"

McWilliams did not disappoint her.

# CHAPTER SEVEN

During the hours that the First and Second Fleets had dueled to the death in the solar system of Sikorsky's Planet, a lone stealth super Raumschiff had been searching for a clue, any residual piece of evidence, which would reveal the final fate of the *Calypso* and her crew. Charles Bennington, the former security officer that had retired and then took a position as chief of the criminal investigation division on Space Station Cy-7, was resolute in his decision that he and his crew would not abandon the search even though there was such a massive conflict occurring all around them. He prayed that the stealth mechanisms of his space craft would keep the two competing forces from detecting their presence.   And they searched and searched until they finally found something.

Doctor Nicolette Rosenburg, who was one of the few living humans that knew how to produce Replicants in mass quantities. She had become Bennington's lover, surprised that a man of action such as he was would be interested in a studious woman like her. She was ecstatic when one of the Garrison clones informed them that they had found something. It was an old-style communication beacon that was floating aimlessly near the binary stars. Bennington immediately ordered that the space craft retrieve the item for closer inspection. Three Garrison clones donned enviro-suits and went out into deep space. Using hand held magnetizers, the Garrison men retrieved the eight-foot-long and four-foot-wide metallic shelled beacon. After ensuring there were no deadly biological organisms attached to it, they brought the beacon back on board the craft where Bennington, Nicolette, twelve clones of Drayton Love Easter, nine other clones of Garrison, twelve clones of Kristen Rosenburg and twelve clones of Nicollete were waiting.

The crew of fifty were all filled with wonder as to whether this two-hundred-year-old canister contained the last words of Robert Richard Andrews. They did not have to wait long to find out. Bennington and three of the Garrison Replicants quickly wired the beacon to the ship computer system. They were all typing on holographic keypads until the computer indicated that it had downloaded all the data and recordings from the device.

Bennington nodded to Nicolette, "Computer, can you play for us the last recording that was found in the beacon?"

The computer did not respond verbally as it normally would. Instead, it began to project images on the wall of the computer room, as if the crew were at an old-style motion picture theater. And they saw that they had found exactly what they had been searching for.

The image had not been corrupted at all from the two centuries it had floated in the protective canister. The quality of the scene was as clear as a blue sky. Nicolette held Bennington's hand tightly as she whispered to herself: "Please let it be Andrews."

And it was.

They saw Robert Richard Andrews on the command station of the ancient ship *Calypso*. There were two seats near the front of that section, one was empty and one was occupied by astronaut Javier Perez Guerrero. Around the section were numerous floor to ceiling computer stations with chairs around them. Six of the chairs were occupied by daughters of Andrews. They were all working feverishly on projects as their father was speaking on the screen. Andrews was dressed in a two-piece light green uniform, with breast pockets and a web belt around his pants. His dark brown boots stood out the white metal floor of the *Calypso* as he paced back and forth.

Perez Guerrero was wearing a dark blue one-piece flight suit with black boots. His dark hair was slicked back and hung over his shoulders. His eyes showed that he was concerned about their situation. He had both of his hands wrapped around the steering wheel of the space craft and was doing his level best to keep the ship under control as it increased speed.

"The *Calypso* was about as large as a Super Raumschiff," one of the Love-Easter clones remarked as he observed that the command room of the ship was only slightly larger that of a current model of the Fenster Corporation version of the Raumschiff.

"She only had a crew capacity of fifty-eight," Jimmy Garrison stated as he viewed the scene before him.

"People of Earth, this is our last broadcast!" Bennington heard Andrews saying with a loud voice. He could hear the strain of the engines of the *Calypso* and what sounded like the outer hull of the ship making painful noises as it was being urged on at high speeds by astronaut Perez Guerrero.

"We were contacted by the Queen of the Akarzdamedians! She has begged for a cease fire and to begin a diplomatic solution. I informed U.N. mission commander Vladimir Sikorsky of the request! He refused to negotiate for peace. I insisted and he declared me and the *Calypso* enemies of humanity! He has fired nuclear weapons at our ship!" Andrews continued as he sat down in the empty seat next to Perez Guerrero. "My daughter, Judy, suggested that we try and outrun the projectiles by using the gravitational pull of the largest sun!"

The stunned members of the ship watched as the recording continued with Andrews and Perez Guerrero trying to control the direction of the space craft. They could see that the two men had strain on their faces. They were grinding their teeth as the *Calypso* was reaching speeds that were not though possible in that time.

"Father! We are over ten thousand kilometers an hour!" A frantic young Judy Andrews screamed out. She was sitting in one of the seats around the computer banks of the command station. Over her head of long dark was a head phone set and a tear drop microphone. She looked so young, Nicolette thought to herself. History had recorded that she had been sixteen years old when she died with her family.

"Keep monitoring everything!" Andrews barked at his daughters. "When those missiles get too close for comfort, we need to jettison all of our communication warning beacons! The world needs to know that we were betrayed by Sikorsky and Tan! Are the canisters ready to deploy?"

"Yes father!" Judy Andrews yelled. Her eyes were wide with amazement. "Daddy! What are all of these colors?"

The audience watching the recording could see that the inside of the *Calypso* had numerous energy bolts, almost like lightening, flickering here and there. There were different shades of pink, red, yellow, orange and white bolts that were flashing throughout the ship. All the crew members had grey smoke rising from their uniforms. Andrews was struggling with the pilot controls as he realized they were experiencing an anomaly that he had never seen before.

"They are so beautiful!" Deanna Andrews called out.

"Launch the beacons!" Robert Andrews ordered as the *Calypso* was dangerously close to being hit by one or more of the nuclear missiles that Vladimir Sikorsky had fired on him.

"They look like Angels!" Judy Andrews gasped as some of the lightening colors began to take shape.

"Launch the recording beacons!" Andrews screamed even louder.

Judy Andrews began pressing several buttons and she was smiling.

Bennington and Nicolette looked at each other in awe as the last vision they saw recorded was that of a lightning bolt taking shape into an angelic form. It was female and was floating above Judy Andrews. The angel touched her face, like a loving mother would caress the face of a newborn child.

The recording ended with the voice of the angel telling young Judy Andrews two words: "Not yet."

The words sounded like an echo and musical at the same time. Bennington felt a chill go through his spine when he heard the colorful being speak, not from fear but from the knowledge that he had just witnessed a being from another world. He was intrigued.

And then the recording ended.

The three Garrison clones that were in attendance looked toward Nicolette and Bennington as they waited for their next orders. There were several Love-Easter's there standing in silence. All eyes were on the couple that commanded the ship.

Finally, Bennington made his decision, "We need to connect with the nearest broadcast satellite in the solar system. Then link all of the recordings of this canister so that the eight solar systems will be able to see this. But we upload this recording first. This should give humanity a little bit of righteous indignation to use against Sikorsky. The history books were all lies. We were all taught in school how the Andrews family and the Calypso were vaporized by the Akarzdamedian armies. All along, it had been Sikorsky that had killed them. The world needs to know the truth."

"Let's do it," one of the Garrison clones agreed and motioned for the other two to follow his lead. "But that angel that appeared at the end of the recording, what was that?"

"I don't know," Bennington responded.

Nicolette watched as the others began to get to work. She wondered how her sisters were faring on their individual missions in other solar systems. She had entered an alliance with Penelope Rosenburg to start a civil war and fight for the elimination of the Sikorsky rule. Although these lost recordings would serve as an excellent public relations coup, it might not resonate with the poor or those that were migrant travelers. They might not care about such events and were more likely than not to shrug their shoulders with apathy regarding their government lying to them. If history was to repeat itself, she knew that the war would ultimately be decided by a small portion of the population. The majority would sit back and enjoy the show as others sacrificed their lives for them.

Nicolette pondered the angelic vision that appeared before Judy Andrews in the recording and looked out at the darkness of space. She recalled the words that the angel told the young girl. "Not yet." Nicolette had heard that phrase recently and she concentrated, trying to recall where she had heard that before. Then she remembered. She had heard it in an interview conducted with Marco Andolini after the Blood Moon Incident. He had been asked by the reporter about his near-death experience. Marco had claimed he heard a voice tell him those two words just before he was ejected from his doomed ship. Nicolette tapped her fingernails on the computer panel in front of her and wondered about the true power in the universe. Had the Andrews family inadvertently captured something on the recording that was not meant to be seen? Or did the angelic figure want to be discovered for some bigger reason that none of them could understand? Nicolette smiled to herself as she compared the events that Marco and the Andrews went through. Each event was over two hundred years apart in time. But the words were the same. Marco even described the voice to sound just as the voice that spoke to Judy Andrews had.

"Damn," Nicolette whispered to herself. "Judy Andrews must still be alive somewhere."

"Excuse me?" Bennington responded.

"That being, angel, whatever it was. I bet that it removed Judy Andrews from the pending doom of her family. I bet she is alive somewhere."

"That would be impossible," Bennington told her. "That ship was hit by several nuclear weapons. The Andrews family was annihilated."

Nicolette shook her head, "We shall see."

# CHAPTER EIGHT

The flight to Dakota Province took less than thirty minutes. During the trip, Reynita Calderon and her crew of rebels devised specific missions for each of them to complete to further their plans to replace the current planetary government. Harumi, Jen Staszko and Else Regehr spent the thirty minutes memorizing the military chain of command in that settlement. They learned that there were ten flight squadrons consisting of forty-two pilots in each pilot was assigned an engineer, two mechanical technicians, two weapons technicians and a computer technician. The pilots were all officers, the majority holding the ranks of Ensign or Lieutenant Junior Grade and the support staff were all non-commissioned officers, holding the ranks of Technical Sergeant or lower. The only exception was the engineer assigned each pilot was a well-paid civilian.

In addition, they learned that each of the squadrons had a squadron leader that had a rank of Lieutenant. The squadrons were commanded by Captain Rendon and her executive officer, Commander Feklisov. Under those two officers were four staff commanders for personnel, supplies, training and tactical. The last tactical officer for the ten squadrons had been killed in an accidental boiler room explosion just two weeks earlier. But the other three would have to be dealt with in some manner if their mission was to be a success.

Reynita had chosen the Dakota settlements as her first target for several reasons. The first was that the original colonists had been native American Indians from North and South Dakota located on Old Earth. Their names had been true to their roots and their chief had been a man named Shooting Star McCabe. Shooting Star and his family grew to be close friends with Reynita's father during the Dinosaur Wars. Likewise, Reynita and her siblings became close to Shooting Star's children, nephews and grandchildren. Reynita was confident that the family would side with her cause and even support the rebellion.

The second reason she selected the Dakota Province was due to the number of former Bragg Gang members that had secured positions in the military ranks there. First Lieutenant Alexis de Vida Brock was the executive officer at one of the Military Intelligence companies located near the capital. Alexis had a brother, Carletto, who was serving as one of the squadron commanders in the province. The Brock's had been loyal Bragg Gang members during their four years as cadets at Clovis Academy. Carletto was the long-time love interest for Lisa

Bragg, who was a pilot stationed in the Dakota Province. Daniella Bragg was in the same squadron as her sister Lisa.

The problem for Reynita and her band of lady rebels was to eliminate the highest-ranking officers so that her friends could rise in rank, take control of the military establishment and back the play of the family of Shooting Star McCabe. The McCabe family support was critical since they were the most financially stable family in the territory and had a vast extended family presence.

Reynita first contacted the patriarch of the McCabe family to secure his blessings in the rebellion. The pleasantries of their conversation lasted longer than Reynita had liked, but she kept calm as she told the elderly man all about how her father and uncle had been doing the past year. She informed the man about the progress of each of her siblings. McCabe pressed Reynita to marry one of his grandsons, which he always did whenever the Calderon and McCabe families would meet. She politely declined the offer, informing the man that she had a boyfriend. The two finally began to discuss the idea of the Dakota's being free of the Clovis City United Nations rule, and the Rosenburg family. McCabe indicated that he would be supportive of such a change as he was weary of the Rosenburg's demands for monetary compensation for this unnecessary program or that. No contract was needed to seal the deal with the man.    The McCabe's word was their bond and Reynita was satisfied that the wealthiest family in the Dakota's was now with her.

She next turned her attention to her friend Alexis de Vida Brock. Alexis had been one of the original Bragg Gang members with the arrest record to prove it. She had been incarcerated in Clovis City three times, Lynott's Land once and the Dakota Province once. Her family hired the best lawyers to get her out of the three Clovis City charges. They were successful and the courts wrote those off as cadets blowing off steam during a bar fight.

The charge in Lynott's Land had been difficult as all the gang had been implicated in that event, save Reynita. The Bragg's crashed a wedding, literally, and caused a major episode of violence and property destruction. Reynita had to help bail out her friends, with the help of her former lover, Les Gillis. Each of the Bragg Gang members had to obtain a thousand Lynott Dollars from their parents to pay off the corrupt General Tan and the charges magically disappeared.

The arrest in the Dakota's was due to a fight that Alexis had not started. One of the McCabe family, a man named Pointed Arrow McCabe, had taken a liking to Alexis. It happened during one of the large family gatherings between the Calderon's, Nour's, Bragg's, McCabe's and Brock's. Alexis had been nineteen at the time. She had found him attractive as well in that Pointed Arrow was a handsome man, tall, with long dark hair and toned body.

As the family gathering went deep into the night, Alexis decided she wanted to see if Pointed Arrow would live up to his name and led him off to the woods for some heavy-duty penetration. Unfortunately for the would-be lovers, another man named Ezekiel Rosenburg had taken an interest in Alexis. The man followed the two lovers and became enraged with jealousy when he watched them begin to make love. Ezekiel attacked Pointed Arrow and the men fought with knives over the chance to mount Alexis. Not willing to allow a knife fight to determine which man earned the right to bed her, Alexis smashed a large rock over the back of Ezekiel's head. The grandson of the powerful Rosenburg family ended up in a coma and both Alexis and Pointed Arrow went to jail. Alfred Rosenburg demanded that the two be convicted and sent to the prison planet Cootron. It took the intervention of Sean Collins to have the charges dropped.

Reynita was gratified that her satellite call to Alexis was taken. Her friend was drinking coffee and wearing her solid black battle fatigues as she answered the call. "You little vixen! Reynita, how in the name of the damned have you been?"

"I have had better weeks, Alexis. How about you? Any Pointed Arrow stories to update me with?" Reynita did not flinch at being called 'little vixen' as that was the name Alexis used for her ever since they first met.

Alexis laughed out loud and shook her head from side to side. "No, he got married to some other woman. Can you believe that? I was ready to let him ride me day and night, but his family found some average looking banker girl from a well to do family and married him off. Too bad, his name was very appropriate as it matched his abilities in the bedroom. I sure miss his shaft, if you know what I mean. And you, are you seeing anyone special?"

"I think so. I mean, it is complicated. I'm in a relationship with my platoon sergeant. Alexis, he is so hot. He has muscles on top of his muscles and he just gets me so turned on by the way he looks at me. I see the lust in his eyes and then he just takes me. I can't say no to him. I know I am his commanding officer and that we shouldn't be doing it, but I just love his hands on my body."

Alexis was still laughing as Reynita spoke, "You still are a little vixen. That is a great arrangement. You outrank him so you can order him to do whatever you want, sexually I mean."

"I don't have to order him. He just takes charge and it feels so good."

"What is his name?"

"Mark Lund."

"Sounds hot. What is he, Scandinavian? Well, I have hit a dry spell in my love life ever since Pointed Arrow married that girl. Do you have any men out there that you can send my way?"

Reynita smiled and nodded her head, "My brother Pepito was always hot for you. He has grown up quite a bit over the last two years and I think you would like him."

"Pepito, huh? He was cute. I think I could give him a try. So what's up, little vixen? What was so urgent that you wanted to contact me today?"

Reynita leaned into her holographic-communication device and whispered to her friend, "Are you alone right now? I need to speak with you off the record."

"Yes, why?"

"Because I do not want anyone else to know what we are up to, that's why."

"Shoot."

Reynita began to tell Alexis everything about the past two days. Alexis sipped her coffee and listened intently to the quick rendition of the events. Reynita covered all the highlights and left out most of the details. But she eventually got down to what she wanted Alexis to do. "I need you to take over the MI forces in the Dakota's and be in command quickly because the proverbial poggie dung is about to get flung."

Alexis finished her coffee and thought of the implications of such an act of treason. If they failed, they would all most certainly be executed. If they succeeded, then the Rosenburg bastards would be gone forever. "You know how fond I was of Lupita. I will take your word for the fact that it was the Royal's that had her killed. All right, you little vixen. I'm in and I know exactly how to get rid of the other MI officers."

Reynita next had to get two of her lady rebels to contact an old friend by satellite device. She had Staszko and Harumi by her side as the person they were attempting to add to their small group had been a Gorski Gang member. Reynita was certain that the woman might have some negative feelings toward her.

"Yes? Who is this?" the voice responded to the holo-com device call. A small holographic image of Aura Lynda Glenn materialized before them. She was wearing her dark blue fatigue pilot uniform; her long hair was pinned up and she had a hand laser fastened just above her left breast where she could grab it for quick use.

"Hello Lieutenant. You may not remember me. My name is Reynita Calderon."

Glenn was silent for a moment as she wondered why an old rival would bother reaching out to her. "Yes, I remember you. You used to run with that ass named Nour and the other one, what was his name? Zerbe? Yes, that was you, right? You were one of the jerks that ruined Dia and Felicia's wedding celebration."

Reynita nodded to each of Glenn's accusations, "You are correct on each account. That was me. But I no longer run with Zerbe or Nour or Bragg and I am very sorry about the wedding and the other fights we got into with you, your brother and the others."

Glenn was silent for a moment as she looked over the three-dimensional image of her former rival. She saw that she was wearing the solid black uniform of the MI branch, "What can I do for you, Miss Militizia?"

Reynita grimaced at the reference to her black uniform. The astronaut corps typically referred to the MI soldiers as Militizia and it was not a term of endearment.

"I am with Jen and Harumi. We want to meet you when we arrive in Dakota's Territory. What would be convenient for you?"

Glenn was again silent for a few moments before responding, "Harumi, you and I have much to discuss. My brother and your husband were serving together under Admiral Weems. I heard that the Admiral was killed and I have lost contact with Frank. Have you heard from Dominic?"

"No, not since he told me they were flying to planet Cootron." Harumi responded.

"That was my last report as well. You know that Frank is a father now? I just hope that nothing bad has happened to them." Glenn sighed, "Are you bringing me bad news about my parents or siblings in Clovis City or Lynott's Land? I have been watching the news reports about the military crackdown. Has something happened to my parents?"

"No, not yet. But it is about them and everyone else that lives on this planet that brought us to you. Lynda we really need to speak in person." Staszko was intentionally vague in her words in case some MI technician had hacked into their communication system.

Glenn realized that the women did not wish to reveal the reason for wanting to meet her. She had a sullen look on her face as she determined that their desire to meet was to discuss a topic best not brought up over live satellite feeds that could be easily recorded by the Militzia. In her experience, such meetings generally were for some purpose that led to no good.

"Okay, I will meet with you. I will be at a restaurant off base called Ojos Locos. It has really good food and the beer is always cold," Glenn finally told them after a long pause. "It had better be good or Calderon will get her butt kicked all the way back to Clovis City."

Reynita waited for the communication line between their ship and Glenn was severed before she addressed the others. "When we land, Harumi and Jen are with me. We will meet

Lynda at the bar she proposed and see if we can add her to our group. Blossom, you stay with the ship and don't let anyone else on board unless I clear it. The rest of you, I want you to survey the hills above the Squadron Command buildings. Find some good areas and set up sniper positions. Once you are ready, notify me immediately. If Lynda is willing to join us, we must take out the commander of the squadrons and her XO."

"If someone tries to come on board the ship, how do I dissuade them?" Li asked as she crossed her arms.

Tamura handed Li a laser pistol, "Shoot them right between the eyes."

"I suppose that is one way to show them," Li took the pistol as she glared at Tamura.

"Shoot as a last resort," Reynita told Li. "You are pretty diplomatic, so I know you will be able to think of something if anyone wants to inspect the ship. If you find yourself in a fix, contact me on my holo-com."

Elsa Regehr was standing in the rear with her hand raised like a grade school student trying to get the attention of her teacher. Reynita pointed in her direction. "What is it?"

"Well, I have never fired a sniper rifle before," Regehr said as she fidgeted. "So, I was wondering why I would be sent off on such a mission. I would not know what to do."

"Elsa, you and Melissa will be acting as spotters for Sara, Miyu and Supreet. They will be relying on you two to locate the two main targets for them. That is why I had you memorize their faces. It is a very important job, Elsa. Can we count on you?"

Regehr nodded her head, "Yes, Reynita. You can count on me."

"Good," Reynita smiled and turned to face Staszko and Harumi. "We will keep up the facade of you two being military enlisted women. If we are approached by any suspicious MI soldiers, let me do all the talking. No shooting or killing unless I act first. Got it?"

"You are the boss," Staszko responded as she sheathed a twelve-inch blade into a hilt on her web belt.

"Reynita, I have an idea," Supreet Patel told her. "If we use our holo-com's, then they will be bouncing off the local transmission towers, go through the satellite system and then to the person we are communicating with. That means that General Tan and her MI spies could tap into our conversations. Elsa and I can alter the frequencies of our devices so that we bypass the satellite system and use the old communication beacons that are all over the planet. They were dropped by the first settlers and Marines about seventeen years ago. They were never destroyed and we can use them. Remember, Elsa?"

Regehr pulled out her own device from her belt pouch, "Supreet is right! We took a class together this semester and learned how to open these and rewire them for that purpose. We will still be able to receive incoming calls through the satellite system, but our personal communications would go through the planetary beacon system."

"And the authorities will not be able to listen in to our private conversations?" Stewart concluded. "How do we do it?"

Supreet pointed down toward the engineering section of the ship. "Elsa and I just need a few tools and some wiring and then we can fix all of the devices."

"How long to do it on all of our communication devices?" Reynita wanted to know.

"About thirty minutes each," Supreet informed her.

Reynita tapped her left foot on the metal flooring of the space craft. They did not have the time for that, even though it was a great covert move. The situation at Clovis City had grown untenable. "What if the sender was on the beacon system but the receiver was not?"

"Then it would have the same effect," Supreet answered quickly.

"All right, Supreet. I want you and Elsa to fix your devices as well as those belonging to Miyu, Sara and Melissa. Do it while you are in route for the hills. Once they are all fixed up, contact me. You can fix the rest of ours later. We cannot delay our mission here. Everything depends on us securing an air attack. Now let's move out." Reynita led Harumi and Staszko toward the walk ramp that led to the planet surface.

Li watched in silence as the other women left her behind. When the last of them were off the rear loading ramp, Li ordered the ship computer to raise the ramp and seal the rear bulkheads. She quietly worried for her family and friends back in Clovis City. She hoped that the plans laid out by Calderon and the other officers that had allied themselves with her worked.

Tamura took the point with her group as she walked briskly across the long landing strip, passing dozens of space craft of varying sizes as she scanned the hills in the distance. She heard the distant sound of the waves of the New Edinburgh Ocean crashing on the beaches. The air smelled fresh and clean. She marveled at the number of men and women that were frolicking in the direction of the beaches, wearing skimpy outfits and carrying towels in their hands. Tamura would never be able to bring herself to go to the beaches on the planet due to the large predators that populated the oceans. It was not uncommon for one of those creatures to get past the water defenses and devour humans. Tamura felt that the care free citizens she passed were taking an unacceptable risk and she would never join them.

One of the muscular men that was heading toward the beach whistled at the women as they passed him by. He tried his best to get them to stop by waving his arms and telling them how much he wanted to see them all naked on the sand.

"He's cute," Regehr whispered to Supreet.

"Ignore him. He's a cute pig," Supreet told her. "We have a job to do. We can get some action later."

Melissa Harcourt brought up the rear of the five-woman team and found the man shouting at them annoying. She put a suggestion in his mind that he should go get drunk at a local bar and leave women alone for the rest of the week. The man stopped his verbal calls at the women and walked away from them, as if in a trance.

Stewart pulled out a small pair of green and black binocular glasses and looked over the hill tops. Some small birds flew by, obscuring her view for a second. She estimated that they had about three kilometers to walk and an additional two to climb. Fortunately, the hills were not too steep and the weather was agreeable. She picked up the pace to walk alongside Tamura.

Reynita led Staszko and Harumi to the beaches, full of fine grained light purple sand and the rows of bars located there. Most of the bars and restaurants were made from thatch materials and had doors that resembled bamboo glued together. The colors were mostly light reds and purples. The beach was full of naked men and women, lying on the purple sand, catching the rays from the sun. There were a few couples that were engaging in sexual acts on the beach. Reynita found herself missing Lund as she saw a handsome looking young man mounting a voluptuous brunette. Reynita was amazed that so many people were willing to have sex out in the open, with a large audience to cheer them on. Although the Glorious Leader encouraged such behavior, her parents had taught her differently. She paused when she noticed a small group of six MI soldiers in the distance. They were patrolling the beaches, most likely to keep the civilians safe from any aquatic predators that might break through the metal wires that were located half a mile into the ocean. It happened rarely, but when it did, bloody mayhem followed.

"Over there!" Staszko was pointing toward a two-story building with a light red thatch roof that was about fifty feet from them. The frame of the structure was light blue with silver trim. There was a black set of letters on the light red walls that said "Ojos Locos."

The three women walked faster and stepped over two women that were kissing and running their hands over each other near the entrance of the establishment. Harumi walked in first and looked around to see if Glenn was there yet. There were two long bars, manned by two bartenders at each, about forty small tables that could comfortably seat four people at each place and restrooms and a kitchen to the rear. There was a flight of stairs going up to the second floor. The business was popular. Harumi quickly guessed that there were over two hundred patron's present, eating seafood and drinking tropical alcoholic beverages. Most of the customers were nude or close to it.

Staszko saw Glenn first. The two women ran to each other and hugged. Reynita breathed a sigh of relief since she had fully expected Glenn to stand them up. Glenn hugged Harumi and shrugged at Reynita, still holding a grudge for what the Bragg Gang had done to the wedding ceremony of Felicia Essex and Dia Cho. She led the three women to a corner table that was near the west wall, overlooking the beach. Glenn sat down and had a pint of ale there that she had been nursing while she waited for the women to arrive.

A waitress promptly arrived and took their orders. Once she left, Glenn leaned over the table and glared at Reynita. The animosity between them was long standing. The Glenn and Calderon families were two of the largest in Clovis City. The clashes between the Glenn and Calderon children had grown into the stuff of legend. Staszko was in the Academy a year prior to Harumi and had seen some of the hatred played out before her eyes. Whenever the Bragg Gang initiated a fight, the Glenn's would take the opportunity to tangle with the Calderon's. Aura Lynda had been involved in some of those incidents. Staszko smiled at Harumi as a non-verbal way of letting her know that, despite the tension in the air, everything would turn out fine.

"I do not know how you convinced my two friends here to join you, Reynita. But I have a long memory. You and your poggie shit friends did a lot of damage all those years ago." Lynda hissed the words at her and pointed her right index finger in Reynita's face.

"Lynda, I did not do anything," Reynita protested.

"Aura Lynda," Glenn corrected her.

"Okay, Aura Lynda. I did not bust up the wedding. I left with Les Gillis when things started getting ugly. Don't you remember?"

"How could I remember anything of the sort?" Glenn paused to drink from her pint. "I was fighting against Nour and Zerbe and your other friends. Besides, I don't believe you. Les is my friend. Why would Les go with you?"

"Because he wanted to fuck me. And we did." Reynita smiled as the waitress delivered her a pint of her own. "We did it in the dark, behind some Raumschiffs on the Lynott's Land space port and he was a hell of a lover, I will give him that."

Glenn finished her pint and motioned to the waitress for a refill. "I still do not believe you. I doubt Les would involve himself with a Bragg Gang member. So, you used my two friends here to lure me to meet you. Why? Why would a committed Bragg Gang bitch want to meet with me after all this time has passed? Why?"

Reynita leaned in closer to Glenn and whispered to her, "Because I want your squadrons of ships and pilots to come with me, Harumi and Jen."

Glenn glared at her for a moment and waited for her new pint of ale to arrive. "Go with you to what location?"

"To a place we have never seen before. I want us to all go to a place called freedom."

Glenn busted out laughing and looked over at Staszko, "Is this bitch serious?"

"Yes, she is," Staszko told her. "Lynda, the new military commanders murdered Sigebert Evart, Admiral Seward, the Warren's and your ex, Captain Hibbert."

Glenn's anger toward Reynita seemed to change as she took in Staszko's words. Her face softened and she grew sullen as she thought of all the people from her schooling that were mentioned. The name that cut into her heart and mind was Hibbert. He had been her main instructor in the astronaut program, her mentor and in her senior year she had a brief affair with him. As with many extra-marital relationships, Hibbert refused to leave his wives and children which left Glenn with unresolved emotional issues and much confusion as to the nature of relationships. Although she had not spoken to Hibbert for over a year, she mourned him and felt as if she had lost a part of her life.

"How?" Glenn finally forced herself to ask. "How did they all die? Who killed them?"

"Seward was shot in the back by a sniper. Evart was thrown from the UN Tower; he was dead on impact. The Warrens were tortured and had their sex organs cut out before they were hung to death on the Academy flagpole. Hibbert and all of the other pilots were mauled by one of those large aliens called Babbcottiatta." Staszko paused and sipped from her beer mug. "I am sorry to be the one to bring you the news, Lynda. There are many others that have been killed. They arrested Colonel Gorski and some of his officers."

"And most of my former gang members are either dead or missing," Reynita informed her. "Many of them were in the middle of the fight that cost the lives of Seward and all of the pilot instructors. They were shot down over the Forbidden Region when they attempted to escape. Six of my brothers were in one of the ships that went down as were John Gauthier and James Cobb."

"Lynda, you know that Marco, Felicia and Dia were with the Second Fleet and most likely among the many casualties of the Glorious Leader's orders to take no prisoners," Harumi added. "The events that are unfolding have influenced all of us."

Glenn leaned back in her chair and snapped at the waitress to get her attention. After the waitress looked in their direction, Glenn used her hands to act like she was scribbling on something to signify that she wanted the check. She leaned forward as she collected her thoughts and faced the three women. "You ladies are considering insurrection? I am an officer in the Space Command and it would be my duty to turn you in for execution. I have a huge extended family that I need to protect."

"I sense that there is a refrain coming our way?" Staszko was leaning in close as well to avoid other patrons overhearing the conversation.

"First, my little brother, Trey, is attending the Academy. Is there any news of where he might be?" Glenn whispered, dreading the answer.

"He is with some of the junior officers that have joined up with me," Reynita assured her. "Trey is safe, but he has decided to join our, as you call it, insurrection. He has decided and the time is coming for everyone to pick a side. You can try to turn us in as would be your duty to your oath to the service. If you do, I will fight you. I would rather have you on my side. The decision you have today, Aura Lynda, is whether you have had enough of the narcissists and sociopaths that make up the Sikorsky Regime. I have. My sister is dead because of them. I may be young and inexperienced as a soldier, but I will kill as many of them as I can before they kill me."

Glenn laughed out loud and then glared into Reynita's eyes, "You do realize that Daniella and Lisa Bragg are a part of my squadron? Carletto de Vida Brock is one of the other squadron commanders. All three were in your little piece of shit Gang. I have tolerated them over the time we have been stationed here together. Maybe it is time I put aside our old differences and see if we can all work together. If I help you, Reynita, and I have not yet said yes, but if I do, you need to do something about Captain Rendon and Commander Feklisov. They command the entire Planetary Defense System Space Command division."

"I am aware of the chain of command," Reynita assured her as she drank from her beer mug. "And I did know that Carletto, Lisa and Daniella were stationed here as pilots. They will join us. Lisa and Daniella are still pissed off that their brother William was killed by assassins sent in by the Rosenburg's. They want blood. Carletto will do whatever Lisa tells him to do. The question for you is this: can you rally all of the other fighter pilots to our side if I can get rid of Feklisov and Rendon?"

"And by get rid of, do you mean arrest them or something else?" Glenn fidgeted in her chair at the thought of the implications if the rebellion moved forward.

"By get rid of I mean I intend to have the two bitches assassinated," Reynita replied in a cold tone of voice. "So, now that you know I intend to commit treason, it is time for you to make a move. Arrest me or join us. Which will it be?"

"Come on, Lynda," Harumi said with urgency in her voice. "We need you. People are dying and we can't stop it unless we have a powerful aerial presence. You have to join us."

Glenn pursed her lips and looked into Harumi's eyes and then turned her head toward Staszko and back to Reynita. "I don't even want to know how you plan on killing my Captain and her Exec. But if you succeed, and I join up with you, what do you want from me?"

"I studied your chain of command and concluded that without Rendon and Feklisov, you and Carletto would be the highest-ranking pilots left. You two would become the de facto commanders of the entire fleet of fighter squadrons."

"Not true, Reynita. Not true. There are five other squadron commanders that are here and then there are the squadrons in Clovis City, Lynott's Land and the Ferro Provinces. What about all of them?"

Reynita smiled and tapped Glenn's arm, "The other squadron commanders are already on our side, they just don't know it yet. Each of them are daughters of people that have been directly affected by the military presence here. One is the illegitimate daughter of the attorney named Goldsmith, so she will join due to how her father was ripped to pieces. Another is from the Essex family and another from the Cho family. The fourth commander is from the Mingjuan family and her sister, Li, was killed by the Ragnarsson assassins, so she will join us. Lieutenant Ryons is sleeping with Daniella Bragg and she has already spoken with him about joining up with us. Wild Horse McCabe is the granddaughter of the patriarch of this Territory and he has already signed on to this rebellion, so his family will do the same. Our intelligence on CeElsa MacAllen is that she is a follower and not leadership material, so she will follow all the others. The last commander is from the Wyclyffe family that was publicly executed by the Rosenburg's so she will be on our side for certain. As for the other squadrons in Clovis City, Lynott's Land, the Ferro Province and Murdock's, they will be formidable opponents for you and your pilots. I never said that this would be easy, did I? You must be ready to take on those other squadrons and beat them in a dog fight. This is a war, Aura Lynda. Many will die and we will have to kill them."

"Lynda."

"Excuse me?"

"Call me Lynda. All my friends call me Lynda. I'm in. You kill Rendon and Feklisov and I will gather up those that I know will be loyal to me. I will ask them to begin recruiting the rest of the pilots. Some will not want any part of this and will try and turn us in, so we may have to, as you say, get rid of them. But I don't want to be killing young Ensigns and Lieutenant Junior Grade Officers just because they are idealistic and patriotic. I will only authorize for them to be stunned and restrained. Got it?"

Reynita nodded her head in agreement as the bill was delivered to the table, "Yes, I agree. We can use stun darts on those that are not willing to be a part of this. I completely agree with you. When can you start reaching out to the others?"

Glenn stood from her seat and drank the remaining ale in her mug. She slammed the empty container down onto the table top and nodded to the three women. "Reynita, you pay the tab. We start right now. Carletto and Lisa have their own apartment that they have been shacking up in for the last year. We get them first and start from there. When do you intend to move against Rendon and Feklisov?"

Reynita pulled out some Clovis City Dollars and began counting them to determine whether she had enough cash to cover the bill. "My people are already on it. With any luck, your Captain will be dead already."

Glenn paused as her holographic-communication device began to make a loud siren noise. She unzipped the pocket over her left breast and pulled the device out and inspected the identity of the person attempting to contact her. She gave the other women a motion to keep quiet before she flipped the device open to speak with Captain Rendon. The red three-dimensional image of the Planetary Defense commander glowed bright red and was about two feet high, towering over the open computer mechanism.

"Yes, Captain?" Glenn spoke to the stern looking Captain.

"Lieutenant Glenn, I know that you are off duty, but an emergency has come up. You are to assemble your squadron for immediate deployment. We have a Class Red Ten emergency on our hands." Rendon's voice sounded as if she were standing right beside them. The new military issued communication devices had fantastic audio reception.

Glenn's eyes narrowed as she heard the orders. A Class Red Ten was an all-out war command, which meant that the proverbial poggie dung had hit the fan. "Ma'am, what happened to warrant a Class Ten?"

Rendon coughed before she could bring herself to speak up. The sounds of other voices were evident over the reception which caused Rendon to turn her head a few times as she listened to other individuals screaming out words, most of which were not clear to Glenn and the others. "Lieutenant, where have you been? It is all over the news! The Battle Cruiser Lysander was hit by nuclear missiles. She was destroyed and all crew aboard her are lost. You need to report to duty ASAP and join your squadron for further orders!"

"Yes, Captain! I will report immediately!" Glenn acknowledged the orders as she closed her holo-com and ended the communication. She looked over the faces of Reynita, Staszko and Harumi and saw that they were as shocked as she was. "Alright, Reynita. It looks like someone from your side has retaliated already. Do you have any idea what this means? The Lysander had been the personal Battle Cruiser of the Glorious Leader for several decades. I can guarantee that you will now get your war."

Harumi had already pulled out her personal satellite-com and checked the news reports to confirm the information that they had received from Rendon. She ordered the internal computer on her device to increase the volume so that the others could hear the female reporter.

"Again, breaking news just in! The Battle Cruiser Lysander was just destroyed by an apparent nuclear missile barrage that the experts are speculating was launched from the Southern Ocean of planet New Edinburgh. The ship was under the command of Admiral CeRae Sikorsky, the highly decorated granddaughter of the Glorious Leader himself. The long-range scans of the impact indicate that the Admiral was attempting evasive maneuvers to avoid the projectiles. The area of space is irradiated with colors and dangerous particles. The satellite news offices are issuing a Class Red Ten alert to all military and civilian occupants of the planet New Edinburgh, Space Station Cy-7 and the lunar base. This is not a drill. The planetary command believes this to be a possible alien attack. All non-essential personnel are to report to the protective bunkers immediately. All military personnel are to report for combat duty and stand ready to repel any alien invasion."

The reporter continued to speak, but her words were drowned out by the fact Harumi muted her device. Her eyes were wide with surprise. "Which of our teams would have been able to do this?"

"Only one group could have been responsible and that is the team led by Arch and Elektra. They were going under the ocean to find Elektra's aunt. They most likely succeeded in getting Admiral Zachariades to join us and they just gave the loyalists a bloody nose," Staszko said as she hugged Harumi and then Reynita. "Now their air superiority is nullified. We don't have to be concerned with any nukes or biological warfare being dropped on us from the Lysander. We are well on our way to getting the revenge we all deserve."

Glenn shushed the girls as the staff at the Ojos Locos had turned on several of the large screens that were showing the destruction in outer space. The Lysander was obliterated, all that was in her place was the radiation that the female news reporter warned about. The reports were indicating that the Planetary Defense space ships from Lynott's Land had already launched to secure the outer atmosphere of the planet from any alien invasion.

"You say that Arch and Elektra did that?" Glenn asked in a whisper. "Little naive Elektra and humble Arch Frazier? Of all the people to strike a big blow to the Glorious Leader, they would have been the last two that I would have predicted to accomplish this. I guess the quiet ones are the ones you should always watch out for."

"Elektra has grown up quite a bit since the last time you came to Clovis City," Staszko said before she finished her beer. "She is pretty kick ass now."

"No kidding," Glenn whispered as she worried that the Glorious Leader would send in one of his deadly Red Javelin weapons to kill everyone on the planet as retribution for blowing up his prized ship. "Arch and Elektra. Wow."

Military Intelligence Major JaCaiver Jenssen loved his position of authority in the Dakota Province. He was kept out of the politics of his family, he could enjoy the purple sand of the serene beaches whenever he wished and there was a plethora of naked women that he could make love to during those times he ventured to the coastal areas. As a Major and a member of the Royal Family, Jenssen could do as he wished. Even the powerful

McCabe family turned a blind eye to some of his actions if they did not harm their interests. Jenssen also loved the fact that the majority of his two companies of MI soldiers were women and that he could use his rank to compel them to perform sex acts without fear of retribution or demotion. The women had no one that they could complain to except for General Tan and she refused to hear any complaints if the Royal Family left her alone in Lynott's Land. It was the perfect set up for Jenssen. Once Jenssen had raped a fifteen-year-old tourist from Planet New South Africa. Her parents had bitterly complained to the local law enforcement due to the lack of arrest or prosecution. The family left the planet at the end of their vacation and no charges were ever filed. Jenssen's family had successfully bribed or coerced everyone up and down the line to avoid justice.

Jenssen had his way with any woman he wanted. Except for the fact that one specific woman had consistently refused to sleep with him.

He had lusted for First Lieutenant Alexis de Vida Brock ever since he laid eyes on her. She had a slender, athletic body, nice smile and long, sexy hair. He had even ordered her to perform sex acts with him on several field training exercises which she refused. Part of him wanted to inject her with a stun dart and rape her, another thought in his mind was to just kill her for outright insubordination and then have sex with her corpse. He could not permit her being held as an example by the other women under his command. If she was such an example, then the other women would refuse his advances and he just would not have that.

Accordingly, he was pleasantly surprised when Alexis de Vida Brock asked his permission to sit at his table at the Officer's Club that afternoon during lunch. She was dressed in her black fatigues, her front zipper was not zipped all the way up to her neck line, as was required by regulation. She had left it in a position that showed off some cleavage. Jenssen enjoyed the view and refused to admonish her as to the failure to properly cover herself. After she sat down next to him she smiled and took a sip from her water glass. The Officer's Club was an exclusive establishment with high ceilings, expensive paintings adorning the white walls, burgundy carpet and white linens on each of the zebra wood tables. The crowd was sparse, as was the norm, leaving ample opportunity for the patrons to interact with little scrutiny.

"So, Major. What plans do we have for today?" Alexis asked and leaned her hips and her shoulder against his. She saw that he was eying her cleavage and breasts, which was the desired result.

"The Company commanders were supposed to meet me here, but I do not see any of them. It is uncharacteristic of them to be late," Jenssen said softly. "You do realize we are under a Code Ten alert?"

"Oh, I am aware of that pesky alert, sir." Alexis purred. What she did not tell the Major was that before arriving at the Officer's Club she had taken a squad of women and killed the two Company Commanders, the other Company Executive Officer, and several of the platoon leaders that were loyal to Jenssen. Aura Lynda had sent in her cat-human hybrid friends to dispatch of many other officers that would not be in support of the coup. All the remained was to eliminate Jenssen himself. "May I speak freely, Major?"

"Please do," Jenssen licked his lips, wanting to take her right there in the restaurant hall, on top of the table where everyone could see him do it.

Alexis slid her hand over Jenssen's leg and ran it up toward his crotch. She smiled at him and watched the reaction in his eyes as she began running her hand up and down. It took only a few seconds to get him to become erect. "You see, Major, I am a woman that does not like to share. You kept pursuing me and I would refuse to sleep with you because you have all those other women. Now that I have made you wait a few years, I have a question."

"Yes? Yes. What is your question?" Jenssen was leaning back in his chair as he enjoyed how she moved her hand over his manhood.

"Are you ready to get rid of all the other women and just have me in your bed? If you are, I will take care of your needs day and night. How about it, Major?" She whispered the words into his ear and continued her slow massage of his erection.

"You mean like marry you?" Jenssen sounded surprised by her proposal.

"No, not today, silly. Later perhaps, after we both sample each other's merchandise. We don't want any, shall we say, buyer's remorse? I just want you all to myself. Think you can handle that? I am a woman with a very strong sex drive and I need a man like you to bed me and take me. I want to be your personal slut."

"Let's go back to my office," Jenssen said with urgency. He wanted her and her hand job was driving him wild with desire.

"To hell with lunch, I wasn't hungry anyway. Lead the way, Major."

Jenssen stood up, not caring if any of the other patrons noticed that he was aroused. He took Alexis by the hand and led her out of the Officer's Club to the front entrance where his personal long black transport was waiting for him on the transparent metal roadway. The vehicle was long enough to support six rows of leather seats behind the driver's seat in the front. His driver was a female polar bear-human hybrid with MI

Corporal stripes on her shoulders and she saluted him as he approached. The back doors opened and Jenssen leaped inside. Alexis slid into the seat with him. Jenssen did not waste any time. He leaned into Alexis, kissing her with great passion and running his hands over her breasts. The transport ship took off as Jenssen began pulling the front zipper of her uniform all the way down.

"You like?" Alexis asked as Jenssen undid the front button of her sports bra and exposed her full breasts. Jenssen responded by licking her hardened, pink nipples and softly biting them. Alexis moaned and ran her fingers through Jenssen's hair as she pretended to enjoy his sexual advance.

Alexis looked out the observation windows to ensure that the Corporal had flown the ship far enough from the ground before she acted. She reached over Jenssen and pulled his web belt off, acting as if she were undressing him for sex. The reality was that she was disarming the lecherous man so that she could kill him. She pulled out his laser pistol that had a pearl colored handle and tossed the rest of the web belt into the seat in front of them. He was so engrossed with enjoying her breasts that he did not notice what she had done.

She pressed the barrel of the laser pistol into his abdomen and smiled, "I changed my mind, Major. I would rather kill you instead."

Jenssen lifted his head up from her chest with a look of surprise in his eyes. "What the hell is this? What are you doing with my laser? That was a gift from the Glorious Leader himself. Give it to me!"

"Gladly," Alexis whispered as she pulled the trigger, sending the sliver of energy into his stomach and blowing a baseball sized hole out of his lower back. The impact of the shot sent Jenssen flying into the roof of the transport and slamming back down onto the seat. He had his hands around the wound in the front of his torso.

"Why?"

Alexis responded to his question by shooting him a second time in the crotch. He screamed as she fired. She quickly fastened her sports bra back and then zipped up the front of her uniform. Jenssen slumped onto the seat in an awkward position and gasped for breath as he gazed at her with disbelief in his eyes. His head slumped over and he was soon dead, his eyes were staring blankly at her.

"That must suck, ma'am." Corporal Arigella Tyner, the polar bear-human hybrid driver, in the front of the transport ship commented. Her white fur could not conceal the smile on her face. Her sharp teeth glistened white in the sunlight.

Alexis inspected the laser pistol and saw that there was an engraving from the Glorious Leader to Jenssen on the side. "What sucks, Corporal?"

"Thinking you are about to get some and then get shot instead. I was watching on the security cam and he was really going to town on your tits. You sure you didn't want to just let him have you before killing him? You know, kind of like a last supper before being executed?"

Alexis laughed and pondered the words of the Corporal for a moment as she placed the pearl handled laser pistol into her own holster. "I never thought of that, but yes. Yes, that would suck. Sucked for him, anyway. Get us to the main Plaza Azul so we can rendezvous with the others. Glad to have you along with us on this Corporal."

"Glad to be a part of the New World Order, Lieutenant. By the way, I am just saying, you really have nice tits. I have a cousin that is part polar bear just like me, but he likes full human women. He would love to get you into his bed."

Alexis smiled, "I have never been with any of the hybrid humans. Does he have fur all over him like you do?"

Tyner nodded, "Yes ma'am. But he has a big shaft, if you know what I mean."

Alexis smiled and looked up into the sky. She had just committed treason and was discussing a possible sexual hook up while she should be worried about being decapitated for her criminal action. "Sure, I will try anything after this. You realize that the Royals are going to come after all of us if we fail."

Tyner shrugged, "The Royals treat all of the human-animal hybrids like second class citizens. I would rather be on your side. We just need to make sure that we don't fail. So, where do you want to dump Jenssen's body?"

Alexis laughed and pointed out toward the ocean, "Out there so he can be devoured as part of the food chain. It is all he deserves. It is what all of the Royals deserve."

The Executive Officer of the New Edinburgh Space Command Planetary Defense, Commander LeJacene Feklisov, had enjoyed her two years on the Dakota Provinces. She had several lovers, consisting of various men, women and Kotek's, that kept her human hormone drug addicted sex drive satisfied. She maintained a large mansion near the beach so that she could enjoy the lovely view of the oceans. The only drawback was the occasional aquatic life form that would crawl from the waters onto her property to find food, either human or animal, and kill one of Feklisov's many dogs. She had imported dogs of all kinds from Old Earth to populate her property with. Unfortunately for the dogs, they were sometimes not fast enough to avoid the quicker lizard-like creatures with powerful jaws and sharp fangs. Feklisov grieved for each of her pets that perished due to the creature's attacks. But in her mind, the loss of the dogs was a small price to pay for her to live on such a magnificent location.

Feklisov received the alert to report for duty due to the destruction of the *Lysander* before Captain Rendon. Feklisov dressed and looked around the large lobby on the lower floor of her mansion at her collection of underage teens that she had taken from one of the local orphanages. She referred to the girls and boys as her personal harem and she used them to pleasure her sexual urges at will. If any refused, Feklisov would kill him or her in front of the others as an example.

She spied one young girl that she estimated to be just over thirteen years old and decided that she would take her along to the command base so she could use her in her military offices. Feklisov rapidly dressed into her dark blue flight suit and zipped the front zipper all the way to her neck line. She shoved her feet into her black boots, holstered her laser pistol and sheathed her knives before descending her granite spiral stair case.

Feklisov grabbed the young girl that she had selected by her hair and made her face the double doors at the end of the hallway. "We are going to my office, my love. You do as I say and want, and you will be fine."

The young girl nodded, the fear in her eyes was evident. The other teens seemed to be relieved that Feklisov had not chosen them for her daily sadistic rituals. As they walked out the front doors together, neither one of them thought to look to the rolling hills that were several hundred yards in the distance. Feklisov's personal Raumschiff was waiting for them near the beach as the teen dutifully followed her cruel keeper toward the rear entrance. There were dozens of dogs, cocker spaniels, Chihuahuas, poodles, mixed breeds and a few golden retrievers running around, barking at the skyline where the colors of radioactive activity could be seen with the naked eye. The kaleidoscope of colors was all that remained of the *Lysander*.

Tamura smiled when Melissa informed her that their target had left the safety of the mansion. The two women were lying prone on the rolling hills and had a clear view of Feklisov and the teen as they walked toward the Raumschiff. They had not been waiting long for the target to come outside. Tamura had expected that they would be waiting for hours before the Commander would leave for work. The destruction of the *Lysander* pushed their timetable up considerably.

On the roof of the mansion were three female private security guards that Feklisov hired to protect her and her dogs from the occasional sea creature that would venture onto the property. They were leaning over the roof, watching their employer as she walked toward the navy blue and white trimmed Raumschiff. The dogs were acting strange as they all suddenly stopped walking. The guards looked at each other quizzically as they were accustomed to the dogs barking or yelping whenever they saw Feklisov outside. What the three guards did not realize was that Melissa Harcourt had been using her powers of mind control over the dogs to keep them calm so that Tamura would have an easier time of killing Feklisov.

Tamura leaned her cheek into the stock of her sniper laser rifle and gazed through her long-range scope with her right eye. She controlled her breathing and allowed the barrel to rest on the tripod she had previously set on the ground before her. She slowly moved her index finger over the trigger. She watched Feklisov slap the teen girl across the face. The teen fell to her knees, crying, as Feklisov stood over her screaming obscenities. Tamura squeezed the trigger.

The head of Commander Feklisov exploded as Tamura's shot impacted just under the chin. The corpse of the abusive officer twirled in circles and collapsed to the ground. The teen that had been with her screamed as she gazed upon the headless body on the ground.

"Great shot!" Melissa praised.

Tamura did not pause to celebrate. She moved the barrel of her sniper rifle up slightly and targeted the three guards on the roof. They were reacting slowly to the death of their employer as only one of them saw Feklisov fall. The other two were still looking down at the dogs. The guard that saw Feklisov fall was trying to comprehend what had happened. Tamura fired three shots, each only a second or two apart, scoring direct hits on each soldier. All three of the security guards were hit in the center of their chests, blowing out a baseball sized hole out of their backs. Their bodies collapsed onto the roof.

"Pack up. Let's go," Tamura instructed Melissa as she slung the sniper rifle sling over her right shoulder. She seemed to show no reaction to the fact that she had just killed four women in a span of under ten seconds.

"We should take that Raumschiff and free the children inside the mansion," Melissa suggested. "We don't want them contacting the authorities."

Tamura pondered her suggestion for a moment. "Can't you use your powers to make that girl forget what she saw? We need to move and have little time now that the Lysander was blown up. We need to go."

"I agree that we need to go, Miyu. But I think that you will find that Feklisov's ship will be quite helpful to our cause."

"How do you mean?"

Melissa smiled at her and pointed at the large space craft. "I read Feklisov's mind before you vaporized it. That ship is loaded with weaponry and the computer memories are full of military information and security codes. Believe me, it has more firepower than the Comen Mierda that we stole in Clovis City. Trust me. Reynita will love it."

Tamura nodded as she listened to the cadet tell her the information. She had no doubt that Melissa's powers were formidable, especially after she had almost singlehandedly taken out the squadron of ships earlier. Tamura decided to trust the woman.

"Lead on, cadet."

Tamura followed Melissa down the hill, running rapidly. As they approached the space ship, the dogs began to follow them.

"We can use the dogs, too." Melissa told her. "I used my mind control to make the dogs ours. The Chihuahua dogs might be a nuisance at best, but the black labs, golden retrievers, shepherds, Dobermans, and some of the other bigger dogs can be used as war dogs if we need them. There are several orphans inside the mansion that need to be told that they are free."

"How do you know what is inside the mansion?" Tamura asked as she kneeled to pet two cream colored cocker spaniels. The dogs were licking Tamura on her hands and cheek.

"I told you, I read her mind."

Tamura laughed as the dogs were surrounding her to get her attention. Melissa found the behavior inconsistent. Tamura killed four people without any emotion and was now enjoying the company of the collection of dogs around her. "Okay, go get the orphans and tell them that they are free. Those that want to go with us can. But we need to go quickly."

Melissa observed that the thirteen-year-old orphan was standing still, in obvious fear of the two women. "Got it, Miyu." She nodded in the direction of the orphan. "You come with me. We need to go inside and let your friends know that they are all free. You think that you can do that?"

The orphan looked down at the headless body of Feklisov and swallowed. "Yes, I can do whatever you ask."

Captain Analesa Rendon had used her offices at the Planetary Defense Headquarters to send out the word to her squadron commanders to go on alert. The destruction of the *Lysander* was an event that was expected. Although the narrative the government was releasing was that it was from an alien attack, Rendon was aware that the real perpetrators were loyalists to Colonel Gorski. Somehow they had gotten their hands on nuclear rockets and have demonstrated that they were willing to use them with deadly accuracy. Rendon had been in her formal Class A blues when the *Lysander* was wiped out and because of the state of emergency, she did not have the time to change.

Rendon used her office computer system to contact all her squadron commanders to go on alert. After completing that task, she had determined that Feklisov was on her way in to the headquarters. Rendon walked out of her spacious office and into the large room adjacent to it. She found that dozens of enlisted

Space Command technicians were at their desks, typing furiously on their three-dimensional keyboards and some were shouting into their communication systems. The stress level was high. Each of the soldiers were in abject fear of a possible alien invasion.

Rendon walked through the outer doors into the landing where she saw several dozen pilots running with a purpose toward the stairs and escalators to get down to the lower levels over forty floors below them. Some others were running up the several flights of stairs to get to the Allen Fighter Type ships that were on the rooftop. Rendon looked around and saw that her personnel section chief, Lieutenant Commander CeRida LeJames, was barking orders to the pilots to get airborne quickly. LeJames saw that Rendon was approaching her out of the corner of her eye and turned to face her.

"Captain, the pilots are all responding well. Lieutenant Wyclyffe already has her squadron airborne and ready for combat. I am still waiting on word from the others.

"Good. Good. Let's get to the landing strips so that we can get in the air as well." Rendon ordered. "I want to direct the battle in my fighter ship. Feklisov can take charge of the ground forces while we are away."

LeJames followed Rendon down the several floors of escalators to the first-floor lobby and then out into the large blue concrete plaza that surrounded the Planetary Defense Command building. It was named Plaza Azul due to the blue concrete, the blue brick walls, light blue glass displays and statutes and the blue flowers that were all around. Rendon and LeJames returned several salutes of the enlisted men and women as they walked west toward the main landing strip that was filled with just under two thousand Allen Type Fighter ships.

On the hilltop overlooking the Planetary Defense Command building, Sara Stewart had her sights of her sniper rifle facing the Plaza Azul. Likewise, Patel had a sniper laser rifle ready as she was in a prone position about thirty feet from Stewart. In between the two snipers was Elsa Regehr, using a set of binoculars to scan the scene of panic below.

"Ladies, I have visual of Captain Rendon!" Regehr reported excitedly. "She just came out of the main entrance with another high-ranking officer."

"I see them. I see them. Supreet, I have the Captain in my sights. Can you take out the officer next to her?" Stewart's voice was steady and calm as she had been trained to be a sniper through the advanced MI courses. In her mind, she kept reminding herself to think of Rendon as just another target.

"I got her, Sara," Supreet said loud enough for the other two women to hear her. "Just give me the word."

"Take her out," Stewart responded.

Both women fired their laser rifles simultaneously. LeJames died instantly as her chest exploded when the laser hit her in the upper back. Her body was thrown several feet into the air and rolled over several times and finally slid to a stop on the Plaza Azul. There was smoke billowing from the massive hole in her chest which revealed parts of her shattered rib cage. Rendon's head was blown off from the nose up. Her body flipped backwards and slammed onto a bed of blue flowers.

Upon seeing their Captain assassinated before their eyes, the soldiers and pilots that were rushing back and forth on the Plaza Azul began to panic. They had all been fed the narrative of a pending alien invasion which led to their paranoia. On the hilltop above, Stewart, Supreet and Regehr could hear the screams and cries from below.

"Mission accomplished ladies," Stewart told them. "Pack it up and move back to the Comen Mierda to rendezvous with the others."

Regehr kept viewing the panic around the building as Supreet and Stewart began to pack up their sniper rifles. Some civilians were trampling over each other as the pilots were shoving their way through them. It was not a pretty sight and Regehr finally turned her head away to see that Stewart was already packed up and ready to leave. She followed the two back over the hilltops at a fast pace as Stewart verbally chastised them to move faster.

"Come on, ladies. Once the initial shock of what we did wears off, they will send in some fighter pilots to investigate. We need to be long gone before that happens. Move it."

Lieutenant Carletto De Vida Brock was in a foul mood. He had been enjoying his day off from work with his long-term girlfriend, Lisa Bragg, when the communication from Captain Rendon came in to report for duty. He had been in the middle of making love to Lisa and cursed that they had been interrupted. Brock rolled out of his king size bed and walked toward his large closet.

"Can't you just finish fucking me before we report? The Lysander is already destroyed, nothing we can do about it now." Lisa was lying on her back, naked and angry that her lover was choosing duty over sex. "Carletto, get back her and nail me."

Brock found his dark blue one-piece Class C uniform and turned in her direction. "Lisa, I love you and would love to finish what we started here, but if we are being invaded then we are needed. Get dressed. I promise that I will nail you after the alert is over."

Lisa leaned up on her elbows and scowled at him. She knew that he was correct, they had their orders and had to go. She slid out of the bed, missing the soft, satin sheets as soon as she was on her feet. "You owe me big time."

She looked around the bedroom for her uniform and heard her holographic-communication unit beeping. She walked over to the table where her device was located, ordered it to respond to the call and sat down in front of it. She looked upon the bright red, green and black three-dimensional image of her old friend, Reynita Calderon.

"Reynita? Is that you?"

"Geez Lisa! Put some clothes on!" Reynita responded with a laugh in her voice. "It doesn't take much detective work to conclude that Carletto is with you."

"Yes, he is with me. As much as I would love to chat, we are in the middle of a crisis. We have been ordered to full alert. Can I call you back?"

"Lisa, my friends and I are the alert," Reynita told her. "There is no alien attack."

Bragg paused and sat back on the bed, "Okay, girl. You got my undivided attention. What do you mean that you are the cause of the alert?"

"Lisa, the people that killed Bill also killed my sister, they killed our church pastor and have taken over Clovis City. Lisa, they killed Admiral Seward."

"What? When?"

"Yes, Seward is dead. Martial Law was implemented, the cadets are being held captive in the dormitories, curfews are being enforced and people are being arrested and executed by the dozens. Some of us got together to fight back. Zoe, Shana and Bret are with us. One of our other teams blew up the *Lysander*. We are going to fight back, Lisa. I need you to help us."

Lisa Bragg shook her head, "My brother and little sisters are with you? What the hell, girl? You blew up a Battle Cruiser? Are you crazy?"

"For probably the first time in my life, I am thinking straight. Lisa, I need an aerial presence to cover for my land troops. Please, I need you and Carletto to stand with me and fight. The time to stand up and fight is now. We just rocked their world by blasting that Battle Cruiser to atoms. Now we need to go finish this and take Clovis City, install a new set of leaders, write our own set of laws and live with true freedom. Are you with me, Lisa?"

Lisa looked at the image of Reynita and then back at her lover, Carletto. He had a serious look on his face, one that she had never seen before. He slowly walked over to her and took her hands in his, gazing lovingly into her eyes for a moment. The lovers had never heard such words from Reynita. They both remembered her as the motorcycle gang member, clad in black leather that would fight someone without a second thought. The person that addressed them now sounded more like a politician.

"What?" Lisa asked him when she saw the look in his eyes.

"You know that I love you, girl, more than anything." Carletto spoke softly to her. "Little Reynita is correct. What did Les Gillis say in his broadcast from the Blood Moon? Remember? He said we live with an illusion of freedom. Someday soon, my hope is that you and I will have children together. Many children. I want them to live in a world of real freedom. For them and for their offspring. Reynita is offering us the chance to fight for our unborn children, for the generations to come, I would fight and die for that. My squadron would follow me; of that I am certain. Your sister will, too. What they did to Bill was wrong. The Blood Moon ambush was wrong. What kind of leaders do we have with that kind of arrogance? They think that killing people as they have is fine? They are supposed to serve us, not the other way around. We must do this. Lisa. We must fight."

"And your sister, Carletto? She is in the MI and would become our sworn enemy if we do this. Can you take that? What if she is killed fighting against us? Your own sister."

Reynita felt that it was time to cut into the conversation. "Carletto, I can assure you that your sister will be with us. After I finish here, I am going to Lynott's Land and taking over the entirety of the Tan's Brigades. She and I were close friends and I know her better than I know some of my own siblings. She will side with us."

"It is up to you, my love," Carletto told Lisa.

She sighed and buried her head in his chest, savoring his smell. "All right, Carletto. All right. We do this for the past and for the future. I never thought of myself as a traitor, but that is what we are all about to become."

Lieutenant Commander LeCheri Fovre La Nour learned of the assassinations of Rendon and Feklisov over her satellite-com device. She cursed and pulled on her dark blue Space Command battle fatigues as she told her lover good bye. Due to the elimination of the Commander and Executive officer, she would be the de facto commander of the Planetary Defense astronauts. La Nour walked briskly to the front of her military housing and ordered her computer to open the sliding metal doors. She had expected to be on her way to the Planetary Defense Headquarters. Instead, she was assaulted by two women in MI uniforms that had been waiting at her front door. One was an Asian girl and the other a taller dirty blonde.

Jen Staszko placed her long knife under La Nour's throat and forced her back into the housing as Harumi Shigeta rushed into the back bedroom with her laser pistol in hand. Harumi found La Nour's female, jaguar-human hybrid lover and stunned her before she could get a word out. She pulled out some plastic twist ties and bound the unconscious woman's legs and arms as Staszko began to explain to La Nour the terms of her remaining alive.

"You are the fourth in command of the fighter pilot defense force, this we know. Due to recent events, you are now in charge. You want to live or die like the others?"

La Nour had tears in her eyes as she listened to the words of the woman with the knife. "I want to live."

"Good, because I really do not want to have to kill you. Now, slowly hand me your laser pistol that is in your holster."

La Nour did as instructed. Staszko tossed the laser over to Harumi who had just reentered the living area.

"Did you kill her? She's an innocent teacher at Preo-School." La Nour directed her question at Harumi.

"No, she is only stunned. Now sit down as we have a few things to discuss."

La Nour moved slowly toward her black silk couch and love seat sectional and sat down in the center, keeping her hands up in the air. "So the MI is making a play? I assume you two are with Tan's Brigades? Is she taking over the planet now? Is that what this is about?"

Both cadets laughed at the suggestion.

"No, we are not Tan's Brigades. We are cadets from Clovis Academy," Harumi informed her as she sat down across from her, keeping the barrel of her laser trained in her direction. "We decided that we have had enough of the Sikorsky and Rosenberg way of doing things. After the Dark October assassinations, the Dust Storm Incident, the Blitzkrieg Attack, the Blood Moon Ambush, the kidnaping of the Fenster siblings and the murder of Lupita Calderon, we all got together and felt a change in leadership was needed. Enough is enough, as they say."

"You are cadets?" Le Nour laughed as she looked at them. "Really? Mere cadets took out that Battle Cruiser?"

"And we plan on doing a whole hell of a lot more," Staszko promised her. "Our co-conspirators have eliminated your Captain and Executive officer. Your Personnel Officer is dead, too. We really do not want to add you to the list of the dead."

"Why spare me? You are committing treason and I would only get in your way. You should kill me." La Nour spoke bravely although her heart was still pounding in her chest.

"No, we will not kill you unless you force us to do so." Harumi pointed to the pictures on the walls of the home that depicted scenes of La Nour with her extended family. "Leaving you alive is more pragmatic than anything. First, the Nour family is extremely powerful in the Ferro Province. If we killed you, then they would want revenge on us. So, by leaving you alive and well, we remove the Nour family from the chess board that is currently in play. But that is not why we are allowing you to live."

"Then why?" La Nour was now breathing normally as she felt more at ease.

"Because you have a reputation for being a decent pilot, a good leader and you are smart, articulate and considered fair minded by your junior officers. When this is all over, regardless of who prevails, humanity will have a need for good people like you to step into leadership roles.  Since you never exhibited any narcissistic or psychopathic behaviors, we decided that the new government, in whatever shape or form it becomes, would benefit with a person like you involved." Harumi paused for a moment as her words were taken in by La Nour. "So, you and your lady friend will be placed in a cryo-sleep tube that will be opened after we take back Clovis City. But we need you to do something for us, first."

La Nour fidgeted in her seat and swallowed, dreading the request that was about to be made of her. "What do you wish for me to do?"

"Contact all of the pilots in the Planetary Defense and instruct them that Lieutenant Aura Lynda Glenn oversees them. Tell them that you have been injured and are, therefore, unable to assume command." Staszko said with a smile. She still had her long, sharp knife in her hand, waiving it in circles as she spoke.

"And if I refuse to do that?" La Nour demanded.

"Then we will have to kill you," Harumi responded. "And we will kill your lover, too."

"I cannot believe that this is happening. Lynda joined up with a bunch of traitors and helped kill the Captain? This is insane!" La Nour was ready to leap to her feet but thought better of it when she saw that the Asian cadet had her finger on the trigger of the laser pistol aimed in her direction. "All right. All right. I'll do it."

"And no misstatements to the pilots, or I will cut your girlfriend into small pieces," Staszko warned her.

La Nour nodded and stood up slowly, "My main computer communication screen is in my study down the hallway. I will do what you want."

La Nour was true to her word. She sent out a verbal command to all the squadron commanders that Lieutenant Glenn was in command of the entire Planetary Defense pilot corps. Harumi stunned her after she had done so. The two cadets took La Nour and her lover to the basement of the military issued home and placed the two sleeping women in the cryo-sleep tubes that were there. After ensuring that the women were safely tucked away until someone came along to revive them, the two cadets left the home to their next destination.

The rest of the fighter pilots across planet New Edinburgh received the news with quiet reserve. They waited for orders from their new commander. The squadron of forty-two Allen Type Fighters under the command of Lieutenant Yessica Wyclyffe-Sorenssen was already in orbit around the planet, searching for any evidence of an alien invasion. The only reason that she had not been killed with her family was due to her use of the last name Sorenssen as opposed to Wyclyffe. She had made that election as a young teen when her father divorced her mother. Her full siblings did the same and never had interacted with their father ever since. When the news reached her that her father had been disemboweled and decapitated on the main plaza surrounding the governmental offices of Clovis City, she did not cry. But when the Rosenberg woman named Rebecca did the same to her half-siblings, she wept for them. Most of them were just children and had been innocent.

Aura Lynda had been one of her closest friends over the past two years. She silently wondered what her first order would be now that the responsibility of the safety of the planet from extra-terrestrial invasion was on her shoulders. Her visor to her enviro-suit helmet was opened, a violation of the protocol and standards found in the Space Command training manuals. She hated flying in space with the transparent metal and the visor separating her from the beauty of the darkness. One level of separation from the void was enough for her.

She heard several of her pilots chatting over the communication system. Sorenssen let them do so, as the events of the past day had certainly been both shocking and unexpected. She smiled to herself as she heard the voice of Glenn finally come to them.

"This is your acting commander, Lieutenant Aura Lynda Glenn, speaking to you from a secure location in the Dakota Provinces." Glenn was smiling as she sat behind Captain Rendon's desk. In the office with her were Reynita Calderon, Daniella and Lisa Bragg and Carletto de Vida Brock, each in battle fatigues and armed with laser rifles slung over their shoulders. Glenn detested the idea of working in concert with the four Bragg Gang members, but they were united due to the current state of affairs.

Also with Glenn were some of her feline-human hybrid friends. The majority of the feline hybrids were terrified of being trapped inside of a metal flying machine. Something about their cat senses that made them feel claustrophobic inside a space craft. Accordingly, the Kotek's or cat-humans as they were sometimes referred to, avoided space travel if possible. But the Bedrosian clan from planet New Edinburgh were not afraid of space craft. On the contrary, they reveled in it, excelled as pilots and sought out employment in that line of work.

Larissa Bedrosian had green eyes, orange and white fur, sharp teeth and Ristina Bedrosian white and black were fraternal twins from a litter of seven. Recent graduates from the Clovis

Academy and commissioned as Junior Grade Lieutenants in the UNSC. Their first assignment was to serve on a flight squadron in the Planetary Defense of New Edinburgh under the command of Lieutenant Aura Lynda Glenn.

Zarnella Bedrosian had quit the Academy after she had killed a Ragnarsson assassin on campus. She had endured the looks in the eyes of many students that indicated that they had feared her, loathed her and even despised her. Zarnella could no longer take the way she was shunned all because she had acted to save the lives of Elektra Frazier and Flora Evart. So, she quit the Academy and took her penance, which was forced enlistment into the military. Fortunately for her, Aura Lynda needed competent mechanics to maintain the Allen Fighters and the Fenster Corporation Raumschiffs in her squadron. Zarnella found herself slapped with the rank of Corporal with orders to join Glenn's squadron in the Army Corps of Engineers. She was a year younger than Ristina and Larissa, and was different from them in many ways. She hated flying in ships and preferred her feet, or paws, on the ground. She was prone to losing her temper faster than her sisters and she was far more athletic.

Each of the Bedrosian sisters had blood on their paw-shaped hands and their furry chins from the victims they had eliminated during the coup. They were cognizant of the officers that would not support Aura Lynda so they took it upon themselves to use their hunter instinct and eliminate those that would not follow the rebellion.

Glenn had paused for a few seconds so that all the many squadrons around the planet would listen closely to her commands. She had Reynita patch in her communication to the lunar base, Space Station Cy-7 and the main military headquarters of Clovis City. "As you know, the Lysander has been destroyed. Several of our top-ranking officers have been assassinated leaving me in command. Like each of you, I have assessed the murders of Major Evart, Admiral Seward, the Goldsmith family, the Ward family, the Wyclyffe family, the Hsu family and the numerous rapes by the coalition of forces loyal to the Rosenburg's. The situation is, in my opinion, a direct contradiction to natural law. I hereby make the following orders so that we can avoid further death, rape and violence.

First, the fleet under Lieutenant Sorenssen will maintain orbit over the planet to protect against foreign invasion. The fleet under command of Lieutenant Dai Yu Mingjuan is ordered to secure the lunar base. To the current commander of the New Edinburgh lunar base, you are ordered to stand down and release your command to Lieutenant Mingjuan. If you fail to do so, her fleet will open fire and burn you out. Your murder of the Hsu family was barbaric and without reason and now you will answer for what you did. If you fail to surrender the base, then Lieutenant Mingjuan and her squadron will kill everyone there.

"The squadron under my command will fly missions to protect the Dakota Provinces from any attempt to interfere with our sovereignty. Yes, General Kimberly Sikorsky, you heard that correctly. From this day forward, the Dakota Provinces are free from the tyrannical rule of the Rosenburg-Sikorsky Axis of Evil. If you or any of your forces attempt to cross the borders of the Dakota's I will have my forces vaporize them. Do not toy with me, General Sikorsky. I am a serious woman and my followers are ready to fight to the death if need be."

Glenn stopped as MI First Lieutenant Alexis de Vida Brock entered the office with a squad of enlisted soldiers. The soldiers had two large black duffle bags in their hands and brought them to the desk where Glenn was sitting. They opened the bags and dumped out the heads of Major Jenssen and the other officers of the MI unit that Alexis and her squad had killed. Glenn motioned to the heads on her desk with her left hand as if she were a game show host.

"You see, General Sikorsky. The MI is under my control as well. You have no further control here. Stay away or die!"

Harumi, Staszko, Regehr, Li, Melissa Harcourt, Stewart, Supreet and Tamura watched the transmission of Glenn from the safety of the Super Raumschiff called the *Comen Mierda*. Several of the dogs that Melissa took from the mansion of

Commander Feklisov were sitting around the women, wagging their tails and happily accepting food and water from them. The stolen Raumschiff that had belonged to Commander Feklisov was parked next to *Comen Mierda*, with the engines turned off and all the security protocols reprogrammed by Patel and Regehr. Reynita had yet to determine if she would utilize the new ship in her plans to move against General Tan.

Blossom Li had taken a seat in the command area and had a small white poodle in her lap that snuggled close to her. She looked over the other women and saw that they were all in a mood to celebrate. She did not share their enthusiasm. Her parents were restauranteurs and generally concerned themselves with business and not politics or military. But the reputation of General Kimberly Sikorsky was well known by both solider and civilian alike. What little Li knew of Sikorsky was enough to convince her that any celebration was premature. "Ladies, you do realize that we just kicked a scorpion and pissed it off."

"Blossom, we kicked ass!" Regehr responded as she knelt to pet a friendly cocker spaniel. "Now we showed them that we cannot be messed with."

Staszko and Harumi understood where Li was coming from. General Sikorsky had thrown Evart to his death and Rebecca Rosenburg personally assisted the executions of the Wyclyffe and Rice families. The two women would not take this setback well. They would react in some fashion that was yet to be seen.

# CHAPTER NINE

The night before the destruction of the *Lysander,* Piotr Gorski, Stella Andolini, Paolo Andolini, Flora Evart and the rest of the Evart and Andolini families safely arrived at the Andolini underground mansion located nearby Ferro Province. The patriarch of the Andolini family was a great host and provided everyone with a feast that would rival that of the Lynott family. Piotr was still angry that Reynita had ordered that he take no part in the war effort. The cold beer provided to him by Stella Andolini helped him relax.

After checking on the current events of the annihilation of the Second Fleet and the alleged declaration of independence by planet Cootron, Piotr followed Stella to the guest room that had been prepared for him.

Piotr was dressed in a black sweater and khaki pants with black shoes. Stella was wearing black shorts with a baggy white night shirt that fell over her shoulder and revealed hints of cleavage. Piotr enjoyed Stella's shapely, firm legs and firm buttocks as he walked behind her. He spent almost his entire childhood with Venus, Giola, Paolo, Lucius and Stella. They were inseparable just like their older siblings had been with Yuri.

"It is getting late," Piotr observed as he looked out the window of his third-floor room. He could see the distant mining communities that were run primarily by the infamous Nour and Hsu families. The war over Ferro Province had occurred early in the history of the settlement of planet New Edinburgh. Others had competed for control of the mineral and element rich land. Many died and their names were forgotten as the Nour's and Hsu's won those wars. Gorski's father had been involved in some way, but he refused to speak of his involvement to his two sons.

"Are you trying to get rid of me?" Stella chimed in as she sat on the king size bed in the room.

Piotr laughed at the thought. She was his favorite person to spend time with and his closest friend. "No, I would never try to get rid of you. Your parents won't be upset if you are here with me? I could be a stalker or some crazy fan after you."

Stella laughed at that, "Ah, Piotr. My parents love you and consider you family. They think that you are the kindest of all the friends we have. They have already had to deal with psycho guys stalking me and my sisters. My parents know better than to think of such things about you. You would be surprised by the amount of fan e-mail my sisters and I get every time we do a bikini poster or some photo shoot. I get naked pictures of guys, propositions for marriage, sex, requests to meet and rude demands to meet. I even get offered money for sex by some rich people. You know I was offered by a guy claiming to be a Brackenridge over ten thousand Empire dollars to sleep with him. Can you believe that?"

He smiled at her, "Yes, I do believe it. You and your sisters are so beautiful. I hear that you three could stop space traffic. Ten thousand dollars? Was that for one night?"

Stella smiled at that, "You don't think I would be worth ten thousand?"

"Stella, you are worth so much more. The man that earns your love will be the luckiest man alive."

"Really? You know my sisters and I think the same of you and Yuri. We knew we never stood a chance with Yuri. He always treated us like his little sisters. Plus, he had that hot red head, Siobhan, hanging on his every word. Then Mary came along and she was so beautiful and nice to us. Then Jen took her place and we all loved all three of those girls. They were so nice to us. But then there was you, Piotr. All three of us wondered why you never asked one of us out. Was it your undying crush on Mia Nguyen? Why didn't you ever ask one of us out?"

He looked away from the window and smiled at her. "Well, there was Mia. But that fizzled out. Before her there was that girl I dated for a short time, Monica Fujita. And before her I dated Lauren Li. I was seeing Therese Fenster just before she was taken. That was the extent of my love life."

"So, you like Asian cuisine? That's why you never asked me out, or Giola or Venus?"

He laughed out loud. "Asian cuisine? Where did you ever hear such a phrase?"

"I just made it up. Look at your love life. All you date is Asian women, well except for Therese. That's okay. I mean everyone has a preference. So, you like sex with Asian women. No big deal. So, what was it like with Mia?"

He shrugged, feeling a bit uncomfortable with the question, even though he and Stella had discussed everything over the years. "I don't like to kiss and tell. But Mia and I were not meant to be. I caught her messing around with Rolf Rhinehard. We argued and broke up. That was a few months ago. I hope she will be happy with Rolf."

Stella threw her head back and began laughing. "Playboy Rolf? Really? She lost you for that womanizer? What a fool. I can guarantee that she is alone now. He is not a serious man, Piotr. Don't get me wrong. I like Rolf. I know he has had Marco and Dominic's backs in several bar fights over the years, but he is not the kind of man that sticks with a woman."

He gave her an inquisitive look, "I don't know Rolf that well. What do you mean by those comments?"

"He uses women and then tosses them aside. His reputation is well known in the cadet community. He is the opposite of his brother. Klaus loves April and would never think of losing her or cheating on her. But Rolf? I think he wants to sleep with every woman in Clovis City. From what I hear he has a good start on that goal."

"I never knew that about him. I feel bad for Mia."

Stella smiled and sat up in the bed, twirling her long dark hair through her right index finger. "Well, Piotr. I was wondering what it would take to get you interested in sampling pasta as opposed to tofu."

He looked over at her with an inquisitive look on his face. She and her sisters were the most attractive women he had ever seen. She was smiling at him as he looked over her shapely legs and slowly considered her sparkling eyes. "You mean you and me?"

"There's no one else here, Piotr. Just you and me. Come on, it makes sense. We are close friends. We have no surprises or secrets from one another. We can talk and joke around about anything. I know I like being in your company. My parents always expected that one of us would end up with you. Besides, I need a good man to help protect me from all those horny business owners, photographers and advertising executives. They are always trying to bed me or screw me during a photo shoot. I am tired of having to fight them off. I need a good man to tell them to back off."

He sat down on the bed next to her. "Stella, I had no idea you thought of me in such a manner. You have always been my best friend. What if we screw things up? I would feel terrible if I couldn't talk with you anymore."

She leaned into him and kissed him affectionately on his cheek. He felt her firm breasts against his arm when she got close to him.

"Piotr, I would rather try with you and take the risks. Personally, I like our chances." She kissed his cheek again. "We are no longer those little children. We are all grown up now. You grew into a strong and handsome man. You are smart and listen to my every word. You laugh at my silly jokes. And me, well, I have nice legs. I have some nice tits for you to enjoy. I think I can make you very happy."

Piotr put his arm around her slim waist and gently kissed her full lips. She kissed him back and put her arms around his shoulders. They kissed gently for a few minutes and soon began kissing passionately. She smiled and pulled off her white top. She tossed the white baggy shirt to the floor. Piotr noticed that she had nothing underneath. He stared at her bare breasts for a moment and ran his hands over them.

"They are really nice," he told her as he continued kissing her.

"You should close and lock the door," Stella told him in between kisses. "Paolo is a light sleeper and he is down the hall. He will be happy when we tell everyone that I am your girlfriend. But he might freak if he sees us having sex."

Piotr stood up and walked quickly to the door and closed it. He locked the latch above the door handle before he turned and faced Stella in time to see that she was shedding her shorts and underwear. He began to undress as he walked toward her. By the time he was at the foot of the bed he was completely naked.

She sat up on her knees and took his hands in hers. She pulled him onto the bed with her and they began kissing again. He ran his hands all over her body and found she had little to no body fat, his hands found her firm and well-rounded breasts and she wrapped her slender legs around his back. He slowly kissed her all over her body and spent time sucking on her hardened nipples. Stella moaned pleasurably as he finally thrust himself inside of her. She buried her face in his chest as he made love to her. She encouraged him with her moans.

Stella had not told Piotr the whole truth behind her desire to become his girlfriend which was that she was in love with him and had been for years. She felt him explode inside of her and kissed him passionately. As a young boy, Piotr never imagined that little Stella would grow and mature into such a desirable woman. He realized that he had just made love to his closest friend. He gazed into her enchanting eyes and she smiled at him. Both were covered in sweat from their love making.

"I really like pasta," Piotr told her in between deep breaths.

She laughed and kissed him, "Then I am your buffet. You can have all the pasta you want."

They made love again and fell asleep together in each other arms.

Down the hallway, Paolo Andolini snuck out of his room just after two in the morning. He tip-toed several doors down to the room where the object of his desire was sleeping. He knocked softly on the door and smiled when Daniella Evart answered. She had been awake for hours, reading a spy novel on her small computer, waiting for him to come to her as they had previously agreed. He slipped into her room and noticed she was wearing a revealing red lace top and matching panties.

Paolo and Daniella had been secretly involved for almost a year. Any chance they found they would meet and have sex. Daniella's fear was that her father would catch her. Sigebert Evart had been extremely protective of his many daughters. Paolo had been growing weary of the arrangement as he preferred things out in the open. Plus, he was proud to have Daniella by his side. She was a remarkable woman, intelligent, pretty and a great lover. He kissed her as the door to her room slid shut behind him.

She ran her hands through his long dark hair, "Paolo, I know you want to have sex, but I don't know if I can enjoy it tonight."

Paolo considered her eyes and ran his fingers through her hair. "Because of your father?"

"Yes," she nodded. "I had always dreamed of the day I could tell him the truth about you and me. I wanted to tell him we are involved because he always thought highly of you. But now he's gone. My father was a good man. He was a wonderful father. He gave me and my sisters everything. He was always there for us. Why did they have to kill him? Why?"

She buried her head in his chest and he held her close. She wept for several minutes. Paolo said nothing as he was certain words could never soothe the pain she was experiencing. He wished he could heal the hurt in her heart, but he knew that he could not. So, he decided that he would just be there for her, let her cry on his shoulders all she needed to, and pay attention to her every word. He had never felt that way for a woman before. Paolo was like his brother Marco when it came to women. Paolo had dozens of lovers due to his skills as a soccer player. But Daniella was the only one that kept his attention. She made him laugh and he always felt appreciated when she was with him. She wasn't a groupie girl. She was a lady and he loved her for it.

"I can't answer your questions, Daniella. I don't know why they would do such a terrible thing. I love you and I will stand by you through this. I will be here so you can cry on my shoulder night and day if you need to."

She looked at him with tears in her eyes. "My father was strict, but he was a good father to me and my sisters. He never abused us. He hardly ever raised his voice at us when we got out of line. He was so patient and caring. I miss him so much."

Paolo nodded and held her close, "Let me stay here with you tonight. I will hold you and we can wake up next to each other. I don't want you to be alone."

"Oui, please, Paolo. Please. Stay with me." She began walking to the bed. "It would mean the world to me to just have you here by my side."

Paolo followed her to the bed and cuddled up next to her. She laid her head on his chest and he wrapped his arms around her shoulders, holding her close. She fell asleep in no time.

In the morning, Piotr woke up to the chime of his personal satellite-com device. He groaned as he had forgotten to turn off his automatic five a.m. alarm setting. He sat up and found the ringing mechanism on the dresser next to the bed and turned it off. He realized that Stella was no longer in the bed with him. He felt badly that she was gone. He had so much to say to her. He loved her in many ways, not just as his closest friend and confidant, but in every way he could imagine. He was happy that she had made love with him. It felt right. He felt in his heart that she was the one for him now and forever. He wanted her to always be by his side and regretted that she did not stay to hear him tell her how he felt. He stood up and walked to the small bathroom and shower in his room and found that she was not there. In the bathroom was a change of clothes, a bath towel, soap, tooth brush, tooth paste, razor, deodorant, and a bottle of cologne. Piotr smiled as he deduced he had Stella to thank for that.

He quickly showered, shaved, brushed his teeth and put on the black sweater and light colored jeans that had been left for him. He was hungry and slowly made his way down the long hallway, passing several closed doors and to the staircase at the end. He could hear voices down below and smelled the aroma of coffee, poggie bacon, sausage and eggs. He quickly descended the two flights of stairs to the end that led to the family entertainment room. He could see two dozen large projections on the walls depicting current events from the news broadcasts. He stopped for a moment and watched some of the reporters speaking about the military crackdown on Clovis City. He gritted his teeth when he heard the reports of how Major Evart was killed. He was even more disturbed by the images of prominent citizens' heads on poles for all to see, all around the courtyard surrounding the United Nations Building.

"Hey, you're up!"

Piotr turned to see Flora Evart standing at the edge of the entertainment room, holding a cup of coffee in her hand. She was wearing a set of blue pajamas and her hair was up.

"Yes. How are you holding out?"

Flora shrugged. It had just been two days since her beloved uncle had been murdered. She was numb and had not been able to fully process the loss due to how everything had happened so quickly. Before she knew it, there was a laser battle in the church where Lupita's last ceremony was taking place and then she and her family were being told to leave Clovis City with the Andolini family. She was grateful to the Andolini's for risking their lives to protect her and all of her cousins. "As well as can be expected."

Sensing that Flora was emotionally drained, Piotr hugged her. "It is good to see you safe. The food smells great."

"It is. Come on. Several of us are already up." Flora led Piotr to the large kitchen of the Andolini hideaway.

He admired the high ceilings, the over three thousand square feet of space that surrounded the kitchen full of a large stove, convection oven, toasters, microwaves, a pizza oven, two large round dark brown tables that had the seating capacity for twelve people on each one, solar powered lighting above, several refrigerators and freezers, and four large pantries for canned food and fresh fruits and vegetables.

Flora directed Piotr to the closest pot of fresh coffee. Overhanging the four pots of coffee were dozens of large ceramic cups hanging on hooks underneath the storage cabinets that held dishes, glasses and other items. He took a large cup and filled it with the enticing coffee and took a small sip. He saw rows of large ceramic bowls with colorful floral patterns painted on the outside. Inside the bowls were various forms of fresh fruit. He found a stack of plates and began to fill it with sliced cantaloupe, strawberries, plantanas, grapes and kiwi.

"Yo! Piotr!" Paolo yelled out from one of the tables. He was wearing his jersey from the Clovis City Rattlesnakes soccer team and some warm up shorts. His long dark hair was pulled back into a pony tail. He was waving his fork at Gorski and motioned for him to sit in the empty chair next to him.

Piotr smiled at his childhood friend and wondered how angry he would be if he learned that he had spent the night lusting for his twin sister. The entire Andolini clan was up and yelling loudly as they ate. The tables had several bowls and plates of meats, bacon, sausage, cheeses, breads and more fruit. There were also several liquid containers with juices. Piotr noticed that Daniella Evart, one of the older daughters of Sigebert Evart, was sitting next to Paolo. She was also wearing one of his jerseys and she was exchanging some knowing looks at Paolo which led Gorski wondered if there was some growing love interest there. Next to the empty chair that Paolo had pointed at was lovely Stella. She had on a set of pink pajamas and her hair was pulled back by several twist ties. She blushed when her eyes met Piotr's.

Sitting at the head of the table was the patriarch of the Andolini family, Anselmo. He had been one of Nikolai Gorski's oldest and most trusted friends. Anselmo was the engineer that had designed and built the Great Protective Wall that surrounded Clovis City. The design had been duplicated for Lynott's Land and other territories on New Edinburgh. Due to the intricate designs and some of the hydraulic engineering and other complicated facets of the walls, the Andolini family became wealthy. It was the fact of the times. Engineers were high in demand and generally could provide comfortable livings for their families.

But Anselmo Andolini and his wife, Valentina, were much more to the Gorski family. When the young Lieutenant

Gorski was fighting the Dinosaur Wars on the planet surface of the "Purple Planet" as New Edinburgh had been referred to, the Andolini's watched over Piotr and Yuri and treated them as part of the family. Piotr and Yuri saw little of their father those first two years on planet New Edinburgh. The two boys were close to all the Andolini's as if they were actual members of the sibling group. Piotr always wondered how he could ever repay the kind family for their hospitality and protection. He knew he never could.

But he also did not want to disrespect the family by sneaking around their home, sleeping with one of their daughters. He wanted things to be out in the open. They were all good people and deserved better than that.

He said his good mornings to everyone as he made his way around the table. There were a few of Sigebert Evart's widows present and several of his lovely daughters. Piotr was certain that had he not fallen in love with Stella, that one of Evart girls would have won his heart.

Piotr set his plate down on the table where Paolo had urged him to sit. All the Andolini and Evart siblings began standing to hug him.

The last to embrace him was Stella. She had left his room after he fell asleep due to the uncertainty regarding her future with Piotr and her feelings of guilt that she seduced him. He was her best friend and she was worried that now that she had used her body to lure him into a sexual relationship that she would eventually lose him forever. Stella had not slept after she returned to her own room as she went over and over in her mind wondering why she did such a thing. She knew that she had sex with Piotr for one reason, and that was because she loved him.

Piotr held her close to him and smelled her perfume. He was amazed at how her body felt so good next to his. It was as if it was natural, it was meant to be. For some reason, his thoughts went to his father. He had always wondered why his father never remarried. His mother had died all those years ago and his father never desired to be with anyone else. At that moment, Piotr understood his father. He felt the same for Stella. If something ever happened to her, Piotr knew he would never feel so strongly for another woman. As the realization of his feelings came over him, Piotr needed to tell her how he felt. "I love you."

Stella pulled her head back slowly and looked into his eyes. She could tell that he was in love with her because his stare was exactly the way her father looked at her mother to that very day. She leaned her head next to his. "You know I love you, too."

"Hey!" Paolo yelled. "You hold my sister that close you better be ready to marry her!"

The Evart girls and the younger Andolini siblings were laughing at that.

Piotr smiled and softly kissed Stella on the lips. She kissed him back. Some of the younger Evart girls began screaming out: "Wooooooo!"

Piotr slowly pulled back from Stella and looked at his friend Paolo and Anselmo Andolini. Even Valentina Andolini, who had been in the back of the kitchen was watching, her mouth wide open with a look of shock. She had always hoped that one of her daughters would find love with Piotr, but she was not sure what to make of the public display of affection that she witnessed between him and Stella.

Piotr looked at the parents first, "I love your daughter. And Paolo is right. Any man that embraces her like I just did should marry her and that is what I hope you both will give me permission to do. She means everything to me and I cannot imagine my life without her in it."

Stella was speechless, a single tear rolled down her left cheek as she heard his words.

Anselmo Andolini smiled as he stood up and approached Piotr and wrapped his arms around the younger man. "Yes, of course! You have always been like a son to Tina and I. We always knew that there was a special bond between you and our Stella. I am so glad that you both finally realized it."

Valentina embraced her daughter Stella and asked her in Italian if she loved Piotr, too. Her daughter responded by only nodding as she was caught up in the emotion of knowing her dreams had come true. She buried her face on her mother's shoulder and began crying with joy.

Daniella Evart smiled at Paolo as the congratulations were being offered to Stella and Piotr. "A Russian boy and an Italian girl? What do you think?"

"I think it will work out great," Paolo told her as he was letting the moment sink in. His best friend was going to marry his sister. He could not imagine ever being happier for Stella. As her twin, Paolo always could tell that Stella loved Piotr. Even as young children she would always follow him around and want to be by his side. "It was always like they were meant to be with each other."

"Well, what about an Italian boy and a French girl?" Daniella prodded him.

Paolo beheld her lovely eyes. He had been sleeping with her for the past year. But the two had been discreet and were never caught. He nodded as he contemplated her question. "Yes, I think that would work out very well. But this is their moment. You and I can come out of the closet much later."

"How much later?"

"Tomorrow later."

"And what will we tell everyone?"

"That we plan on having a few dozen children together," Paolo smiled. Daniella had always loved babysitting her younger sisters and seemed to possess natural maternal instincts.

"Let's say a baker's dozen, yes?"

"How many in a baker's dozen?"

She took a piece of cantaloupe from her plate and bit into it as she watched Piotr and Stella holding hands. They were smiling. Stella's cheeks were radiant with color and her eyes beamed with joy. Daniella turned her head back toward Paolo. "A baker's dozen is when your wife lets you knock her up as many times as you can until she tells you she has had enough children."

Paolo shrugged at that, "As long we get to keep having fun when that is finished."

Daniella laughed out loud and realized some of the Evart's and Andolini's looked over in their direction. She smiled back at them.

It was a joyous moment for three families that had shared much tragedy. Each of the younger Evart girls were clapping for the happy couple and for just a few hours, they all put out of their minds the losses that they had suffered.

Unbeknownst to all of the occupants of the secret Andolini hideaway, the Sikorsky military, through the advanced scanning technology on board the Battle Cruiser *Lysander*, had launched small one foot around, dark metal devices onto New Edinburgh. The round objects flew down toward the surface of the planet and began to search for signs of life, heat and human emissions to round up all the missing traitors.

Several of the objects soared over the location of the hidden Andolini property. As they photographed the area and scanned for signs of life the Andolini's, Evart's and Piotr Gorski were dining together in peace. The scans produced no positive hits over the hidden mansion. Anselmo and Valentina Andolini had been prepared for such an attempt. They had the roof area of their home covered with wild forest trees and the metal of the base and walls were made from a special material to absorb heat and to reflect scans away from it so that no life signs would be detected. The last safety measure that the Andolini's had devised was the location of their secret home. They were in the southern province of the Forbidden Region. Outside they were surrounded by thousands of Verburgt, Dozal, Jumpers, and other deadly indigenous creatures.

Anselmo purposely chose that location just in case he ever needed to escape persecution from the government that he knew was unjust. Even if they located his home, the soldiers would have to fight thousands of aggressive creatures that loved the taste of human flesh and bone before they could gain entry.

The scanning devices photographed the area and continued to other locations to investigate. The Andolini's went undetected.

# CHAPTER TEN

MI General Kimberly Sikorsky did not take well to the threats she had received from the lowly Lieutenant Aura Lynda Glenn. In fact, she was infuriated that such a junior officer would dare challenge her in such a brazen and open manner. The General was cognizant of the fact that many civilians and all the military had been privy to the one-sided conversation and would be watching to see what Sikorsky's reaction would be. As a descendant of the Glorious Leader, she could not allow Glenn or her fellow rebels to survive. Weakness was provocative. The people of New Edinburgh and the rest of the planets in the eight solar systems were watching. It was as if all the eyes of humanity were focused on their planet, waiting to see the drama play out through the vast system of satellite broadcasts. If Sikorsky failed to crush Glenn, McCabe and the rest of the rebels in the Dakota Territory, then more rebellions would be encouraged to follow their example. If she killed them all, as had been done to the Second Fleet, then the certainty of death would discourage the people from further acts of treason. She had to be decisive.

She had taken over the office of Colonel Nikolai Gorski and turned it into her own. She had removed all of his plaques and pictures of his long-lost wife and replaced them all with pictures of her children, grandchildren and great grandchildren. She had been sent by the Glorious Leader to rid the planet of Sean Collins and his legal team, Gorski, Evart and about a dozen elected leaders in the United Nations. She had succeeded in about seventy-five percent of her duties. Evart, Goldsmith, Wyclyffe and Rice were dead. While the others were either on the run or in jail, awaiting their public execution. The two that angered her the most were Collins and Gorski. They were the highest profile targets and they had, thus far, eluded her assassins and soldiers. She glared across her desk at the other two women sitting in the plush, black leather chairs. One was her daughter, Major Katherine Sikorsky of the MI and the other was the newly appointed U.N. Security Council Secretary General Rebecca Rosenburg. Katherine was quiet and reserved throughout Glenn's satellite-com broadcast while Rebecca was cursing and screaming obscenities to the point that the General had to have her office computer system replay portions of Glenn's words that she had not heard the first time around.

The General had to tell Rebecca to keep her mouth shut several times due to her propensity to blurt out things. It was a fact that the entire purge of the planet would never have been necessary had it not been for the idiotic behavior of the Rosenburg's. They attacked the cadets on the space station, then dispatched the Ragnarsson assassins against them and then concocted the ill-advised ambush on the Blood Moon. All the mess that the Sikorsky Regime had been brought about due to the sniveling Caine Rosenburg's sociopath acts and the attempt to cover them up by his mother and father.

"She will burn us down? No! We should invade and kill every single man, woman and child in the Dakota's right now! I am ordering you, General! Send in the entire military and kill everyone!" Rebecca was screaming loud enough for the other officers and clerical staff down the hallway to hear her. The cadence of her speech grew more and shriller as she spoke, pounding her fist on the table top to accentuate her orders. She was, without a doubt, a spoiled brat.

General Sikorsky was not accustomed to having mere civilians dictate how to handle a military operation, especially ones that had no combat experience. She glared at Rebecca and thought for a moment about the need to remain civil with her. The General decided that it was best to be blunt with the petulant girl and put her in her place, to remind her who was truly in command of the planetary operations. "I have had just about enough of you, Rebecca. You and your entire family are to blame for this entire situation. By your actions, we may very well lose this planet and die here in the next few days. The Glorious Leader gave you this planet to rule over and all you have done is to continuously cause good men and women to talk of separatism or cessation. Dark October should have cleaned up all the loose ends and your family should have learned from their ways to act differently. But you Rosenburg's continued to treat the people badly and new civilians revolted against us. This is all you're doing, you damned Rosenburg's. I have half a mind to take all of your family over to the Dakota's and turn you over for the decapitations you each deserve."

Rebecca squirmed in her chair as she took the verbal lashing from the General. It was evident by her demeanor that she was no longer willing to tolerate the games the Rosenburg's had played in the past. The General was now in command and would not bow down to Rebecca's family as past commanders had done. The best play for her and the rest of the Rosenburg's was to be apologetic, submissive and helpful.

"General, you are correct about my father and many of my family. Caine was a cancer and I warned my father many times about him. Now they are both dead, which is good for all of us here. I can control what is left of my family, General. I guarantee that they will not cause any further scandals. My sole purpose here is to assist you in bringing about the status quo for the Glorious Leader so that New Edinburgh will never hint at rebellion again."

The General smiled sarcastically at Rebecca and stood up, wagging her index finger at her direction. "You are little more than a child! You are perhaps the youngest of your siblings and you expect me to believe that you can control the others? Most of you family was in jail when I arrived here! And for what? One was a pedophile, another a murderer and others were worse than those two, which I still cannot see how that was even possible! The people of this planet were right to turn on you. When this is over and it will be over soon, you and the rest of your siblings will retire to the Rosenburg Ranch and stay the hell out of the other Territories forever. We will not be coming to clean up your messes any longer. You understand me?"

Rebecca bit her lip and nodded in response. She was intelligent enough to realize that she had best keep her mouth shut.

"Mother, what shall we do about the Dakota's? We cannot allow them to secede." Katherine asked softly.

"Yes, you are correct. I am going to send in the squadrons from Murdock Territory to bomb the Dakota's into submission. The squadrons from Ferro Province will be split between defending the lunar base and Clovis City. We will send in the attack immediately. This Glenn seems to be an astute officer and would have most likely rose in rank quickly but for her treasonous actions. She must be killed, which is unfortunate. Good officers like her are hard to come by. Katherine, use encrypted communication channels to relay to the Murdock and Ferro squadron commanders my orders. Do it immediately."

Katherine stood up and sharply walked out of the office, leaving Rebecca alone with the General. For several seconds, there was an uncomfortable silence between them before the General addressed her. "I have read all about your family, Rebecca. I know that your father and mothers used several enhancement drugs on you and your siblings while you were each gestating in the womb. The steroid use continued after birth, making each of you stronger and smarter than the average human. But there were negative side effects in the usage of all those chemicals. Caine was a prime example of that. I know that you are brilliant, Rebecca, otherwise you would never have been sent by your father to represent him here in Clovis City. Because you are so intelligent, you may very well have a place here in the future. But I should inform you that the rest of your siblings are not welcome here any longer. I know that Carla, Nydia, Juliana, Peter, Thomas, Joseph and Joshua have high rise apartments that they own in Clovis City. After I eliminate Glenn and her rebellious pilots, all your siblings that I just named will be asked to leave and to never return. You understand me?"

"Yes, General."

"You can stay, most likely not as Secretary General, but we will find a role for you to match your talents. Now that my cards are all on the table, do you think that you and I can co-exist within those parameters?"

"Yes, General. I can work with you."

"Good to hear. Now on to business. If I were Glenn, I would be preparing for a direct attack on Clovis City. If she is doing as I would, then we need to prepare. Your new lover, Angus McWilliams, did a fantastic job assassinating Admiral Seward for us. I want you to take his snipers and place them on the rooftops and the upper level floors of each high rise building in the city. Concentrate the majority of the snipers on the Rosenburg-Ragnarsson law firm skyscraper. It is perhaps the tallest building in the city, and since it is owned by your family it will cause the least displacement of civilians than the others. We want the people to be on our side, to embrace our position and to remain stupid enough to believe our narratives and talking points to the media. I will send Captain Susannah Murdock from the MI branch with McWilliams to organize the most strategic locations to place our shooters. She is without empathy to others and views the common citizens as you and your siblings do. Once you accomplish that task, I need for you to draft a speech condemning Glenn for her actions. Before you give the speech, I want to proofread it to ensure that it is within the bounds of acceptable public discourse."

"Yes, General."

"Get on with it!" The General waived her hand in a dismissive manner at Rebecca.

Rebecca leaped to her feet and ran out of the office quickly. She hoped that the General was true to her words and would not send her away to the purgatory of Rosenburg's Ranch if she proved her worth. To avoid that, Rebecca would do anything that the General asked of her.

Alistair Feklisov Murdock had been an officer in the Space Command for several decades before retiring with the rank of Admiral. He had grown weary of war and combat over the years of his service and longed for the day when he could settle down in a quiet community for a stress-free life. As a member of the Royal Family, he had been offered a plot of land on planet New Edinburgh. He readily accepted the land, moved his several wives there and began a large colony. The Murdock settlement was a little over two hundred kilometers wide and three hundred kilometers from north and south. It was, as the other territories on the northern continent of New Edinburgh, surrounded by the jungles. The settlement had a protective wall around it, just as the others that were land locked, and had a military presence to keep the peace.

The main force in the Murdock Territory was five fighter squadrons of small Allen Type ships, just under five hundred of them, and just under two hundred pilots in the units. Alistair Feklisov Murdock commanded the squadrons from his mansion home while he delegated the civic management to his daughters and sons. All his pilots and engineers were members of the Royal Family. Until recently, he never had to ask his pilots to fly any missions of import. When he received the order from his half-sister, General Kimberly Sikorsky, to send in all his pilots to annihilate the Dakota settlements, it had been the first time he had to authorize combat. He delegated the orders to a Space Command Captain named Melodia Ginn while he relaxed in his mansion, enjoying the company of his younger wives as the pilots rushed off to go to war.

But the pilots never made it to their destination. The new commander of the pilots in the Dakota settlements, Aura Lynda Glenn, had been ready for such an attempt by General Sikorsky. While the Murdock squadrons prepared their Allen Type Fighter ships for lift off, Glenn had two squadrons racing in to thwart their orders. Dakota Squadron Commanders CeElsa MacAllen and Arturius Ryons led just under ninety pilots in their Allen

Fighters. Their mission was to ambush the Murdock squadrons in a pre-emptive strike. They flew in at speeds more than ten thousand kilometers an hour and attacked without warning since the Murdock defenders had never found a need to activate long range scanners. This oversight by Murdock allowed the enemy pilots into the territory undetected.

The defeat was complete. Each of the small Allen Fighter ships in the Murdock land were destroyed by the unmerciful barrage of lasers and R-5 rockets that rained down upon them from the squadrons from the Dakota's. The explosions shook the grounds and caused many casualties in the process. Metal was tossed into the air with the torn bodies of the Murdock squadron pilots and mechanics. Ryons led his squadron to hit the other landing strips that had several military style Raumschiff space craft as MacAllen's squadron finished off the towers and anti-aircraft weapons in the outer major military posts. Ryons' and his pilots wiped out forty Raumschiff space crafts while MacAllen's squadron annihilated the Allen Fighter ships.

When the attack was over, Ryons squadron had lost only one pilot while MacAllen had zero casualties. They left behind a complete destruction of every military space craft in the region. When Alistair Feklisov Murdock learned of the attack, he was dumbfounded. His entire territory was left defenseless and his corps of pilots went from two hundred to seventeen. He found his way to his liquor cabinet and took a few shots of vodka before he could bring himself to contact General Sikorsky and give her the news.

MI Lieutenant Colonel Clea Sowa and Marine General Elizabeth Murdock began setting up the ground forces defenses of Clovis City. The two officers place additional soldiers in the Great Protective Wall, armed with shoulder launched anti-air missiles and laser canons that were being mounted onto the top of the wall. They placed hundreds of slave Babbcottiatta and Saharakaree around the main plaza surrounding the governmental offices as well as in strategic locations such as the major landing strips and some of the main supply buildings. They concentrated many humans around the main United Nations buildings in the center of the town, ready for any ground forces that might attempt invasion. Metal and concrete barricades were placed all around the plaza so that the soldiers would have places to hide behind as they engaged the enemy.

Most of the forces were from the soldiers that had been brought from Sikorsky's Planet in the *Lysander*. General Murdock accomplished the redesign of the main city defenses in just under forty-eight hours of work.

Admiral Zara Sowa had ten squadrons of Allen Type Fighter ships at her disposal in Clovis City. One of the squadrons had been sent out to shoot down a stolen Rosenburg Raumschiff named *Comen Mierda*. The fact that a single Raumschiff could wipe out the squadron vexed Sowa to no end. Sowa had studied military tactics more than her cousins and relatives that were in command of the military establishment of the planet. Sowa quietly assessed the situation that she found herself in. She and her allies were now cut off from any potential aid from Sikorsky's Planet due to the destruction of the Red Javelin weapons and the resulting distortion that followed. The loss of the *Lysander* and the talented squadron pilots stationed in the Dakota's were a concern. If the civilians around Clovis City were to be encouraged to confront the military, the conclusion would be a bloodbath. Sowa wanted to avoid slaughtering the people that she and her family were meant to command.

But now she was down to nine squadrons full of pilots of lesser talent than the ones in the Dakota settlements. There were the pilots in the Murdock and Ferro territories as well as the brigades and pilots in Lynott's Land. The other planetary settlements had little military presence to be worthy of consideration in her plans to mount a feasible defense. While General Kimberly Sikorsky engaged in a course of calumny against the Rosenburg family for the predicament they found themselves in, Sowa schemed and devised several scenarios of how the situation would eventually play out.

Sowa ordered Captain Karl Schneller to send five of the Clovis City squadrons on alert and had them flying cover around the city. She learned that Schneller had the pilots and pit crews of the other four squadrons go to bed and rest so that they would be fresh when the attack eventually came.

Sowa was certain that the attack was coming. She and her family members had killed too many people when they arrived and the result was plenty of angry citizens. She concluded that her best option to mount a defense was to impress the cadets that were being held in quarantine in the dormitories at Clovis Academy. Releasing the cadets would be risky, as several had shown rebellious tendencies and the murder of Seward and the Warrens would be a negative against the Royal Family. The fact that several of the female cadets had been raped by the soldiers guarding them was a disgrace and Sowa had advocated for corporal punishment of the offenders only to be rebuffed by the General.

But the power and ability to bribe the cadets rested in her family. Accordingly, Sowa ordered Army Captain Brisen Jenssen, Army Captain Alain Feklisov and Army Major Jenessie CeAkin to work on a plan that involved either impressment of the cadets or outright bribery. The bribery option would turn the cadets into mercenaries, which Sowa always believed the Space

Command to be full of, while the impressment option would allow the cadets to be patriotic and fight for their Glorious Leader. Sowa additionally brought in a recent graduate from the Clovis Academy, Space Command Lieutenant Junior Grade Johann LeSkaysner, to offer positions to the cadet pilots. LeSkaysner seemed to hold some influence over the cadet juniors and sophomores due to his past status as a student.

CeAkin reported to Sowa that there were over eighteen thousand cadets being held in the numerous dormitories and under two thousand that were either unaccounted for or dead. Most the cadet casualties occurred in the failed attempt to rescue Admiral Seward and his pilot instructors. Sowa instructed CeAkin to work with the people with the money and get them to be ready to pay.

CeAkin brought in Carla Rosenburg, who seemed to have been the de facto member of that family to control the money since the death of their patriarch on the Blood Moon. Carla was a smart girl and had little empathy for others. But she cared about her own survival and maintaining the family power base. She assured CeAkin that the Rosenburg monies would be made available for any cadet that agreed to fight on their side. Carla instructed CeAkin and her officers to offer the cadet twenty-five thousand Empire Dollars in return for their services.

CeAkin agreed that fee was more than equitable and sent Captains Jenssen and Feklisov along with Victoria Rosenburg to the campus dormitories to begin making the offers.

Carla contacted her four brothers that were residing in Clovis City, Thomas, Peter, Joseph and Joshua Rosenburg, to return to the Rosenburg Ranch to secure the funds from their family banks. CeAkin wondered if the Rosenburg's could be fully trusted and sent some of her enlisted soldiers along to keep an eye on them, just in case.

While Carla Rosenburg was doing her part to build up an army, she received a Satellite-com request from her sister Nydia. Carla excused herself from the others and found her way to an office that was not occupied. She ordered that the computer in the room seal the door shut behind her so that she could converse with her sister in private.

"Nydia, what is going on?" Carla blurted out when the door was sliding shut behind her.

"Carla, listen to me. Boris and I found out who is behind leaking his pictures."

"Who?"

"Klaus Rhinehard, one of the Gorski Gang cadets. We dug into his background and found out that he is at the main hospital while his wife is in labor. I am taking Boris, about two dozen assassins, a few of the slave Babbcottiatta and Saharakaree and some MI soldiers to take Rhinehard out. If we can, we'll kill his bitch wife and his children. But I also learned something else when I hacked into the hospital computer system."

"Spill it, Nydia. I am really busy over here."

"Cara Perez Guerrerro is in the hospital, too. She was the one that stole a lot of our money in that bullshit lawsuit over the Blood Moon Incident. Remember?"

Carla sat down in the office swivel chair that was behind the lone desk that was surrounded by shelves of files. "Yes, I remember that our brother Alfred encouraged us to pay her off. What is it that you are thinking?"

"I am going to force her to sign over the money to us before I kill her and her twins," Nydia hissed. "From the security cams, the woman is sedated and will be easy to manipulate. I will get our money back from her and then slit her throat."

Carla shook her head as she realized how much Nydia was like their father, "Nydia, leave it alone. We are trying to recruit cadets to help us out here. If you go over there and start killing them, then the other cadets that might be willing to help us will back out. Let it go."

"But they outed Boris!"

"Then perhaps Boris should have been more careful with his identity when he helped kidnap the Fenster brats. Nydia, just get a new boyfriend and be done with Boris. He is a drug addicted half-rate pilot and will never amount to anything more. Cut him loose and find another man. Do not go to that hospital."

Nydia remained quiet for a moment as she took in Carla's harsh words. Nydia loved Ilyasova, despite his faults. She decided to lie to her sister. "All right, Carla. We will stay away from the cadets at the hospital. I will wait for your next instructions."

"Good, Nydia. You are making a wise decision in this. There will be time to kill the Gorski Gang members after we stop the small rebellion here on the planet. Once we have our position solidified, we will kill all of them. But for now, let it go."

When the image of Carla faded away, Nydia turned her attention to Ilyasova and glared at him. "We go in, kill Rhinehard, Mejia and their children and then leave. You got that?"

Ilyasova sharpened the blade of one of his knives as Nydia addressed him. He said nothing in response.

# CHAPTER ELEVEN

Captain Rafer Tierney was speechless after he learned of the destruction of the Battle Cruiser *Lysander*. Although the cadets with Elektra seemed optimistic regarding their attack on the larger ship, Tierney fully expected that some of the counter measures in the defense section of the *Lysander* would have repelled the missiles. Based on the nuclear explosion, the defenses failed and now the advantage that the Sikorsky loyalists once had was eliminated. Tierney had been alone for more than twenty minutes in the weapons section of the Raumschiff that Juliana Rosenburg gave to him and Colonel Gorski to facilitate their escape from the planet. The woman had spent almost the entire trip in his lap and Tierney found that he loved the attention. She was smart, beautiful, a bit childish in her outlook on some things, but she professed her undying love for him and she liked kissing. Tierney found that he could not stop thinking about her and he longed for her to return.

She finally did come back to the weapons area, wearing a change in clothes that included a white sweater, black shorts that revealed her shapely legs and flip flops. She was carrying a tray that had some fresh food, a glass of water and a large metal cup of coffee on it. She slid into the seat next to Tierney and laid the tray on top of the computer table top in front of him.

"I cooked you up a fresh white fish, blackened, some rice pilaf, steamed broccoli, grilled some tomato slices, prepared some coffee and made a pitcher of freshly squeezed orange juice. I hope you enjoy." Her voice sounded like music to him.

Tierney inspected the tray and turned to kiss her. She picked up a metal fork, cut a piece of fish loosed and fed it to him. "That is damn good," Tierney told her as he chewed.

"Glad you like it. You hit the jackpot with me, Captain. I have great legs, I can cook and I am rich. What more could any man ask for?"

Tierney kissed her again and then took a drink from his coffee cup, "So why me? A dynamite looking woman like you must have had many men begging for your attention. What was it that turned your head in my direction?"

"I told you already, I like a man in uniform. Your broad shoulders and muscular chest and arms helped a little, too. I think the main thing that attracted me was that you were not a man that could be bought. My family tried to marry me off in the past to worthless politicians that were on the take. I wanted a man with principles, with dignity and self-respect. You have those qualities and let me tell you, they are very hard to find in this universe. When if first saw you, I knew that you were a man that would never be bought."

Tierney was about to respond to her when they heard the voice of Jericho Griffin come over the ship communication system. "All right, folks. We are five minutes away from Space Station Cy-7. We are cleared by the landing security to enter the docking bay, so if you are going to change into civilian clothing, then do it now. And I do recommend that you do so."

"I don't have any civilian clothing," Tierney commented as he stuffed some broccoli in his mouth. "I suppose that they will have bounty hunters looking for the Colonel and me all over the station?"

Juliana smiled and thought for a moment about his question, "First, there are several quarters below stocked with men's clothing. You and the Colonel can find something incognito. Secondly, they would never expect you two to come here, to Cy-7, of all places. You are in more danger from your own people than my family. I think that this is a bad idea, coming here. You may think that your military officers will join you, but what if you are wrong? If we must try and escape this station under fire and pursued out into space, if we are lucky? I just have my intuition telling me that we should leave. I have property on other worlds. We could leave New Edinburgh behind forever, live on another planet, make children of our own and have a family. Please, think about that for me."

Tierney kissed her again and then stood up, lifting her in his arms. "When this is over, there is nothing I would love more than to go away with you. But I have lost friends and there are others that need me back in Clovis City. I cannot abandon them or the Colonel. Like you said, I have principles and because of that I will not walk away from this fight. But I can also tell you that, even though we are just getting to know one another, I feel in my heart that we are meant to be together. Probably crazy for me to feel that way, but I do."

Juliana wrapped her arms around his neck and kissed him on the lips, pushing her body against his. She paused for a moment staring into his eyes, "It is not crazy. I know I am in love with you and, because I feel that way, I will not leave your side. If you are going to try and free the people of Clovis City, then I will be right by your side through all of it. Now, come on. Let's go get you out of your uniform and into some more, shall we say, less conspicuous clothing."

Nikolai Gorski and Jericho Griffin had been fed by Juliana earlier. Their empty food trays were sitting in the co-pilot seat of the upper level of their space craft. Gorski looked at the station in the distance and grunted as he considered his next move. The *Lysander* was destroyed and that would mean that the Rosenburg controlled army would be in disarray. General Sikorsky was a great commander, but her soldiers would be experiencing a level of anxiety at this point, others would be demoralized due to the most powerful chess piece, the *Lysander*, being removed from play.

"I want for you and Juliana to remain on board while Tierney and I meet our people. If something goes wrong for us, I want you to get out of this station, find the Frazier's and tell them that we were caught. After that, you two should get as far away from here as this ship will take you," Gorski told the pilot.

Griffin listened, concentrating on guiding the ship safely onto the docking platform that had been extended from the space station for their ship to land on. The procedure was the same across the eight solar systems. After landing on the platform, the space craft would be drawn into the space station outer docking airlock for a decontamination procedure and then moved into the oxygenated docking area. The procedure was such that the outer bulkheads, the outer airlock bulkheads and the last interior bulkheads could smoothly transition the ship inside without disrupting the commerce inside the space station.

"Sir, I would recommend that you at least change into civilian clothes. If you step out onto the docking area in that uniform you will be recognized in a Sikorsky City minute," Griffin looked at the Colonel out of the corner of his eyes.

Gorski nodded, patted him on the shoulder and then descended the ladder. He walked briskly to the lower level of the ship and began searching the numerous quarters for any sign of clothing that had been left behind by previous passengers. In the fourth room, he saw Tierney and Juliana going through a plastic desk with six levels of drawers that was full of men's sweats and t-shirts.

"Any in there that would fit me?" Gorski asked to announce his presence.

"Yes, Colonel. I found a set of grey sweats down the hallway that will fit you nicely." Juliana walked over to him and took hold of his arm and led him into the circular hallway. "It is down this way."

He followed her to a room that was many doors down and she pointed out several long sleeves sweat shirts, sweat pants and t-shirts lying on the queen size bed in the center of the room. "These belonged to my brother, Matthew. He was about your size, he had less muscles than you, but they should fit. His shoes are in the closet, most of them were the form fitting slip-ons that athletes use while training, so you should find something suitable."

"Thank you for all your help, Juliana. We will never forget what you have done for us," Gorski told her as she was leaving the room to rejoin Tierney.

"You can thank me by not getting yourselves killed, Colonel. When you find a set of sweats that you like, come find me. All the clothing here was manufactured by my family. The clothes all have some hidden pockets where you can hide laser pistols, daggers, stun or flame darts and other small weapons. I have a feeling that you will need them."

Gorski nodded and began pulling out the sweats that she had pointed out to him. He settled on a dull grey top and black bottoms, believing that they would attract little to no attention from the crowds of civilians and soldiers on the station.

After Gorski and Tierney had changed into the sweats, they met Juliana and Griffin at the lower level of the Raumschiff. The docking procedure had been completed and they were cleared to enter the docking bay and explore the space station. Juliana took a few moments to show the two men the hidden pockets on the pants legs, two torso pockets and one on each sleeve. She showed them how to rip them open, explaining that they were held by a hybrid of Velcro and an alien gel type substance that they discovered on the space craft buried under the Rosenburg Ranch. Gorski and Tierney hid a few stun darts, a laser pistol and a few small knives in the pockets, just in case.

"Ready, Captain?"

"Ready, Colonel." Tierney affirmed.

"Then let's move out."

Gorski pressed the large red circular button on the side of the wall to lower the ramp to the rear loading dock of the Raumschiff and open the bulkheads. He waited patiently as the double enforced bulkheads slid open and the ramp lowered to the metal floor of the space station. Gorski walked quickly down the ramp, followed by Tierney, as the two men rushed to find one of the service men that they mutually hoped would help them raise an army. Griffin and Juliana watched them leave, not saying a word out of fear that the MI soldiers might have listening devices and hidden cameras the size of a tear drop scattered about the landing area.

Gorski did his best to not look anyone in the eye in the docking area. He observed a few dozen MI soldiers to his left and another five at the exit tunnel. There were several hundred-people walking in different directions, rushing to destinations or space craft on the metal landing ramp. Gorski deduced that the civilians were from various planets as some had the dyed hair coloring that was prevalent on planets Athena and Cootron while others had brands of designs on their bodies which were popular on New Sao Paolo and Sikorsky's Planet. He noticed that a large family of Kotek's were being questioned by a civilian port officer to his right. Gorski acted as if he did not see anything as he walked out of the docking area and into the wide tunnel that led to the main wheel of the space station.

He let out an exhale of relief in that none of the MI soldiers stopped him or Tierney as they made their way out of the docking area. The two men kept their eyes focused on the people in front of them as they made their way through the light crowd of tourists, soldiers and civilian employees.

"Which way?" Gorski whispered to Tierney.

"Level Five to a Bar called Lucky Sevens," Tierney responded. "Friedmann and some of his friends play poker there regularly. We might find them there."

Gorski walked toward the solar powered escalators that were straight ahead. The rapid rising and descending escalators were the fastest way to go from level to level on the station. He paused to let a family of six step onto the escalator in front of him before stepping onto the metallic stairs that lifted him upward at a forty-five-degree angle. He remained on the metal ramp until he saw the step off for Level Five. He leaped off the moving stairs onto the stable and solid metal floor of Level Five. He heard Tierney land on the floor behind him.

The two men kept moving, not wanting to stand still for too long and allow someone to get a good look at them. They observed the red glowing sign on the facade of the far wall that had the words "Lucky Sevens" in bold letters. Without a word, Gorski and Tierney walked rapidly toward the entrance and passed several groups of prostitutes on their way through the large open doors. They ignored the offers of sex for money as they passed by the ladies and men of the night. As they scanned the large bar and casino, they saw dozens of tables where patrons were playing poker and many other tables for faro. There were some dice games being played on other tables further away, toward the back wall. The two officers could hear the shouts of glee from winners and the groans of losers as they looked around. Gorski wrinkled his nose to the smell of people that probably had not showered or wiped themselves with disinfectant wipes. The body odor was atrocious, he thought to himself.

A female Kotek wearing a bright red tuxedo uniform approached them and asked them loudly if they wanted a drink from the bar. Gorski politely declined the offer and noticed that Tierney had seemed to locate someone he knew. Gorski followed the Captain as he waded through the crowd of people toward a female in civilian clothes that was sitting at a poker table. She was attractive, with dark hair, wearing a sleeveless white top and shorts and did not have any of the tattoos or branding on her body.

Tierney sat down in the empty seat next to her and whispered into her ear, "Anna, I need your help."

Lieutenant Anna Tatum had been off duty for the last few hours and hoped to win some cash at the poker tables. The last thing that she thought she would see was her friend who was now a wanted fugitive from the MI. Tatum looked at Tierney and her eyes widened when she realized who he was. She had worked with Tierney closely over the past few years and had considered him a good friend. Part of her was happy to see him alive, the other part was angry that he would come to her and put her freedom and life at risk.

"Shit," Tatum whispered to herself and turned back toward the dealer. "I'm out. Cash me out."

Tierney waited patiently as Tatum turned in her chips for cash and stood up from her seat. She motioned to a small table near the bar that was empty. "Let's talk over there. You have a lot of guts coming here."

Tierney nodded, "Yes, I do."

Tatum moved toward the table and sat down and smiled at Tierney as he sat down. Her eyes widened again when Gorski joined them, taking a third chair.

"Shit," she muttered to herself again. "You two are crazy, no offense, Colonel."

"None taken," Gorski assured her. "We came to find out if we could get some help."

Tatum was about to answer when a female in a red tuxedo and pink hair stopped by their table and asked if they wanted drinks. Tatum quickly told her to bring three large ales and waited for the waitress to leave. "Colonel, the Rosenburg's upped the price on your head to a million dollars, cash. You two need to get the hell out of here before someone recognizes you."

"I am not going to leave the people of Clovis City," Gorski responded to her warning. "I swore to protect them and I will. I intend to take the fight to the Rosenburg's and their new military leaders. Is there anyone on this station that we can trust?"

Tatum pondered the question for a moment and smiled at the waitress when she delivered the three ales. "Maybe Doctor Terajima will help. She has no love for the Rosenburg's, but after her, I cannot guarantee anything."

"What about Darby and Dante?" Tierney pressed her.

Tatum sighed and looked up at the ceiling, "Maybe. They are both on their way here to meet with me. My advice is for you to leave before they come."

"Why?" Tierney asked as he sipped from his glass of ale.

"Because they will not be coming alone. They hang out with some of the Tech's and civilians that might want to cash in on the millions you two would bring."

Before Gorski could respond a woman approached them, laughing and clapping her hands. She was wearing a maroon tube top with a black mini-skirt and black high heeled shoes. She wrapped her arms around Tatum's neck.

"Anna! I was looking all over for you!"

Tatum pointed with her thumb at the newcomer, "Gentlemen, this is Erica Lee Coker from the civilian computer technician branch."

Coker had a slender figure, pink hair with purple highlights and some nice features. Her skin pigmentation was light pink, which suggested she was third or fourth generation Cootronian. She smiled and ran over to Tierney and Gorski, hugging both tight, telling them that they were handsome, before sitting down in the last chair at the table.

"So, Anna, what up? Are we gonna do a foursome?" Coker smiled at Tierney. "You are so hot."

"Thank you," Tierney responded with little enthusiasm in his voice. He did not want to encourage her foursome idea.

"No, Erica, we are not having sex with them. At least not right now. Have you seen Dante or Darby?" Tatum asked her.

Coker pointed to the far-left corner of the bar, "They are both over there. Darby is hitting on Amanda, like he always does, and Dante is throwing dice. Why? What is up?"

Tatum forced a smile at her friend, "Wait here, Erica. I need to go speak with them. I will be right back."

"Fine with me!" Coker said as she stood up and forced her way onto Tierney's lap. "I can do things to you that will make your toes curl."

"Of that I have no doubt," Tierney told the woman as he watched Tatum walk over toward the back-dice table where Friedmann and O'Neal were located.

Tatum walked sideways through the crowd and finally made it to the side of Dante Friedmann who gave her a hug when he noticed her. Tatum smiled at Darby O'Neal who had his arms around Technical Sergeant Amanda Zaldivar. The two men were wearing short sleeved shirts with casual slacks and slippers while Zaldivar was dressed in a half shirt and tight jeans. They had a few off-duty MI enlisted women and some other female computer technicians, all of whom Friedmann and O'Neal had been sleeping with off and on, standing nearby. Tatum exchanged greetings with the group and finally broke the news of her surprise meeting with the wanted men to O'Neal, Friedmann and Zaldivar.

"Colonel Gorski is here with Tierney," Tatum said loud enough for them but low enough to avoid any eavesdroppers from listening in.

"What the hell are they doing here?" O'Neal wanted to know, glancing quickly in the direction of Gorski.

"They want to raise an army and go fight the Rosenburg's. Tierney asked for each of you specifically and wants to speak with you."

Zaldivar had an excited look in her eyes regarding the news. "Aren't the military and the Rosenburg's paying a million each for them?"

"Yes they are," Friedmann responded and smiled at O'Neal. The two men had already accepted bribes from the Rosenburg's to help them sneak the Fenster kids off the planet as well as being involved in the takeover of the space station. They were up to their eyeballs in guilt for siding with the Rosenburg family over their friends. "The question is what do we do now?"

"We stun them and get paid, that's what we do," Zaldivar said boldly.

O'Neal pursed his lips and paced over to Tatum's side, "I know you and Tierney had a fling a while back. If we make a move, I need to know that you will back our play."

Tatum looked at the floor and then back at O'Neal, "We all took money to help with the Fenster kidnaping, Darby. If that ever got out, we would be court martialed if Gorski gets his way. They are both good men, but they are on the losing side of this war. We have no choice but to take Gorski and Tierney down."

"You sure?" O'Neal pressed her.

"Positive."

O'Neal looked over to Zaldivar and Friedmann, "Olivo was coming to join us here, but he knows nothing of what we did with the Fenster kids. We need to wrap this up before he and his friends arrive. We should act like we are going to help them, lead them outside and then use stun darts on them. Once we have them down we can contact General Sikorsky and have her arrange for a pick up and our pay off. Two million dollars, that's five hundred thousand each. Not a bad pay day."

"Not bad at all," Friedmann agreed.

"Follow my lead, let me do all the talking and wait until we get them outside before we take them." O'Neal instructed the group and then turned to the eight women from the MI and technical departments that were present. He explained to them that he needed their help in helping him with two men that owed him money for an old gambling debt. He pointed out Gorski and Tierney and lied that they owed him the money. The women agreed, willing to do anything for Friedmann and O'Neal.

O'Neal instructed the eight women to leave the bar, wait outside and back them up if things got rough.

Tatum followed behind O'Neal, feeling guilty about betraying Tierney. But as her friends had pointed out, the money was too good to pass up on. She passed a few solid white furred Kotek's with blue eyes as they walked. She always found the human-feline hybrids creepy and tried not to make eye contact with them. Zaldivar stood beside her, telling her how she could quit the service and buy a large area of land so that she could start her own farm with her share of the reward money. Tatum nodded and pretended to be interested in Zaldivar's dreams.

Tierney learned that the Coker woman was quite aggressive as she was trying to slide her hand underneath his sweat pants to grab his crotch. He had to stop her several times which brought a scowl on her face as she was not accustomed to men rejecting her advances. Tierney was relieved when he saw that Tatum was returning with another woman, Friedmann and O'Neal following next to her.

Gorski stood to greet the officers.

"Colonel, you are looking good," Friedmann shook his hand. "Anna tells us that you need us to help you build an army."

"Yes, we need a small group to make a precision strike at the UN Building." Gorski spoke so that the group could hear him, "If we can get to General Sikorsky, Admiral Sowa and Rebecca Rosenburg then we will have an excellent chance to get the army to stand down. I believe that most of the officers will follow my lead if I can secure the building and eliminate the three I mentioned."

Friedmann gazed at O'Neal and Tatum for a moment as he thought of a response to the statement made by the wanted man. After a few seconds, he looked Gorski in the eye, "Sir, we would love to help out. But this bar is not safe with all the rogues and off duty MI soldiers that are all around us. If someone recognizes you, they will try to collect on the bounty and all hell will break out. I suggest we move to another location quickly."

"I agree," Tierney told Gorski.

Gorski grunted and looked around the bar at the so called "rogues" as Friedmann referred to them. Most of the customers were from the downtrodden and the lower economic groups of the society created by Vladimir Sikorsky. Gorski was not so sure that the patrons would try and turn him in as Friedmann claimed. On the contrary, Gorski felt that the people would join him and his cause.  But, to avoid any arguments with Friedmann and the others, Gorski nodded his head in agreement and stood up from his chair.

Friedmann led the group toward the exit, with Tatum behind him, followed by Tierney with Coker still trying to get his attention, Gorski was next with O'Neal and Zaldivar bringing up the rear. One by one, they exited the bar and walked out onto the fifth floor of the space station and moved toward the protective metal rails. The drop from the fifth level of the space station walkway was over one hundred feet to the lower level floor which was metal covered with white and black tiles. The transparent metal hull of the station was visible when standing next to the rails with the view of planet New Edinburgh for all to see. The eight women that O'Neal had previously requested to wait from them outside were there, acting nonchalant, but watching the events carefully, ready to spring into action against the two men if necessary.

Gorski kept himself alert as he walked with the group, watching the faces of all the employees and visitors that moved past him on the walkway. There were several dozen people around, some were posing at the protective rails for pictures with loved ones, others relaxing with friends and the majority walking by them to some destination elsewhere on the station. He noticed the eight women to his right and concluded that they were military off duty personnel in the way that they stood and were looking around. He made a mental note to keep an eye on them. The Colonel checked under his sweats to make certain his hidden laser pistols were accessible in case he needed to defend himself.

His sixth sense warned him that Griffin might have been correct in that docking on the station had been a bad idea.

Tierney was not as vigilant as Gorski. He fully trusted his friends Tatum, O'Neal and Friedmann. He was talking about some soccer game that they had all attended together many months earlier when Dominic Andolini scored an amazing goal by leaping and twisting his body into the air and kicked the ball at an awkward angle, right through the outstretched hands of the opposing team's goalie and into the net. O'Neal was fully involved in the conversation as he and Tierney reminisced about that game.

Gorski stood back from the main cluster of Tierney, Coker, Friedmann, O'Neal and Tatum. He was aware that the woman named Zaldivar was standing behind him which made him more uneasy. His Spetsnaz training had taught him to keep his eyes looking in every direction, knowing exactly where each person was standing always had become like second nature to Gorski.

As Friedmann was about to address the group, Technical Sergeant Esteban Olivo called out to them from down the hallway. Gorski noticed that Friedmann and O'Neal exchanged some odd looks as Olivo and twelve women and three men approached them. They were all co-workers with Olivo and were wearing civilian clothes. Gorski recognized Olivo of one of the survivors of the now infamous Blitzkrieg Raumschiff attack led by the deceased assassin Junior Ragnarsson. Olivo was asking something about why they were all outside the bar, or something along those lines. It was difficult for Gorski to hear the exact words due to the buzz of conversation from the other people on the walkway. The reaction to the arrival of Olivo and his employees was not what Gorski would have expected.

Without warning, Anna Tatum thrust a stun dart into Tierney's neck, causing him to stagger for a few seconds before he slumped to his knees and fell face first onto the walkway. Coker shrieked when she saw what had happened and leaped at Tatum, demanding an explanation as to why she did such a thing. Simultaneously, O'Neal and Friedmann had drawn laser pistols and began firing in the direction of Olivo and his friends. Several of the off-duty technicians were hit by the rapid fire lasers before the remainder could scatter for cover.

Out of the corner of his eyes, Gorski saw Zaldivar raising her right hand and was about to plunge the needle of the stun dart she was holding into him. Gorski reacted by blocking her arm, flipping her to the metal floor and broke her right wrist in one fluid motion. Zaldivar screamed out in pain and was writhing on the metal floor, holding her injured wrist with her left hand. Gorski was already kneeling and drawing his laser pistol before O'Neal or Friedmann could react.

Gorski heard screaming from the patrons and employees of the station due to the laser shots and the number of injured falling to the floor. There was mass panic as people ran for cover, parents trying to protect their children and Olivo and his remaining technical workers running for cover. Gorski cursed due to his knowledge that the MI security soldiers would be descending upon them in seconds. He fired his first shot and hit Friedmann in the center of his chest. Friedmann fell to the floor without making a sound.

The eight off-duty women began charging at Gorski, drawing hidden laser pistols from underneath their blouses and leather jackets. Gorski knew they were coming by the manner that they were moving and he pivoted to his right and fired eight bursts from his laser pistol in under three seconds. He hit each of the women in the chest sending each one sprawling backwards onto the metal hallway. Unfortunately for the off-duty women, they had not been warned that their prey was a Spetsnaz graduate and a veteran of the Dinosaur Wars.

Gorski moved back to his left and faced the threat of Tatum and O'Neal.

Tatum, to get rid of the emotional Coker, fired her laser pistol point blank into her abdomen. Coker staggered and Tatum impatiently shoved the woman toward the protective rails to get her out of the way. Unfortunately for Coker, her momentum spun her over the rails and she fell one hundred feet to the floor below. She landed face first on a round, four seat table in the food court, splitting her skull and snapping her neck. There were several dozen patrons eating at the lower level food court and they all began screaming and running in different directions after Coker made her fatal fall.

O'Neal fired two shots in the direction of Gorski, who was now rolling to his right, prone to the floor, and returning fire as he rolled. He hit O'Neal in the stomach and the off-duty officer fell to the floor, lying next to Friedmann and Tierney. Tatum was the last combatant, firing her laser pistol wildly at Gorski. Most of her shots were not even close and some even hit some innocent passersby. Gorski continued his defensive roll on the ground and tried to get a good shot at Tatum. Before he could, he felt the sting of electricity hit him in the back. Gorski dropped his laser pistol and his head dropped to the floor of the walkway as he was rendered unconscious due to a laser shot fired from behind him by an MI soldier that had arrived on the scene.

"That mother fucker broke my wrist!" Zaldivar screamed as Tatum ran toward Gorski's prone figure.

"Freeze!" Tatum heard from an MI Lieutenant.

Tatum did as ordered and put her hands up in the air. She looked in the direction of the MI squad that was running toward her, with laser rifles pointing in her direction.

"Lieutenant!" Tatum called out to them and pointed at Gorski, "My friends and I want to claim the bounty on Colonel Gorski. We recognized him in the bar and brought him out here to apprehend him. This is our catch and we should be paid."

Olivo walked over toward the area and glared at Tatum and Zaldivar. He was justifiably angered at the way he and his friends were fired upon by O'Neal and Friedmann. He looked down at Gorski and Tierney and shook his head. Olivo knew that any chance of getting rid of the Rosenburg's ended with the capture of the Colonel. From his view, there were no other officers savvy enough to mount a serious attack to free the people. The fact that Gorski had come to the space station to attempt to seek out some of his old officers indicated that the Colonel did not abandon the people as the fake news reports claimed.

"And so it ends," Olivo whispered to himself as the MI soldiers descended upon them.

# CHAPTER TWELVE

Klaus Rhinehard wondered if every father felt as he did at that magical moment when the nurses handed him his newborn son and daughter. He looked at their innocent faces, their eyes closed and their tiny bodies wrapped up in the warm blankets. He knew that he would fight to give them the very best in life. They would forever be his number one priority. He was overwhelmed with the feeling of love he felt for them, seeing how defenseless they were, so unaware of what life meant for them both. The twins were more than he had ever hoped that he would be blessed with in life.

"Thanks to Odin, they are so healthy." Klaus mumbled to himself and turned toward his exhausted wife, April Mejia.

She was lying on the hospital bed that she had spent the entire time of the birth process on. His wife was drenched in sweat from her several hours of labor. He looked into her eyes that looked as if she were ready to pass out but had a sparkle of hope in them at the same time. He could see a tear of joy roll down her cheek as he walked over to her and showed her their children for first time.

"They are so beautiful; I love you so much." April told him as she reached out with her hand and gently touched the cheek of the closest child to her.

Klaus leaned closer to her and kissed her on the forehead, "I love you more."

One of the nurses touched him on the shoulder. "We have to take them now. You can come with us, Mister Rhinehard."

"Watch them close," April said with a weak voice. Earlier, she had succumbed to the pain of child birth and had been given some medications to make the delivery easier on her. At that moment, seeing her husband with her two children, she was happier than she had ever been in her life. She had created two healthy children with the man that she loved more than any person she had ever known. The children were healthy and had no defects, at least that was what the doctor had told them. She had followed the regimen of vitamins and advanced human enhancement drugs as prescribed by Doctor Patel and had avoided all alcoholic beverages during the gestation period.

Klaus followed the nurses as they took the children to be weighed and measured in one of the back rooms of the maternity ward. He swore by Tyr, the God of War, that he would not let them out of his sight. As he walked down what seemed to be an endless set of hallways, he wondered why his brother, Rolf, had not returned from his trip to Space Station Cy-5 to witness the birth of his niece and nephew. Klaus feared that something had gone very wrong for his brother as it was not like him to miss such an event.

Mejia was cleaned up by two nurses that were using bacterial cleansing wipes. After she had been wiped down, they placed in into a new bed with fresh sheets and wheeled her to her hospital room. When she arrived, Doctor Patel was waiting for her with more drugs.

"You did wonderful, April. I am going to give you an injection that will deaden the pain, relax your muscles and allow you to sleep."

"When will my children be brought over to me?" Mejia asked, her voice sounded fatigued.

"When you wake up they will both be here. The couch in the corner will fold out into a bed for your husband. Get some rest, April. You will need it. Your twins will require an awful lot of your attention." Patel said with a soothing voice as she injected the drugs into Mejia's arm.

Mejia nodded and felt as if she were floating on the clouds in the sky. She slowly drifted off to sleep.

Klaus watched every second of the process of weighing his children. The boy was nine pounds ten ounces and the girl was nine pounds one ounce. He watched the DNA scan be taken of them, their footprints and the measuring process. At some point, he realized that he was crying from the joy he felt. He wondered if his father felt the same when he had been born. He pondered the question as to whether every man felt as he did at that moment. He had known many cadets at the Academy that had come from the orphanages, most of whom had fathers that did not want them. He could not fathom why any man worthy of honor would allow their child to be sent to such a place of despair.

"You will both be safe. I swear that to you," Klaus whispered to himself.

Cara Perez Guerrero woke up in a strange room. Her eyes slowly opened. She heard her own breathing and the monitor in the room that was regulating her life signs. She had tubes in each of her arms, dripping liquids into her veins due to the loss of blood she had suffered from her wounds. She felt dehydrated. She focused her eyes on the white ceiling above her and then turned her head to the right and then the left to see the white walls of what she concluded was a recovery room at the main hospital in Clovis City. She slowly slid her right hand down toward her abdomen and felt bandages.

"My babies," she said with a voice drained of energy. "Please, God, let them be okay."

She could hear footsteps approaching from the hallway outside her door. She tried to sit up in anticipation of receiving visitors, wondering if it was her mother or her siblings. She watched the two figures walk into the room and begin checking the computer monitor on the foot of her bed.

"You are finally awake. That is a good sign, Cara. You are a very strong woman," Doctor Freya Doernitz told her gently. "Your surgery was a success. We were stopped all of the bleeding. We had to remove you twins to save your life. You will be happy to know that they are both fine and healthy. Welcome to the sorority of motherhood."

Cara felt a wave of relief wash over her. Her children were alive and well, which was all she cared about. She nodded as she found she could not respond verbally due to the dryness of her throat.

The other woman with Freya addressed her as she sat down next to the bed. She had a cup in her hand full of chunks of ice and a spoon in her other. "Cara, here. I am going to give you some ice chips. Do not swallow them, just suck on them and let them melt in our mouth. Okay?"

Cara nodded and opened her mouth as the woman put a few ice chips in. She focused on the face and recognized her as a medical student named Lynn Goldsmith. But her silver hair had been dyed black, as if she were trying to disguise herself for some reason. Cara had not learned that Goldsmith's family had been practically wiped out by the Rosenburg backed military so the attempt at disguise confused her somewhat. Lynn and her family did not seem like the other world colonists that colored their hair or put wild looking tattoo's all over themselves. Cara gave Goldsmith a weak smile and sucked on the ice. As it melted, the water felt soothing as it ran down her throat.

"Your life signs are stable. You lost a lot of blood from that explosion. It looked like the soldiers were sent in to arrest our neighbor, Sean Collins. He fought back and escaped. Now I don't want you to worry about what is going on in the city, Cara. We need for you to recover so that you can take your children home. We want you to rest, Cara," Freya told her gently. "I was afraid that I was going to lose you, girl. Ever since I lost Porfirio and you lost Pierre, we have become good friends. So, you rest, get your strength back and we can catch up later."

Cara smiled at Freya and closed her eyes. She felt drained and was quickly falling asleep.

Freya led Goldsmith from the room and out into the long, winding hallway. They walked together in silence until they saw Doctor Patel at one of the elevator lift entrances. She waved at the two women to join her as she held the door open for them. After they entered the elevator, the doors closed behind them and they felt the machine lowering them.

"Time for a late-night snack, coffee and to put our feet up," Patel said to them. "With the military causing all of their crap around the city it has been non-stop in the ER. Rapes, beatings, laser wounds, knife wounds and I even had a civilian that had been attacked by a Saharakaree. We barely saved her life."

"The same for me, Priya," Freya leaned against the wall of the elevator. "I really think these new military commanders are turning more people against them by being so brutal. But it has always been the way of the Glorious Leader, resist and die."

"And because my father tried to put some of the Rosenburg's in jail, they killed him for it and my mother and most of my brothers and sisters." Goldsmith said sadly as she looked at the two women. "All my life I wanted to be a doctor and help people, just like each of you. Now I am a criminal, hiding out in plain view, waiting to be found and killed like the rest of my family. It isn't fair. Some of the ones that they killed were so young. Too young."

The elevator stopped and the doors opened to reveal the large basement cafeteria. There were several nurses and doctors taking a break at some of the round tables, drinking coffee and eating fruits and pastries. The three women walked in slowly and toward the buffet counter.

"Lynn, keep your thoughts to yourself. There is a reward on your head and some of these people here would love to collect on it." Freya whispered the warning to her as they walked. "We will do all we can to protect you and your two siblings, but if anyone hears you speaking in such a manner, they will turn you in. Count on it."

Goldsmith nodded and smiled at a male nurse that was checking her out as she passed by. She had found a hospital outfit that was bit tight in her chest and the nurse was eying her in that direction. "Thank you for the consultation, Doctor."

The three women picked up trays and grabbed some apple pastries, some bear claws, three cups of coffee, some juices and some plantanas to munch on while they relaxed. They found a table in the corner of the cafeteria that was away from the rest of the crowd and sat down. They each grabbed a bear claw and began to eat them as if they had been starving to death.

"This will not do well on my hips, but who cares?" Freya said in between chews. She sipped on her coffee and smiled at Goldsmith. "That handsome nurse was giving you the eye."

"He was giving my rack the eye," Goldsmith responded quickly. "Which I suppose is okay with me. If I get caught I am dead. I have half a mind to let him take me to an empty room so I can at least get laid one last time before they kill me."

"Stop sounding so defeated, you are not dead yet." Patel told her. "He is handsome, though. I bet he would be fun. The other night I did just that with one of the new student interns. He is one of the seniors at the Academy and full of muscles, good looks and stamina. He mounted me like I was the last woman on the planet."

"You two are unbelievable. You never cease to amaze me, Priya." Freya commented as she drank some coffee. "Just wait until you have children, your whole outlook will change."

Patel smiled at her friend and leaned forward, "Freya, it has been many months since Porfirio died. Look at you, you are pretty with a nice body. Heck, every time you gave birth your body just snaps back to its original form. All the other women get surgery to remove the excess weight, but not you. There are several doctors here that would love to do an examination on you behind closed doors. Know what I mean?"

Freya's mood soured at the mention of her deceased husband. It had been months, but every day she would remember him with fondness. He had been a good man, a fantastic husband and an even better father. She missed him every day. "Priya, I doubt I will ever be ready for anything new. I will just live vicariously through you and your adventures. You know that your little sisters all watch you as an example? You should be more discreet in your mating practices."

Patel smiled and then laughed for a moment. She drank some orange juice and then pointed at Freya. "I think that my sisters are far more adventurous than I am when it comes to sex partners. And they did not learn it from me. Come on, Freya. The Glorious Leader has all his floating billboards encouraging sex. He has flooded society with sexualized ads and drugs to increase the sex drive. If anything, I am more reserved than most women."

Goldsmith finished her bear claw and chased it with some coffee. She was enjoying the conversation and it almost made her forget that just several days ago her entire family had been essentially targeted for extinction. She kept eating as she listened to the two doctors continue their debate on the morality of sexual acts.

Everyone in the cafeteria grew quiet when the hospital intercom announced a new round of ER patients arriving. Patel, Freya and Goldsmith drank their coffee cups dry and took and apple pastry each as they rushed toward the elevators. Several other doctors and nurses did the same. At the rate injured people were coming in, they would run out of hospital beds in a few hours.

When the elevator stopped on the first floor, Patel led them out into the lobby that was full of injured civilians and military personnel. Most were sitting in the metal seats with leather covered cushions on the backs while others were being brought in on stretchers. Goldsmith had all the medical scanners and instruments on her uniform and stepped in to assist a woman that was lying on the floor, her left leg broken in three places. Goldsmith hoped that her first year of medical school and her pre-medical school courses would serve her well in impersonating an actual doctor. She checked the vital signs of the injured woman and motioned for a nurse to take her in for immediate surgery.

Goldsmith turned to the next victim and her heart sank. Being held up by her arms was Cadet Jeanna Natalia Carteri. She was unconscious with bruises on her face and torso. Goldsmith knew the cadet pilot well from some of her classes the previous year. Carteri's dream was to become a Search and Rescue astronaut, which required a better than average understanding of medical treatments and survival techniques while in deep space.

Goldsmith knew that it was only a matter of time before Carteri would be awake and that she would recognize her.

Cadets Shanna and Zoe Bragg were holding her upright as Goldsmith scanned the victim. Goldsmith did not recognize the sisters and hoped that they did not recognize her with her disguise as a medical doctor.

"She was raped?" Goldsmith determined out loud. "It looks like her attackers hit her in the face several times."

"Yes, Doctor. She put up a fight. We got to her as soon as we could and brought her straight to the hospital. She needs help." Zoe said with desperation in her voice.

"Nurse!" Goldsmith called out to the handsome man that had been giving her the eye in the cafeteria earlier. "Get her to the eleventh-floor trauma ward. Have the technicians do an immediate scan of her brain for any blunt force trauma and hematomas."

"Yes, Doctor." The man smiled at Goldsmith and motioned for an orderly to bring a stretcher over to take Carteri for treatment.

As the orderlies were gently placing Carteri on the stretcher, Goldsmith saw more cadets approaching them. She recognized one of them as a senior in the Geology section. Dempster Harang led Bret Bragg and Ye Yibing toward the doctor that was helping Carteri. Goldsmith pursed her lips as Harang moved closer to her. She had been in some of his classes when she was a senior. Since they had been in a study group together he would recognize her despite the different color hair and doctor uniform. She was about to be found out and there was little she could do about it.

Fortunately for Goldsmith, Freya Cardenas must have realized that she was in danger. She approached her quickly and took her by the arm. "Doctor, we need to get to the trauma ward, right now."

Goldsmith turned her back on Harang and the other cadets and followed Freya and the orderlies that were wheeling the bed with Carteri resting on it. She got to the elevator and heard the familiar voice of Harang calling out to her.

"Doctor, is she going to make it?"

Goldsmith gave Freya a look of fear. Freya understood that the cadet was a man that could identify her, so she responded to the question. Freya turned and faced Harang, smiled at him and his friends and went to shake their hands. "Thank you all for getting this girl in to us so quickly. Your actions just might have saved her life. We must get her to surgery right away. Wait here in the lobby and I will personally find you after surgery and let you know how she is doing."

Harang shook her hand and glanced over her shoulder at Carteri and the mystery doctor that had her back to him. "Thank you."

Freya turned away from him and ran to the elevator doors that were opening. She joined the staff with the injured Carteri and waited until the doors slid shut behind her before she exhaled. She looked at Goldsmith and shook her head at her. "Who was he?"

"Dempster Harang. His friends call him Demps for short. He's a Geology Explorations Major. Good student, stand up kind of guy. Every one of the other cadets respect him." Goldsmith whispered to her so that the orderlies would not hear. "Thanks for the assist, Doctor."

"Don't mention it," Freya said as the elevator made it to the trauma floor. "Let's get this girl into surgery and save her life."

Harang stared at the elevator doors for a few moments as he wondered about the other doctor. He was certain that he had seen her before, but could not place the face. He had only gotten a quick glance at her. He put it out of his mind, deciding that she was probably someone he saw at a bar once or some other past meeting.

"Demps, what's wrong?" Yibing asked him.

"Nothing, Ye. Nothing at all." Harang turned and faced her. "Klaus and April are here; we should go visit them."

The three Bragg's glared at him for the suggestion.

"You mean Klaus Rhinehard, the leader of the Gorski Gang?" Bret demanded.

"Hey, I am in the Gorski Gang!" Yibing reminded them sternly.

Harang put his hands up in a defensive manner and stepped in between Yibing and Bret. "Cool it, Bret. We're all on the same side now, right? Come on, Bret, relax."

Zoe hit her older brother on the shoulder. "Yeah, Bret. Cool it. Besides, Klaus is so hot. He is tall and had muscles on top of muscles. Too bad he married that girl."

"Zoe has had a crush on Klaus ever since she first saw him," Shanna told the others. "I have to admit he is dreamy, but he only has eyes for his wife."

"Yes, and now he is a father. Bret, I know that Klaus has been the leader of your rival gang since Yuri graduated, but you need to put that behind you. We have a common enemy now and we should work together. Got it?" Harang put his arm around Bret's shoulders as he spoke to him.

"It's just that Klaus really kicked my ass once. I mean I was hurting for a week from the beat down he gave me. It is kind of hard to let things like that go." Bret told them. "I will play nice.  Besides, I love kids. I hope to have a few dozen of my own someday."

"Good. Then let's go congratulate the happy parents, kiss their babies and be friends. Come on, Klaus will be okay when Ye and I vouch for you."

"Yeah, come on. I want to see the babies," Zoe told them. "We've seen enough bad stuff for one day. I bet they are beautiful kids."

"You don't want to see the babies; you want to see Klaus!" Shanna hit Zoe on the shoulder playfully.

Zoe gave her a disapproving look.

Yibing was reading the computer screen on the ceiling and pointed at it. "Maternity is on floor ten," she told the other.

Bret motioned with his hand and pointed to the elevators. "Lead the way, Demps."

Little did they realize; they were all in imminent danger from the hit team assembled by Ilyasova and his Rosenburg lover. They were soon to be in the middle of a fight to survive.

**TO BE CONTINUED**